THESE
Rugged
CLIFFS

THESE
Rugged
CLIFFS

Michelle Ford

TATE PUBLISHING *& Enterprises*

TATE PUBLISHING
    & Enterprises

These Rugged Cliffs
Copyright © 2006 by Michelle Ford. All rights reserved.

Book design copyright © 2006 by Tate Publishing, LLC. All rights reserved.
Cover design by Lynly Taylor
Interior design by Leah LeFlore

Published in the United States of America

ISBN: 1–5988653–0-7
06.09.28

To my parents who taught me to dream
and my loving husband who encouraged me
to make my dreams a reality.

PROLOGUE

Kent, England 1884

Rain fell in sheets outside the window as I pressed my nose against the glass, trying to catch a glimpse of the person I loved most in the world. When I could stand it no longer, I sent the groom to see if he could find my father, who had gone earlier to see a horse one of the neighbors had bought. The tension in the house was becoming unbearable, for I had expected him home long ago.

"I'll be back as soon as I can, Miss," Grady had said as he headed out into the rain. My housekeeper asked what to do with dinner. Without removing my face from the window, I told her to hold it until my father came back.

My eyes were burning from the strain of staring out into the dark, when I suddenly spotted Grady returning on his horse. Another horse followed; the rider's body lay slumped across the saddle, feet and arms dangling.

My worst fears were realized. I rushed out into the rainy night and met the groom as he came up the drive. He jumped down to try to intercept me, but I sidestepped him and rushed to my father's side. His body hung limp. I wiped at the blood on the side of his face. His cheek felt icy, and my fingers went numb as I touched it.

"Papa!" I cried, flinging my arms around the figure lying across the saddle. "Papa, wake up!" My brain told me he was dead, but my heart wouldn't accept it. I don't know how long I stood sobbing in the dark, clinging to my father's lifeless body. The next thing I remember, I woke up in my bed, a fire blazing in the fireplace.

CHAPTER 1

When my maid drew back the curtains, letting bright sunlight fill the room, I groaned and covered my eyes.

"Good morning!" she said. Her voice sounded stilted, overly cheerful, and I knew she was trying to sound that way for my benefit.

"It's a beautiful Sunday, Miss." Her slight emphasis on the word Sunday was not lost on me.

"What will you be wearing to church today?" she asked.

I closed my eyes to keep back the tears of pain and regret; I needn't have put forth the effort. I hadn't cried since the night my father had died. What made me think I would be able to cry now? I opened my eyes to find the maid looking hopefully at me.

"I'm not attending services today," I said quietly.

"I know it's not my place to say, Miss, but this'll be the third Sunday in a row. We're worried about you."

"Thank you, but you needn't worry. I'll be fine."

The words sounded insincere, even to my ears. My

maid frowned and left the room. I got up and walked to the window. I looked out on the lush green grass and rolling hills of the Kent countryside. I hated the fact that it was such a beautiful day. The sun continued to shine just to spite me. The weight of the house seemed heavy on my shoulders—memories jumped out of every corner, every room. Except this one, I told myself. My father had rarely come in here, and I felt safer here—shielded from the emotions I felt everywhere else.

I could not walk down the grand staircase without seeing my father at the bottom, waiting for me. I could not walk through the dining room without seeing him feasting on his favorite meal. And I could not go to church without him, not right now.

I knew the servants were worried; I was worried, too. I had never before felt so numb, and I had no idea what to do about it. I knew I should pray or read my Bible—call out to the Lord for help, but I wasn't speaking to Him right now. I was full of self-pity, wondering why a loving God hadn't kept my father from dying.

I moped around for a couple more days, but Tuesday morning a visit from Mr. Cabot, my solicitor, forced me to go downstairs to the drawing room. When I entered the room, Mr. Cabot rose, and I noticed he looked rather uneasy. He looked like he had something important he wanted to say to me, but was not looking forward to it.

We exchanged pleasantries, and he helped himself to the tea and cakes, which my housekeeper had quickly brought, but I couldn't bring myself to eat anything. He watched me with a wary expression. Finally he seemed ready to speak his mind.

"Kaitlin, I have kept in touch with your housekeeper, and what she has told me has been alarming, indeed. The servants say you have hardly left your room since your father passed away. You're not eating. And you don't seem to realize how despondent you've become."

At the concern in his eyes, I felt my face turn red, and I looked away. I bit my lip and looked down at my hands. I had been carefully folding and unfolding the napkin I held. I knew he was speaking the truth, but what was I to do about it? It seemed a hopeless situation. Finally, I looked up at him with tears in my eyes.

"I'm grateful for your concern, Mr. Cabot. I know I haven't been myself lately."

"I hardly feel as though I should tell you this," he continued solemnly, "but your servants are even worried that you are in danger of ... of doing yourself some harm," he broke off, slightly embarrassed. My breath caught in my throat. I knew I hadn't been giving a very pretty picture of Christian courage and faith the last few weeks, but I didn't think it had gotten *that* bad. Suddenly, I was very ashamed of myself.

"I'm sure that you would not *purposely* do yourself any harm, but the truth is you *are* wasting away."

I looked down at the food I hadn't been able to touch. It was true; my clothes were fitting more loosely, and my cheeks had grown pale.

"Your father was a great man and a great friend, Kaitlin, and I feel responsible for you. I refuse to let you grow more and more depressed with each passing day. You must not stay here, isolated and without family or friends, when there is a better solution."

"A better solution?" I asked.

"You could go and stay with friends."

"You mean for me to go away somewhere?" I asked.

"Yes. That is, I have already purchased a train ticket for you. I have spoken to Mrs. Peters, and even now your maid is packing a few things for you to take on your journey. She will send the rest of your things along tomorrow."

"But where am I to go?" I asked, my voice cracking and the astonishment showing in my face.

"Your father specified for his estate and your inheritance to be under the control of a certain Mr. Fitzpatrick until you turn twenty-one. Mr. Fitzpatrick is the nephew of one of your father's greatest friends, Mr. Edward Williams. Have you ever met either of them?"

I shook my head no, unable to imagine what could possibly cause Mr. Cabot to suggest such a thing. What could he mean by telling me to leave immediately so that I could be with "family and friends"? These people were neither. My father had spoken of Mr. Williams as being a wonderful man, and I seemed to remember the name Fitzpatrick, but I did not *know* them. I blanched at the thought of showing up unwanted on their doorstep. I stood up and walked over to look out the window. The gardens used to be bright with fall color, but now only a few hardy chrysanthemums still bloomed red, yellow, purple, and orange. The apple trees, just visible to the left and up a small hill, had long ago been picked, and the leaves had mostly all fallen off. Usually I loved the view from this window, but while I saw all these things, I was too preoccupied to enjoy them. My heart was beating fast, and I was possessed by a strange desire to laugh. I tried to take several deep breaths. When I spoke, my voice sounded amazingly calm.

"I can't just show up at someone's house—uninvited, unknown. I'm sorry, Mr. Cabot, but I don't think that's a possible solution."

"I've already thought of that," he said, shoving my protests aside. "Mr. Williams passed away a few years ago, but I'm sure his nephew would be happy to have you stay with his family. I have a letter here for you to give Mr. Fitzpatrick. It explains everything, including my reasons for wanting you to be among friends. I'm sure any friends of your father's would be happy to extend you some love and hospitality. Mr. Fitzpatrick has a large country home by the sea. It will be a nice place for you to get away from your pain. Please allow me to help you, Kaitlin. I feel as though I owe it to your father to do so."

He had gripped my hand in his old bony fingers as he said this. I recognized that same numbness creeping back over me—shutting out this new turn of events. I welcomed the feeling after the gripping fear I had felt moments ago.

"You mean for me to leave right away?" I asked, still not quite able to take it in.

"Yes. I must admit I'm afraid that if I leave you to think about it for too long, you will come up with all manner of excuses as to why you can't go. I want to see you safely on that train today, before you have a chance to change your mind. I know you'll feel better as soon as you get away from this house."

I chanced to look over at the big chair by the fireplace. I pictured my father sitting there with me on his lap, telling me stories on a cold winter's night. Perhaps I did need to get away from such powerful memories. I shook my head, as if to erase the pictures in my head.

"I don't know," I said weakly.

"Splendid," he said. He went out into the hall and came back with my cloak. "Your trunk is right here, and the carriage is waiting out front. I'll ride with you to the station."

I started to speak, but the fear was back, and it choked me. Was I such a sight of hopelessness and despair that he would act so strangely? Was he afraid that I would be so overcome with loneliness that I would throw myself from some balcony? I thought about the way I had been acting and decided that it was probably not surprising that the servants would think I just might do that. And they had felt it their business to contact Mr. Cabot. I smiled wryly. If there was anyone to blame for the unimaginable situation I now found myself in, I supposed I would have to blame myself. If I had not been so absorbed with doubting God and pitying my circumstances, I might have been saved the embarrassment of Mr. Cabot's attention.

"Please, Mr. Cabot, could I have a moment to myself?"

He nodded and said softly, "I'll be waiting for you outside."

When he had left, I took a moment to glance around the room, trying to remember every detail. I was careful not to let my eyes dwell too long on the big chair by the fireplace. I walked out into the hall and looked up the grand staircase. I wanted to see if I was still overwhelmed by memories.

Was Mr. Cabot right? Would time away ease my pain, or just make me homesick? Part of me wanted to visit my father's room, take one last look at his things, but I blanched at the thought. I loved my home, but I couldn't live here. Later, I would cherish the memories, but not now.

With one long last look, I left the hall and closed the great front door. Mr. Cabot stood by the carriage, watching me carefully. As he helped me into the carriage, I felt a slight sense of anticipation and adventure that had been quite foreign these last three weeks. Perhaps a vacation was just what I needed. I allowed Mr. Cabot to put me on the train, fuss over my belongings, and kiss me on the cheek.

He made sure I had my packet containing a copy of my father's will and his letter to Mr. Fitzpatrick then he smiled at me and left the train. As the train began to move, however, my sense of adventure failed me, and a new sensation almost overwhelmed me. I was terrified of meeting these people, worried that they would not accept me into their home.

When I finally got off the train at Oberly it was almost four o'clock. At the small station, I asked where I might find the Fitzpatrick residence.

"Why would you be wanting to go there?" the station manager asked with a raised eyebrow.

"They are friends of my father's and I am here on a visit," I said, rather uncomfortable.

"I see," the man said in a strange voice. "Would you like to hire someone to take you out there?"

I told him I would and he motioned for one of the boys to put my trunk on a wagon. Then the youth jumped up on the seat and helped me up. The station man tipped his hat to me as we rode off.

"My name's Bill, Miss," the boy next to me said.

"Nice to meet you, Bill," I said. "My name is Kaitlin Howard." After that, we road on in silence. He didn't say anything more, and I wasn't in the mood to be talkative.

Soon I could see the sea in the distance, and I could smell the spicy scent of the ocean. Finally we pulled up in front of a large manor house. Bill jumped down and set my trunk on the ground. He helped me down and then tipped his hat.

"See ya, Miss," he said.

He jumped back in the wagon and was off. As I looked up at the house I tried to stifle the urge to call for Bill to take me right back to the station.

It was not quite accurate to describe the house as large—monstrous was more like it. As far as I could tell, it was simply a large rectangle jutting up from the ground with no gables or turrets to soften the stark gray stone. There was a certain elegance in the huge mansion, but at the same time, it loomed over one, a grotesque figure silhouetted against the sunlight. It looked as if it were staring, crouching, waiting until the right moment to pounce, and then …

I shook my head, trying to rid it of those fantasies that were so apt to creep in. I was twenty years old, for goodness sake. Much too old to be letting my imagination run wild. I couldn't help it, though. I had always been very concerned with the "what ifs" and "if onlys" of life. I had been a sensitive child. Every so often I could be found cowering in a corner somewhere because I had scared myself silly, dreaming up all sorts of terrible things.

Though it was a struggle, I was able to find the courage to go up and knock on the door. At first no one answered, and I felt incredibly relieved. Maybe no one was home. I knocked again, a little louder.

While I was pondering whether or not to walk back to the station, a little old man with shaggy white hair opened the door. When I finally noticed that the door had been opened, I felt close to tears. I hadn't realized just how much I was hoping no one was home.

"Yes?" the man asked. For a moment, I just stared at him.

"Yes?" the man asked, again. I took a deep breath and prepared to repeat the speech I had been practicing in the wagon all the way from the station. Before I had the chance to utter a word, however, I heard a very loud, tinkling female laugh, and a second later a very beautiful woman came into the hall.

When she saw me, she stopped short. I could only imagine the sort of picture I must make. I had spent several hours on a train getting there, plus the ride in the wagon, and I knew I was dusty and disheveled. The woman stared at me for a few seconds and then spoke.

"Jeffries, who is the young person at the door?"

I don't know what it was about the tone of her voice, or the way she spoke the words, but I felt as though I were 10 years old and had just been caught in some kind of mischief.

"I don't know madam. I have been trying to find out the

young lady's reasons for arriving on Mr. Fitzpatrick's doorstep, but have been unsuccessful."

The woman turned her lovely gaze back to me and tilted her head when she spoke.

"What can I do for you, miss?"

I wanted to tell her that I needed a ride back to the station so that I could catch the first train back home, but I didn't. Instead, I continued to stand there looking like an idiot, my prepared speech forgotten.

Finally, I blurted out "My name is Kaitlin Howard. My father died and Mr. Fitzpatrick is … well … sort of my guardian. My solicitor thought I should come." The woman stared at me, seeming to be confused.

Just then, a man entered the hall. He looked at the butler, who was trying to remain dignified after my shocking little speech, at Mrs. Fitzpatrick, and then at me.

At the sight of my bedraggled appearance, he raised an eyebrow and a smile passed quickly over his face. It was hidden the next moment. My face turned an unbecoming red, but I wasn't sure if it was due to the uncomfortable situation or the piercing stare of this gentleman.

"Mr. Fitzpatrick, may I introduce you to Miss Howard, your … uh … ward," the butler said.

I was prepared for a look of shock or an expression of indignation, but was not ready for the cold appraising look he gave me.

The butler continued. "Miss Howard's father passed away and her solicitor sent her to us, it seems."

I realized then that the butler did not like me. He didn't

believe that what I said was true, and he was waiting for his master to dispose of me.

Instead, Mr. Fitzpatrick continued to stare at me. "So you're Thomas Howard's little girl," he finally said. "He talked a lot about you."

I felt at a loss. My father had not talked much about Mr. Fitzpatrick.

"My father died three weeks ago. He was a good friend of your uncle's, I understand, and since your uncle is gone, my father left the care of my estate in your hands until I turn twenty-one. I suppose that sort of makes you my guardian. My solicitor thought it best that I come right away. You see, uh, he seemed to think I was grieving too much for my father and … uh, in danger of jumping off a balcony or something." I gave a little laugh that was much too close to being hysterical. "He thought a visit to friends would be good …" My voice trailed off, and I realized I had been rambling on. "He said I was to give you this. It explains everything." He looked at the envelope and finally took it. "Inside is a copy of the will and a letter from Mr. Cabot."

Instead of replying, he turned and yelled "Mrs. Parks!" toward a door leading off from the hall. A woman emerged from it so quickly it was obvious she had been listening. "Please find a suitable room for Miss Howard." He eyed my bags. "And find someone to take her things to her room. Miss Howard, please follow me."

"Edmund," his lovely wife said in a silky voice, "surely the little thing would like a few minutes to catch her breath before you discuss any important matters. Why don't you have Mrs. Parks show her to a room?"

"No, madam." Mr. Fitzpatrick said, looking closely at me, "Miss Howard's father was a good man and a friend. I will waste no time discovering the details of his death."

I wanted the floor to open up and swallow me whole. I did not care to discuss my father with a complete stranger. And, though I had already taken somewhat of a dislike to Mrs. Fitzpatrick, I was thankful at least that she was worried about my comfort.

As I followed Mr. Fitzpatrick to his study, I was not too dazed to notice something of my surroundings. There was a grand staircase in the exact center of the great hall, with rooms on either side. Mr. Fitzpatrick led me past the staircase to a room that, as near as I could guess, must have been in the center of the back of the house. It overlooked the sloping gardens and meadows that led down to a cliff above the sea. The view was one of the most beautiful I had ever seen. The sun had gone under a cloud, and the wind had picked up. I was glad, because it seemed to match my mood.

Suddenly I realized that Mr. Fitzpatrick was directing me to a chair facing the large mahogany desk. He sat down behind it, opened the envelope and started to read the will. I took a moment to study my host's appearance. He looked much younger than I had expected him to be, probably not yet thirty. His dark hair was thick and wavy, his eyes a piercing blue-gray. I supposed that one would describe his features as "strong," and most women would probably call him handsome. I noticed this all in a brief moment, then I looked away again, not wanting him to catch me staring at him.

While he looked over the will, I fidgeted. I tried to enjoy the view from the large window, but I was ill at ease. Finally,

I looked up to see Mr. Fitzpatrick staring intently at me. He had finished reading the will and the letter. I summoned some hidden inner strength and matched his gaze with my own.

Suddenly, he spoke. "What can you tell me about this letter from Mr. Cabot?"

I was a little surprised at the question. "The solicitor advised me to come here right away. He wanted to get me away from the memory of my father's death." I wondered if I should have spoken so freely. "Mr. Cabot said he would explain everything. He wanted me to leave this morning, and so he made arrangements to send my luggage on after my maid had packed it." I paused for a moment and then went on.

"Mr. Fitzpatrick, I want you to know that I do not intend to stay here for very long. My father left the estate in trust for me until I turn 21, and I will do that in eight months, and by that time Mr. Cabot will hopefully agree that I can safely return to my home without grieving hysterically. I would not even bother you now if Mr. Cabot had not been so worried about my health and well-being. I am sorry I have to inconvenience you and your wife for awhile."

I had been talking mostly to the window, and when I looked back at him he was staring at me, a slight smile on his lips.

"Is something wrong, sir?"

"I'm afraid you are mistaken, Miss Howard. The woman you met is not my wife. She is Mrs. Colton, a widow. She endeavors to keep me amused."

"Oh," I said, feeling my face turn red again. "I'm sorry, I didn't know."

"Don't worry. I'm sure there are lots of things you don't know."

I felt certain he was mocking me, and I did not like it. I was trying to think of a stinging retort when he spoke again.

"Now, pleasantries aside, I should like to hear the details of your father's death. That is, if it does not trouble you too much."

I took a deep breath, looked out the window and tried not to let the pain I was feeling show. The incident was still fresh in my mind and the grief felt like an open wound, raw and infected, tearing my insides to shreds.

"It's a little hard to remember the exact details. It was all a little overwhelming. Of course, it all came as a shock, and the last weeks have been horrible ..." I stopped talking for I realized I wasn't really saying anything. I felt myself trembling and tried hard to make my voice steady as I went on. I looked up at Mr. Fitzpatrick and I could feel the tears in my eyes. For a moment I thought I saw my obvious pain reflected in his face, but then his features took on their set look again, and I thought I might simply have been seeing things.

"Forgive me, Mr. Fitzpatrick. This is harder than I thought it would be. I'm not making much sense, I know. I'll start over. As you know, my father had a great love of horses, and for many years raised some of the finest horses in the country. Shortly before his death, he sold off almost all of his stock. I learned from his secretary, Mr. Johnson, that he was helping to set up a much needed missions hospital in Australia. My father had gone to that country as a young man and made his fortune. I think it gave him a great sense of accomplishment to help fund this project. I would have thought it would kill him to give up his horses, but he was very happy with his decision to retire from raising them. He only kept three horses—one for his carriage, his favorite, King, and Misty, the horse I had grown up riding on.

"Then one night there was an accident. My father was driving his carriage home from a neighbor's. The road is fairly rugged at one point; it goes through some woods and along a riverbank. That night, it had been raining ... he was a good horseman, but the path must have been slippery. Anyway, the carriage overturned and my father was thrown. He hit his head on a rock." My voice broke. I closed my eyes for a moment, remembering exactly how I had felt when the groom had ridden up to the house, leading the horse that carried my father's body.

I closed my eyes to try and ward off the tears that were threatening to flow. When I felt a hand on my arm, they flew open. Mr. Fitzpatrick was kneeling beside my chair with a glass.

"You sounded quite calm as you told your story, but you've gone rather pale on me. Drink this. I'd rather not have any young ladies fainting in my study, if you please."

I took a swallow and grimaced as it burned its way down my throat. I pushed the glass away and glared at the man who assumed I was planning to faint for some sort of dramatic effect.

He took the glass and smiled.

"That's better. You're not looking quite the wounded kitten anymore. Though, I must say that when one finds such an animal on the doorstep it is rarely turned away. I was a little afraid this all might turn a bit theatrical, but I can see that I may have been wrong."

I listened quietly to his little speech, but couldn't believe what I was hearing. Had he really thought I would play a part just to gain his sympathy? Before, I had thought him a little callous, but now, I wondered if he were human. I stood up rather shakily and looked him straight in the eye.

"Excuse me for appearing like a dying animal on your doorstep, but you can be sure I won't continue to appear so. I would have hoped that you could understand my obvious discomfort at having to show up unannounced to a household I know little—if anything—about.

"My father had talked about you and your uncle as being the best of men, but I can't for the life of me understand why he would have left you in charge of my estate. I won't trouble you any further, since you seem to be dreading my stay here. If you would be so kind as to have someone drop me off at the station, I will take the first train back home."

With that I turned and strode toward the door. I tried to look proud and dignified, but my mind was swirling with astonishment at what I'd just said.

"Miss Howard."

He spoke the name softly, but there was a note of steel in it. I was being commanded, albeit nicely, to stop and turn around. I did.

When I had lashed back at this man, I felt I had done so with a great amount of determination, but the look he gave me now was more determined by far. I knew then that it would be dangerous to play games with this man. The set of his jaw proved that he was quite used to getting what he wanted.

Part of me wanted to run out the door, but I knew I would have to go back and face him. I paused, indecisively, my fingers grasping the door handle. Mr. Fitzpatrick sat on the edge of the large desk and regarded me mildly. He no longer looked quite as arrogant; he was waiting to see what I would do. I slowly walked back to stand in front of him. After some moments, he spoke.

"Miss Howard, I am afraid I have judged you rather harshly. Your coming was indeed a surprise, and since I have had very little to do with young, grieving females, I'm afraid I was at a loss. Forgive me."

I wondered at his enigmatic speech. It wasn't exactly an apology, but I assumed it was all I would get. I nodded slightly and he continued.

"I understand, Miss Howard, that your father was a God-fearing gentleman. Do you share his sentiments?"

My throat tightened as I tried to find an answer to his question. My first thought was of my father and me chatting over a cup of tea, discussing the heroes of the Bible. Deep down, my trust in the Lord was strong, I knew that. But my faith had been shaken when my father had died, and I hadn't quite recovered. I chose my words carefully.

"I am a Christian, sir, though in many ways I haven't been showing my faith." I blushed slightly at the thought of my little outburst a few moments ago. "I am sorry if I was rude to you earlier. I was a little distraught. It won't happen again."

He grunted as if to say he was not so sure about that.

"Are you a God-fearing man, sir?"

He looked a little startled at the question, then his eyes narrowed and his mouth set into a firm angry line.

"I have two good friends who buy into that, but not me."

For a moment, I was looking into a face that had borne much pain. He had a haunted look.

"Is Mrs. Colton a Christian?"

"Oh no, not her. She's about as cynical as I am. She helps my perspective. She keeps Nathan and Amelia from brainwashing me too much. And you must admit that she is very beautiful. Certainly the kind of woman a man would like to have around."

Had I detected a note of sarcasm in those last words? I didn't have time to ponder that, for he spoke again.

"Now, Miss Howard, you are looking very tired. I'll have Mrs. Parks show you to your room." He rang a bell to summon the housekeeper.

"Very well, sir."

"Mrs. Colton and her cousin will be dining with us this evening."

"Yes, sir."

"I'll have a maid bring you down to the drawing room when it's almost time for dinner."

"Thank you, sir." I had decided that for the time being it would be better for me to show a little reserve until I got to know these people better. I knew I had a tendency to show my emotions in every blink of my eyes. I thought it might be better not to show what I was thinking. This whole household seemed entirely foreign to any I had ever been in, and I knew it was all due to this strange, cynical man who was its head.

"Oh, Miss Howard," Mr. Fitzpatrick said as I got up to go to the door. "I'm glad Mr. Cabot thought to send you here. Your father and my uncle were great friends and it will be the least I can do for them if I can give you a change of scenery and a chance to get over your father's death."

I could hardly comprehend the changing moods of this man. One moment he was callous, the next he was compassionate. I did not have time to do anything but stare at him, then Mrs. Parks appeared, and I followed her out of Mr. Fitzpatrick's study and up the grand staircase. She led me past several doors, and finally entered one of the rooms.

An enormous bed with a pink counterpane and dark pink pillows made the room seem smaller than it really was. The carpet was luxurious. I was disappointed that the windows did not overlook the sea, but they still gave a beautiful view of the tall graceful trees lining both sides of the front drive. I told Mrs. Parks it was beautiful, and she left me alone to unpack—not that I had too much to take care of.

My trunk was sitting by the large wardrobe, and as I opened it, I saw that my maid had packed my old Bible right on top. I was touched by the gesture. I knew I would have to find comfort within the well-worn pages—and soon. Perhaps that was the only source of the peace I longed for.

I carefully unpacked my dresses, nightgowns, and under things. I had only four dresses with me for now. One was a light green morning dress, and I had two more dresses that were appropriate for dining, one in a darker green shade, and one that was cream colored with little blue roses embroidered on it. I also had the simple gray dress I wore now. It was a sorry selection, but it was all my maid had taken time to pack. I hoped the rest of my belongings would arrive on the train tomorrow. I felt slightly guilty for not having dark colors for mourning, but I knew my father would not have wanted me to mourn for him like that.

I slipped off my shoes, washed my face, combed my hair and sat down in a pink chair that was not nearly as comfortable as it looked. I tried to imagine what would happen this evening when I was once again in the company of Mr. Fitzpatrick and his beautiful friend.

CHAPTER 2

I must have fallen asleep in the chair. I awoke to a knock at my door.

"Come in," I called, rubbing my stiff neck.

The door opened and a girl of 17 or 18 entered. She curtsied and told me in a quiet voice that her name was Sara and that she was to be my maid.

"Hello, Sara," I said as gently as I could. I noticed that the girl was almost trembling. I smiled and tried to set her at ease.

"My name is Kaitlin Howard," I said by way of introduction.

"I know, Miss. Mrs. Parks told me who you were. It was she who sent me to bring you down to supper."

"I would have waited to have you help me unpack, but as you can see, I have just a few things. The rest should come on the train tomorrow." All this I said as I took off my traveling dress. I chose to wear the dark green gown. It complemented my dark hair and blue-green eyes, and I hoped it would flatter me. Besides, even though my father would have never wanted me to wear mourning clothes, the dark color seemed appropriate.

When I pulled the dress over my head, I turned my back to the young maid. She obviously had no idea what to do, so I thought to give her a clue. She immediately set to buttoning the endless buttons. When she finished, she asked shyly, "Would you like me to fix your hair?" I simply stared at her. I couldn't believe she had had any experience.

I looked at her closely, saw the hope and fear that mingled in her eyes and then went and sat in front of the mirror.

"Do what you like," I said with another encouraging smile.

While she worked, she opened up to me and began to talk a little about herself. I found out that she had not been employed for long in the Fitzpatrick household. She told me she had a younger brother and sister and parents in the village of Oberly, just a few miles away. She asked me if I had met Mrs. Colton and Mr. Denson who would be dining here this evening. Then, she seemed to think she had overstepped her bounds and fell silent. When Sara had talked about her mother and father, I had felt a stab of pain in my chest. The pain of losing my father was fresh and new, but I could also feel a much older pain that I had lived with all my life. I had never known my mother. She had died of some type of lung disease when I was about a year old, and I remembered nothing about her. Although my father had tried to make her real to me, I found it hard to imagine what she must have been like. Sometimes when I was being stubborn, my father would say, "Ah, Kaitlin, you sound just like your mother." Even though I knew that stubbornness was not a virtue, it always comforted me to know that I was something like my mother. For the most part, I took after my father. However, I had inherited my mother's high cheekbones, and I definitely had her eyes. Sometimes I would imagine what she might have said in a certain situation. I romanticized that she had the internal strength that I often wished I had. Right now, if she were here, she would probably be telling me not to pity myself, to get on with my life.

My reminisces were interrupted when Sara sighed and said, "There, I hope you like it."

As soon as I opened my eyes, I was ashamed that I hadn't given her more credit. I couldn't believe what she had done. She had teased my dark, coarse hair into small curls which she pinned in a charming pile on top of my head. A few small strands had been allowed to escape and frame my face and fall along my jaw line and onto my neck.

"It's beautiful, Sara," I commented, "Where did you learn to do this?"

"Oh, it's nothing," she said, but she was beaming.

I admired the job she had done a second more, and then gave her a grateful smile. "Thank you, Sara. I'm ready to go down now."

Although I would never be as beautiful as Mrs. Colton, at least I thought I looked good enough not to embarrass myself in her presence.

Sara led me downstairs to the drawing room. I wished, irrationally, that she could go in with me. Mr. Fitzpatrick and Mrs. Colton were already in the room. There was another man there, too, who rose as soon as I entered and gave me a speculative look. Mrs. Colton introduced me to the man. She referred to me lightly as the "rich young orphan."

"Good evening, Miss Howard. My name is Miles Denson, Mrs. Colton's cousin. To be sure, my cousin shouldn't refer to you as an orphan. That makes you sound like a little girl; yet you are very much a woman."

"I'm pleased to meet you," I said and blushed as he took my hand and kissed it. I had lied. I could tell that I was not going to like this man one bit.

"Are Nathan and Amelia joining our little party?" Mrs. Colton asked.

My ears pricked at the mention of their names. I was looking forward to meeting these Christian people, but Mr. Fitzpatrick shook his head. "Nathan and Amelia are in London right now, visiting her mother."

"How sad," Mrs. Colton said, though what she meant seemed to be quite the opposite.

I had been so preoccupied with meeting Mr. Denson and finding out about Mr. Fitzpatrick's mystery friends that I hadn't noticed much else. Now I saw that Mr. Fitzpatrick looked quite elegant in evening dress, and Mrs. Colton was breathtaking. I knew then that even with Sara's talents I could never come close to the sort of perfect beauty Mrs. Colton possessed. I felt clumsy and dowdy just looking at her. Her blond hair and light blue eyes gave her an almost angelic look, and yet, hers was a cold sort of beauty. Although she presented an almost perfect picture, I didn't think there was much compassion or warmth in her pretty smile.

When Mr. Fitzpatrick came and offered her his arm, I

noticed that they made a striking couple, he—tall and dark, she—light-haired and slender. "Now that we're all here, shall we go in to dinner?" he said with a smile.

Mr. Denson rushed over to offer me his arm. I tried to look at him more closely without embarrassment. He was rather good-looking in a way. He also had blond hair, light eyes and a sensual smile. When he smiled at me as though he were attracted, I blushed and turned away.

Mr. Fitzpatrick sat at the head of the dining table, I sat on his right, and the cousins sat opposite me. Rarely did Mr. Denson's eyes leave my face. I found his scrutiny unnerving. He kept trying to meet my gaze, but I kept my eyes mostly fixed on my food.

Mrs. Colton carried the conversation for the most part. Mr. Denson was happy to share in the task by telling several amusing anecdotes, but Mr. Fitzpatrick was rarely drawn into the conversation. I did not know if he was usually so taciturn or if it was my presence that made him so.

"So Miss Howard is gong to be sharing this big empty house with you?" Mrs. Colton said, as if she had read the direction of my thoughts. Her words finally roused our host from his thoughtful stupor.

"Uh, yes. What with her father's death and all, her solicitor thought it would be best."

"But don't you think you should at least have your aunt come and stay with you?" she asked, smiling innocently at him.

Mr. Fitzpatrick gave her a hard look, but she just raised her eyebrows. Mr. Denson seemed to find something funny and was sniggering into his napkin.

"That might not be a bad idea," Mr. Fitzpatrick said.

"Of course," Mrs. Colton purred, "perhaps it would be even better if you had a wife to help you deal with your new responsibilities."

I finally caught on to what she was saying. She was implying that it was somehow improper for me to stay here alone with Mr. Fitzpatrick. Of all the ridiculous assumptions!

For a moment I felt pity for him, because I thought she was making him uncomfortable. Then he opened his mouth.

"It will not be a problem, as Miss Howard's solicitor, with whom I am in full agreement, has already suggested that she get married as soon as possible."

I choked on my roll and Mr. Denson nearly spit out a mouthful of water.

That man smiled a little mockingly and said, "Then allow me to be the first to put in my bid at the chance of courting her." He smiled at Mr. Fitzpatrick, then winked at me.

Mr. Fitzpatrick looked over at me and said, "We'll see."

I had been squeezing the yeast out of my roll, but now I threw it onto my plate and stood up.

"The two of you can kindly stop talking about me as if I'm not here. I am not interested in being married 'as soon as possible'—if at all—and if I was, it would be my decision to make, it would have nothing to do with you," I said firmly. I stared hard at Mr. Denson, until he looked away. I tried to do the same with Mr. Fitzpatrick, but the stubborn man continued to meet my gaze. I thought we would be stuck staring at each other indefinitely, but ironically, it was Mrs. Colton who came to my rescue.

"I think it's time the ladies retire to the library," she said. She took me by the arm and led me away from Mr. Fitzpatrick's domineering stare.

"Don't be long," she said looking back over her shoulder at Mr. Fitzpatrick.

She led us to the library and settled us on a sofa.

"I'm sorry if Miles upset you, Kaitlin. May I call you Kaitlin?"

I nodded.

"He usually has impeccable manners. It must be his attraction for you that made him speak so freely. You do forgive him, don't you?" she asked looking sideways at me.

I had calmed down since my little outburst in the dining room, and I was feeling ashamed of myself. "Of course I forgive him. But I don't really think he's that attracted to me."

"Then you must be blind. I saw the way he looked at you all through dinner. I think you would make him the perfect wife."

I took a deep breath. "I'm sorry, Mrs. Colton, but I don't think I would make anyone the *perfect* wife."

"Oh, you know what I mean. It would be so nice, wouldn't it," she said clinging to my arm, "you and Miles, Edmund and me. We could make it a double wedding."

"So, you and Mr. Fitzpatrick are planning to get married?"

"Well, Edmund isn't planning anything, but *I* am. He has been so good to me since my husband passed away.

Sooner or later, though, he will find out that he can't resist me and that he just *has* to have me as his wife."

I don't know what it was about this little speech, but for some reason it resembled a warning. She seemed to be telling me that I had better not set my sights on Mr. Fitzpatrick. Nothing could be further from my mind, I thought. Not that I could compete on her level, anyway.

"Are you sure Mr. Fitzpatrick shares your views on the subject of matrimony?" I asked innocently. A sudden glint of anger flashed in her eyes, but she controlled it.

"He'll come around," she said confidently, "though he does not get much encouragement from some quarters."

"Oh?"

"Dr. Nathan and Amelia Fenton. I don't know why Edmund bothers with them except that he and Dr. Fenton grew up together. They call themselves 'Christians,' and they're terribly prudish. They've tried to prejudice Edmund against me, but luckily he's not listened to their lies."

"Mr. Fitzpatrick told me he had friends who believed the way I do," I said, hardly believing I could be so bold.

"Oh, so you … ?" She was silent for a moment, her lips pursed. "I see. I hope I've not offended you."

"It's all right. Until a person really understands what it's like to have a personal relationship with Jesus Christ, it's hard to understand Christianity."

An awkward silence followed that statement. I couldn't quite figure Mrs. Colton out. On one hand, she seemed so arrogant and sly, yet sometimes she seemed almost unsure of herself.

I was saved from trying to continue the conversation

when the gentlemen came in. Mr. Fitzpatrick poured himself some more brandy when he came into the room. My father had never been fond of strong drink, and I was glad. It made me nervous to think that a person could drink too much and not know what they were doing.

"I see you two have been getting to know each other better," Mr. Denson said. When he spoke, Mrs. Colton rose.

"Sit here, dear Miles, and get to know Miss Howard. I think I will play for us. Do you play and sing, Miss Howard?" she asked, looking at me out of the corner of her eye.

"A little," I said.

I noticed a small pianoforte along the wall. Mrs. Colton went over and began to play softly. Mr. Fitzpatrick took a seat by Mrs. Colton.

"I haven't had a chance to say so, yet, Kaitlin, but I am so sorry about your father," Mr. Denson said. He put his hand over mine where it lay in my lap. "You must be very lonely."

I looked at his hand laying on mine and felt a rising anger. What was this man trying to do? Had they been discussing the fact that the best thing for me to do would be to get married as soon as possible? To this man? I looked over at Mr. Fitzpatrick. He was sitting by the pianoforte; his features were masked. I could not imagine what he was thinking. I looked back at Mr. Denson. He was waiting with an expectant look on his face. He had a look of innocence, but I was not deceived.

I needed to do *something* to let this man know that I was not interested in his attentions and did not appreciate his informality. I carefully removed my hand from his and stood up. I looked him squarely in the eye. My stomach churned, but I spoke as firmly as I could.

"Mr. Denson, please be assured that I appreciate your compliments but I am not interested in such attentions."

Mr. Denson rose gracefully from his seat. "Miss Howard, I am afraid you have misunderstood me. I am offering you the kindness of friendship, nothing more. I would not dream of making you uncomfortable." He smiled at me innocently and I wanted to choke. I noticed that Mr. Fitzpatrick was watching our little scene intently.

I gave Mr. Denson a weak smile and walked over to look out the window. All of a sudden, Mr. Fitzpatrick was standing next to me.

"How is your young friend doing?"

"What do you mean?" I asked. I was embarrassed, upset, and still tired from my journey.

"Has he upset you?" he asked. I could not tell by the look on his face whether he was teasing me, or whether he was concerned.

"I'm fine," I said. I made up my mind that I was not going to let suave Mr. Denson bother me. It was not as if I had to take him seriously. I hadn't realized it but Mrs. Colton had stopped playing. She came over and stood near us.

"It's a beautiful evening, isn't it?" she said, holding Mr. Fitzpatrick's arm. She looked over at me.

"My dear Kaitlin, you do look tired. We won't be offended if you leave us and go to bed."

I looked up at Mr. Fitzpatrick.

"Of course you may go to bed if you are tired."

I wanted to stay there. I didn't want to give up—retreat. But, I did.

"I guess maybe I am a little tired."

Mrs. Colton took my arm and led me over to the door.

"Try to get a good night's rest," she said.

"Thank you for your concern," I said, and I left the room without saying goodbye to either Mr. Fitzpatrick or Mr. Denson.

I was feeling very unsure of myself. I didn't understand Mr. Denson's interest in me. I supposed I was somewhat attractive. My eyes were probably my best feature—blue-green in color, and my father always said he loved my smile, but I was no real beauty. Not in the sense that Mrs. Colton was, anyway.

I changed my clothes, then lay in bed, unable to sleep. Sometime later, I heard the rumble of a carriage heading down the drive away from the house, and I knew the guests had left. A few minutes later I heard footsteps pass my door. How quiet the house is, I thought.

Finally I drifted off. I had a fitful night's rest. I dreamed mostly of my father.

CHAPTER 3

When Sara came in the next morning, I was getting dressed. It was still early and she was surprised to see me up and about. She fixed my hair and asked if I would like to breakfast downstairs or if I would like a tray in my room. I told her that I would go down for breakfast.

When I went into the dining room, I found Mr. Fitzpatrick there ahead of me. He looked up, surprised, when I came in.

"Good morning," I said.

"You're up early," he said and waved his arm toward a buffet table where I could take my pick from several dishes of food. "Help yourself."

I filled a plate and poured myself a cup of tea. When I sat down, Mr. Fitzpatrick said, "After you've finished your breakfast, I'll have Mrs. Parks show you around so you'll be able to find your way without getting lost."

"All right," I said.

He rose to go.

"Mr. Fitzpatrick?"

He paused and looked down at me—one eyebrow cocked.

"Um … Mr. Cabot said that he would be sending my luggage along today. Do you think it … well, I mean would it be possible …"

"I'll send someone along to get it."

"Thank you," I said gratefully, surprised that he had seemed to read my mind. He walked out the door, but then he stepped back into the room.

"Do you ride, Miss Howard?" he asked.

"Yes, of course," I said quickly.

"I have several horses in my stables that would be suitable for you to ride. My groom, Martin, will set you up. Feel free to ride into town or anywhere you please. There is a beautiful view from the path by the cliffs." A shadow crossed his face. "Just be careful."

"Thank you. I haven't ridden since my father's death." It was my turn to frown.

"Then you must do so without delay. Mr. Cabot sent you here to force you out of your deep depression and I can't help but think that your father would also insist that you ride."

"I'm sure he would."

He left then, and soon after, Mrs. Parks came in to see if I was ready for a tour. There were four floors, and she started on the top floor. She showed me the servant's wing and the nursery. Next, she showed me bedroom after bedroom. When I thought I was thoroughly confused, we came down the main staircase to the front hall and I finally got my bearings. Mrs. Parks took me through the large dining hall at the front of the house, through the kitchens, through a smaller eating room, and finally we were in a hallway toward the back of the house. On my left was the library. She opened the door for me and I stepped inside. It was a gorgeous room, and I loved to read. The back of the house looked out toward the ocean and the view was marvelous.

Next to the library was Mr. Fitzpatrick's study. We walked along and Mrs. Parks was leading me to a large room that led into the front drawing room, when I noticed a door next to Mr. Fitzpatrick's study.

"What's in there, Mrs. Parks?" I asked, reaching for the door handle. She quickly stepped in front of me.

"I'm sorry, Miss Howard, but that room is not used anymore—Mr. Fitzpatrick's orders."

I was perplexed, but I let her lead me into a large room overlooking the gardens and then back into the drawing room. There she left me to sit and contemplate what I would do with all the time on my hands. I finally decided to take Mr. Fitzpatrick's advice and go for a ride. I wished I had taken the time to pack riding clothes, but Mr. Cabot had whisked me away from the house so quickly I hardly had time to think straight. My gray dress would have to serve the purpose until my clothes arrived on the train. Taking an apple from the kitchen, I headed out. When I got to the stables, I saw a man working there and I assumed he must be Martin.

"Excuse me," I said nervously. The man looked up and came over to me.

"Hello, miss. My name's Martin and I'm the groom."

He sounded very nice and helpful, so I began to relax.

"Mr. Fitzpatrick said that you might find a horse for me to ride."

"Have you ridden much?" he asked.

"I'm quite an experienced rider," I told him.

"Then I have just the horse for you. His name is Spirit, and he's a fine mount. As you can tell by his name, he's a spirited horse, but I think you'll enjoy him if you've had experience with horses."

"I think he sounds perfect."

Martin saddled the horse, and I stood talking to Spirit for a while before I even tried to mount. I offered him the apple. He took a few bites, but didn't want anymore.

I patted his head. "You are a fine fellow. You won't be won over with little gifts, will you?" I said gently.

He whinnied and nudged my shoulder, and I felt he was ready for me to ride him.

Martin helped me to mount, and I walked him around the back of the stables to where I could see the sea in the distance. Spirit acted like he wanted to run, but for now, I held the reins tightly and led him to the edge of the cliffs. The wind blew in off the ocean, whipping my hair about my face. I breathed in the scent and sighed. Whether it was the refreshing air or the fact that I was riding a horse again, I don't know, but I felt more alive than I had in a long time. I kept Spirit back from the edge, but I could see that it was quite a steep drop to the rocks below. There was a large pile of rocks just to my left, and I thought that would be a nice spot to come and sit and think.

Spirit was getting restless, so I led him to a path about 20 yards inland that ran parallel to the cliff's edge. Then I let him gallop to his heart's content. There was a long stretch of rolling hills and grass before the trees got closer and closer together and we came to a small forest. I slowed Spirit, and we walked for awhile through the woods. The path went on, and I wondered where it went. Through the trees on my right, I could still see the sea. Here and there were scattered other piles of large rocks. Suddenly, I was surprised to see a small hut some distance inland. It looked uninhabitable, but I saw smoke coming from a makeshift chimney. I followed the path a little farther, until it came out of the woods, and again there was more rolling hillside. Not far away, to my left perhaps a hundred yards, was a large manor house. I wondered who lived there.

I realized then that I had been gone longer than I thought. I led Spirit back the way we came. He seemed content to trot along, and before long, we reached the house. I felt very refreshed after my ride. I took Spirit back to the stable, and Martin was there to greet me.

"How was your ride, miss?"

"Just what I needed," I said grinning. "Spirit is a wonderful horse."

"He wasn't too much for you to handle, was he?" he asked, nervously.

"Of course, not. I told you I was an experienced rider."

"Glad to hear it," he said, leading Spirit back into the stable.

I wondered why he had seemed worried about whether or not I could handle the horse. I didn't have to wonder for long. It was time for luncheon when I got back inside. Mr.

Fitzpatrick was in the hall when I came in, and he led the way to the dining room.

We had hardly started eating when Mr. Fitzpatrick asked, "Did you enjoy your ride?"

"Yes, very much. Thank you for letting me ride one of your horses."

"Martin tells me he let you ride Spirit."

"Yes, he is a fine horse."

"Are you sure you can handle him? He can have a mind of his own sometimes. I would hate to see him take off on you and run you into a tree or something."

"I'm sure that won't happen," I said feeling a little annoyed.

"You never know."

"Are you saying you don't want me to ride him?"

He looked down at his plate for a moment.

"Please forgive me, Kaitlin. I'm sure you can decide for yourself whether or not you should ride Spirit. I shouldn't be so concerned for your safety, but I feel I have a responsibility to your father to see that you are well taken care of."

"Please don't feel that way," I said, surprised at his use of my first name. I supposed that it would be silly for us to go around calling each other Mr. Fitzpatrick and Miss Howard, but I couldn't bring myself to call him Edmund, like Mrs. Colton so easily did.

"I'm afraid I must feel that way," he replied. "Your father chose to put me in control of your finances."

I didn't know what to say to that, so I chose to remain silent. Before too long, I was finished. I stood up and excused myself and went back out to get my coat.

As I had nothing else to occupy my time, and since it was a beautiful day, I decided to go for a walk. I had an idea that I might make my way into town. So far I had only seen the train station, and I was curious as to what the rest of the town looked like. I asked Martin where the town was, and he pointed out which direction to go on the main road. After I had traveled for about five minutes, I heard a rider approaching and I turned to see Mr. Denson coming. My spirits fell. After last night, he was the last person I wanted to see.

"Hello, Miss Howard. It's a beautiful day, isn't it?"

"Yes," I said and kept walking.

He jumped off his horse and started walking alongside me.

"Please allow me to apologize again for my behavior last night. I can only say that I was so distracted by your beauty that I took leave of my senses. I'm afraid I have a tendency to be arrogant and presumptuous—especially when I'm nervous."

I warmed towards him slightly at this apology. I knew *certain* people who were not nearly so sincere or eloquent when apologizing. Mr. Denson led his horse and walked beside me, telling me more about himself, wondering about me. I was worried that he would stay with me as long as I walked, so I finally turned around to head back to the house.

"I'm sorry to cut our talk short, Mr. Denson, but I think I'm going to head back. I had a nice ride this morning, and after this walk, I find that I am getting rather tired."

"Of course, of course," he said sympathetically. "Would you like me to walk you back home?"

"Oh no," I said quickly. "I wouldn't dream of holding you up from whatever business you have."

"All right, then," Mr. Denson said sadly. "I will take my leave of you now, but I hope to see you again soon."

With that, he rode off, leaving me to head back to the house alone. I hadn't lied to him. Since I hadn't been doing much since my father died, I realized that I was not used to getting so much exercise. I really was tired. By the time I reached my room, I was ready to lie down and rest. I needed to build my strength back up; I saw that now. Perhaps Mr. Cabot had been wise to send me on a little "vacation." Maybe a change of scenery and a little rest would help me to be my old self again. When I came down to the drawing room that night, Mr. Fitzpatrick greeted me with a sympathetic look.

"You'd better sit down, Kaitlin," he said. "I have some bad news."

I sat down on the sofa. He poured himself a drink.

"I sent a man into town to pick up your bags, but they did not arrive. In fact, he waited until the last train came, but your luggage was not on it."

"Mr. Cabot said he would have it sent today," I said.

"I'm afraid it must have gotten lost somewhere along the way. Perhaps it will come tomorrow."

"Yes," I said, brightening, "I'm sure it will. They must notice the mistake and send my things on, right?"

"Most likely," he said. "Until then, I'm afraid you'll have to make do. I know how you ladies are when it comes to fashion. I do hope it won't send you into an even deeper depression to not have your fancy dresses here."

I gave him a disdainful look. "I don't care that much for

clothes," I said severely. "I'm not that vain. Besides, I don't even own a very fancy dress."

That evening after dinner, Mr. Fitzpatrick asked, "Do you play chess, Kaitlin?"

His words brought back an image of my father, his forehead furrowed in concentration, staring at the game board.

"Yes, I do," I told him.

"Then let's play. It will make a long night less dreary."

He set up the chessboard and invited me to make my first move. My father was the only person I had ever played chess with, and it seemed strange to be playing against this man. My thoughts were rather distracted that first game and Mr. Fitzpatrick won easily.

"Kaitlin, you'll have to do better than that if you want to be a worthy opponent," he said with a cynical smile. I felt he was trying to bait me, so I didn't answer. Instead, I set up the pieces for a second game. That time, he didn't win quite as easily. I was glad to see he had to concentrate. At one point he said, "Well, this is more like it."

Finally, I was defeated, and we called it a night. It was nice doing something to occupy my mind. I hadn't thought of my father at all during that second game.

"Did you enjoy that?" Mr. Fitzpatrick asked as I was getting ready to go upstairs.

"Yes," I said honestly, "It was nice to do something to get my mind off . . . things."

"I know what you mean," he said enigmatically, and I went to bed.

When Sara came to my room the next morning to bring me some more wood for my fire, she informed me that Mr.

Fitzpatrick was up and gone already. Apparently he had some pressing business in London and wouldn't be home for several days. I tried not to feel disappointed that my host had left so abruptly, but the days ahead felt long and dull.

As Sara busied about getting me fresh water and pulling back my curtains, I noticed she kept looking at me out of the corner of her eye and smiling. I wondered what she was hiding. Of course, I thought, she must have had her first taste of young love. I smiled wryly to myself. I did not think I would soon share that emotion. I had not known very many young gentlemen and the behavior of many that I did know turned my stomach. It was not that I wanted for admirers. I had often had a young man trying to call on me, but it was usually because they knew my father was wealthy. I had decided not to fall in love easily. I did not want to make a foolish marriage to someone who cared only for the money I might bring him. Actually, I enjoyed my independence.

After I ate breakfast, I decided to go for another ride. The sun was shining, the birds were singing, and I was filled with a sense of hopefulness. Perhaps the change of scenery had done me good. I was no longer dwelling on the loss of my father. Instead, I was filled with an interest in my new surroundings and a desire to explore to my heart's content.

I went out to the stable and Martin saddled up Spirit. I headed off down the road in the opposite direction of the town. I wanted to save the pleasure of visiting it until later, so I headed off in search of other interesting sights.

I had ridden a good distance past small cottages and dwellings. Several of Mr. Fitzpatrick's tenants were out and about. I rode a little farther and came to another large manor house. I thought it was the house I had seen from the cliff path yesterday. I led Spirit farther along the path, when I happened to notice the dark clouds on the horizon. It looked like a storm might be brewing. I turned around to head back up the cliff path to the house. Spirit and I had just entered the wooded area when the storm began in earnest. I was a good distance from the house, and I risked getting thoroughly drenched. I did not want to spend days in bed with a cold like I had after my father's death. I had all but given up hope of not getting soaked, when I spotted the small hut I had seen the day before, just 50 yards away. Spirit picked his way carefully toward the shelter. The drops of rain were coming down harder and the wind was picking up as I dismounted and tied Spirit to a tree.

"Sorry, boy, there's no shelter for you," I said softly to the horse, patting him on the neck.

I knocked on the door of the hut, but there was no answer. The rain was coming down hard, so I tried the door. It opened easily. I stepped into a small one-room dwelling. It was obviously lived in. A fire was slowly dying on the hearth, and I welcomed the warmth. The slight chill I had felt was disappearing and my eyes were adjusting to the dim room. Curious, I looked around, trying to get some clues as to the strange person that must live here.

All of a sudden, Spirit let out a loud whinny, and I froze. Every nerve in my body screamed danger, but I wasn't sure what to do. I just knew I had to get away from this eerie place.

When I got to the door, I was shocked to see a little man untie Spirit from the tree and slap him on the back. Spirit whinnied and bucked and then raced off out of the woods, thoroughly spooked.

The little man crept over behind the woodpile. My heart was pounding wildly. The rain was still pouring, but I knew I had to get away from this place. I stepped outside and stared hard at the woodpile. Two eyes stared back at me through the wood. I took a step away from the hut. The eyes didn't move. I took a few more steps. The eyes followed me but didn't budge. I began to wonder if the little man was as afraid of me as I was of him. Then why did he spook my horse and send him running, I wondered. Was he just trying to scare away intruders? I was certainly scared.

I had been easing myself across the clearing, watching carefully to make sure the man stayed put. When I was a good distance away, where the trees grew more thickly, I began to run. I heard a cackle of laughter behind me, but no sounds of chase. I ran hard through the woods. The rain was pouring down, the sky was black, and the wind was whipping my skirts around, but I ran blindly up the path. Once out of the woods, I stopped to try and get my bearings. I looked up then and was startled by what I saw.

All around me was dark, wet, and windy. But as I looked out across the sea, I saw a slight break in the clouds, and there, on the horizon, a rainbow. It was as if God Himself spoke to me in that moment. The promise was there; a miracle in the clouds that He would never leave me or forsake me. Raw emotion threatened to overwhelm me as the tears began to fall. Salty drops mixed with raindrops and flowed down my face. It was the first time since that awful night that I had allowed myself to cry for my father. I had been afraid that if I started, I would never stop, and that fear was with me now. Eventually, the tears slowed, and I knew that though the grief had been powerful, it had not mastered me. I knew then that I would heal. I don't know how long I had been kneeling there when I heard a voice.

"Hello there," a woman called out.

I looked up to see a woman coming toward me, a worried frown on her face. In the distance, I saw a pretty little cottage.

"Are you all right?" the woman called to me. "What are you doing out here?"

She probably thinks I'm daft, I thought to myself. I struggled to my feet, hampered by my muddy skirts.

"I'm Kaitlin Howard," I said. "Thank you for your concern. My horse got away from me and I'm trying to walk home in the rain." For now I decided to leave off the part about the scary little man and the rainbow.

"I'm Ellie Singer. Let's get you indoors before you catch cold."

We stumbled together back to her little cottage. The inside was as nice as the outside. What's more, it was clean and dry. She set me down in front of the wood stove, wrapped me in a quilt, and went to change. When she came back, she was followed by a large, burly man I took to be her husband. Two sets of eyes peeped down from the stairway and I realized Mrs. Singer was a wife and a mother.

"What are you doing out on a day like this, young lady?" the big man said to me. I'm not sure what his intent was, but his tone was rather frightening.

"Hush, Jake," Mrs. Singer said. "The poor thing's horse ran away from her and she had to walk home."

"Well, if she'd have used her head, you'd wouldn't of had to gone out in the rain to fetch her," he said to his wife as though I weren't there.

"Where are you from, girl? I haven't seen you around."

"I'm staying with Mr. Fitzpatrick."

Mrs. Singer gasped and a look I couldn't quite understand passed between husband and wife.

Mr. Singer frowned. "Ah ... well," he said more kindly, "Horses can be flighty creatures. I'd best go up to the big house and let 'em know you're safe. They'll be worrying about ya if'n your horse has come back. You stay here and I'm sure they'll send someone for you in a carriage."

After he had left, Mrs. Singer busied herself getting me a cup of tea. She set it before me and said, "We had heard there was a young woman staying with Mr. Fitzpatrick, but we didn't know it was you."

I thought about my bedraggled appearance and could understand why not.

She frowned, and her eyes avoided me. "Please forgive my husband. He can be ill-tempered at times. I hope ..." she trailed off, wringing her hands nervously.

"Don't worry about it," I said putting my hand on her arm. "As far as I'm concerned, it's forgotten."

Her eyes flew to mine, a puzzled look on her face. Did she expect me to have Mr. Fitzpatrick do something to her husband because of his rudeness? As if I could!

Soon, I heard a carriage pull up. Martin, himself, had come to get me. He and Mr. Singer helped me into the carriage. Mrs. Singer had given me another dry quilt to wrap up in.

"Thank you," I told her.

Martin drove us back to the house. He helped me out at the door. Mrs. Parks met me with a disapproving look. "You worried us greatly, Miss Howard. I don't know what Mr. Fitzpatrick will say."

I had been hoping we wouldn't have to tell him.

The groom frowned at me. "Perhaps you shouldn't be riding Spirit, Miss. Perhaps he is too much for you."

"No!" I cried. "It wasn't that at all. I was in the woods looking for shelter from the rain. I had tied him to a tree, but he was startled and he came back here." It was a garbled excuse that was true—I just hadn't told them everything. I didn't know what they would think.

"Well, we can discuss that all later," Mrs. Parks said firmly. "Right now we had better get you into some dry clothes before you catch pneumonia."

I let her lead me to my room where we were met by Sara. She helped me dry off and get into clean clothes—not that I had much to choose from. She dressed me in a warm nightgown, wrapped me in a blanket and set me in front of the fire. She dried my hair as best she could and went to get me something warm to eat. She came back with hot soup, tea, and crusty bread. She helped me into bed and kept watch until I had eaten most of it.

"Now, Miss," she said, "You had better get some rest. We don't want you to catch cold."

"I don't think there is any danger of that," I said and then sneezed. She left then, a somber look on her face. I did feel rather tired; my eyes felt puffy from crying. I wondered why no one had noticed—perhaps they had been too polite to comment.

I slept soundly for a long time, only waking when Sara brought me some supper. I had developed a bit of a cough, and she piled more blankets on me and rushed off to get me something she called her mother's secret cold remedy. She was back in awhile with a warm, strong drink. It burned my throat and made me quite sleepy.

Having said that I wasn't going to catch cold, the next two days were a bit of a blur. I had a fever and Sara fussed over me like a mother hen. Between feeding me bits of soup, pouring her mother's cold remedy down my throat, and wiping my face with a cold cloth, she was very busy. Her care was wonderful, though. There was talk of calling for a doctor if I wasn't better the next morning. There seemed to be some difficulty about that. It seemed Mr. Fitzpatrick's friend was still in London, and Mrs. Parks didn't have much respect for the old man who was filling in for him.

Thanks to Sara's nursing, however, the doctor didn't need to be called and the fever broke that night. I awoke Sunday morning feeling rather groggy. It seemed ironic that now that I was feeling spiritually sound and ready to go back to church, I was unable to attend services. Sara was pleased to see the fever was gone. She fed me and brought me some more of her mother's famous medicine just to be on the safe side. Once again, I slept long and hard, rarely dreaming, wondering if I would ever wake up. When I finally opened my eyes, I knew it was evening. A few candles gave the room an eerie glow.

Just then the door opened and Mr. Fitzpatrick came right into my room. I pulled the blankets up to cover my nightgown. I tried to smooth back my hair, which lay wildly across my pillow. My cheeks felt hot, my embarrassment showing.

All I could think to say was, "You're back!"

"Yes. I see you've managed to make yourself quite ill while I was gone. I told you Spirit was not the horse for you. It's a wonder you didn't get thrown off and dash your head against a rock—" at the look on my face, he froze. "I'm sorry—I didn't ... I wasn't thinking—I didn't mean to remind you of your father. Forgive me."

Tears pricked my eyelids. "I'm all right. I think I may have gotten over pitying myself. Something about being out in that storm and seeing that rainbow reminded me that I can trust in my God—that I'm not alone."

He gave me a puzzled look, and I realized he must think I was crazy. Strangely, I felt too tired to explain.

"Whatever the case, I told Martin to find you a gentler horse. I hope you will be better soon." He turned to go.

"Please, Mr. Fitzpatrick. It wasn't Spirit's fault. I had dismounted—I wasn't holding his reins and—he was startled. That's why he ran home without me. I wasn't in any danger. If I stop riding him now, he'll wonder why. It might hurt his feelings."

Mr. Fitzpatrick grunted. "You put a lot of stock in a horse's feelings. It's just an animal."

"Well, it would hurt my feelings," I said softly.

"Fine," he said gruffly. "Just be careful. I have a duty to take care of you, and I'm not one to shirk my duty."

"I'll be careful," I said meekly.

After Mr. Fitzpatrick left, I found it hard to rest. Now that he was back, the atmosphere in the house seemed different. Just knowing he was here gave me a strange feeling in the pit of my stomach that I couldn't explain. Since I couldn't sleep, I slipped out of bed and retrieved my Bible from a drawer. I had missed so many days of reading it that I decided to do some catching up. I turned to my favorite part of scripture, the book of Psalms. As I began to find that peace I had craved for so many days, I thought of Mr. Fitzpatrick. Perhaps he was so hard to understand because he kept a mask firmly in place to hide the pain he had suffered. Now that my faith was recovering from its testing, perhaps I would be in a position to share that faith with Mr. Fitzpatrick. The first thing I would need to do was pray for him. I fell asleep that night in the midst of a long prayer time.

Late the next morning I felt well enough to get out of bed. Sara pronounced me cured, and I was thankful to be up and about. It was a chilly day, though, and I was admonished to stay indoors. Not sure what to do, I went in search of Mrs. Parks to see if she could help me find some needlepoint or something to embroider.

"Oh, well, yes, I think I can find you something to do," she said when I found her in the kitchen discussing dinner with the cook.

I followed her upstairs and down a long hallway and into a large bedroom decorated in pale blues, mauves, and creams. It was beautiful.

"This was Mrs. Fitzpatrick's bedroom. She loved to embroider." She opened a bottom drawer in one of the large cupboards, and I was astounded by the assortment of colors of thread and the various materials she had worked on. There were pillowcases, handkerchiefs, and other linens.

"Is Mrs. Fitzpatrick still living?" I asked, wondering why I had heard nothing about Mr. Fitzpatrick's family.

Mrs. Parks looked at me, surprised. "Mr. Fitzpatrick didn't tell you?" I shook my head. "Oh, well, she died about 14 years ago …" her voice trailed off.

"I'll leave you to look through these things. It would be good for you to use them; it's a waste for them to stay here," Mrs. Parks said. "Just be sure to close the door when you leave."

"All right," I said, getting down on my hands and knees to look more closely at the materials. The embroidery threads were beautiful. I chose a pair of pillowcases and a few handkerchiefs. I picked some dark colors of thread with the idea of embroidering some handkerchiefs for Mr. Fitzpatrick for a Christmas present. The pillowcases I wanted to do for myself, so I chose some yellows, light blues, and pinks for those.

Satisfied that I would be able to spend an enjoyable afternoon sewing, I went down to luncheon. I took my materials to the drawing room then went into the dining room. Cook had prepared a light luncheon with cold meat and salad. Mr. Fitzpatrick was not there; I didn't know where he had gone. After I ate, I went back to the drawing room. It took me awhile to plan what kind of design I wanted, but I was soon busy working on a handkerchief. When Sara came in a few hours later, she found me still bent over my embroidery.

"Are you feeling better?" she asked.

I smiled and nodded.

"Do you think you should rest for awhile this afternoon?"

Her motherly attitude was endearing. "I suppose it wouldn't hurt," I said, getting up and rubbing my eyes. I could use a break. I set my sewing on a small table and went up to my room. The day was bleak and dreary, but it also seemed peaceful. Rain had begun to fall, and I watched for awhile from my window until I began to feel a little sleepy. I lay down on my bed to rest for awhile and fell asleep.

When I awoke, it was growing dark, and it would soon be time for dinner. I lit a few lamps and sat down to read my Bible for awhile. Sara came in just before dinner to tell me that Mr. Fitzpatrick was wondering if I was well enough to go down to dinner. I smiled to myself. Apparently he wasn't aware that I had been up and around all day.

I grimaced as I looked at my scant wardrobe. I would have to ask Mr. Fitzpatrick if I could get a local seamstress to make me some clothes. I had never cared much for fashion, so I stared vanity in the face and chose not to change for dinner. The light green muslin dress I was wearing would do just fine.

When I came into the drawing room, Mr. Fitzpatrick was already there. He smiled and asked how I was doing. I told him I was doing fine.

"Shall we go in to dinner?" he motioned toward the door. I followed him into the dining room.

"How was your trip to London?" I asked as we started eating.

"I took care of some pressing business matters. I was

very sorry to have to leave you so soon after your arrival. You mustn't think I deserted you."

"It's not your responsibility to keep me entertained."

"I suppose not," he said with a slightly mocking grin, "but Mr. Cabot did send you here to get over your father's death. I'm afraid I do bear some of the responsibility."

"Are both of your parents gone?" I asked, changing the subject.

"Yes."

"Mrs. Parks said your mother died 14 years ago. What happened?"

"It's none of your business."

"But, I—"

"It doesn't concern you, and I'd rather not talk about it."

"It was just a simple question, yet you seem angry."

"If I seem angry, it must be your imagination. You asked a simple question, I gave a simple answer. I don't want to talk about it anymore. Eat your dinner."

Now it was my turn to be angry.

"I can't for the life of me understand why Mr. Cabot talked me into coming here. I honestly don't know if you're trying to be callous, or if that's just your normal personality."

I was surprised when he threw his head back and laughed out loud.

"Kaitlin, you don't know how good it is for me to be able to bicker with you like this. It takes my mind off my troubles."

I pursed my lips to keep from saying any more. I didn't want him to take what I said lightly, or to assume I enjoyed bickering with him. After I finished eating, I rose and would have gone into the drawing room, but Mr. Fitzpatrick stopped me.

"I got a little something for you when I was in London. It's in your room."

I stared at him, my mouth slightly open. I couldn't believe he would have thought to bring me a gift.

"Go take a look," he said, smiling at my confusion. "I want to see if you like it."

I walked upstairs and opened the door to my room. My jaw dropped open and I stared at the pile of boxes and bags on the bed. I hurried over to the bed, but I could only stare at all the packages. I heard a sound and looked up to see Sara hovering in the doorway.

"What … ? How … ?" I sputtered.

Sara grinned and came quickly to the bed. "Mr. Fitzpatrick had me give him a list of the things you'd need and your sizes. I told him I could make any alterations you might need." She looked at me shyly. "I hope that was all right …"

I nodded at her, a lump in my throat.

"Would you like to help me open these?"

We tore into the boxes like two little girls at Christmas. We found everything needed for a fabulous wardrobe—and many things that were just plain frivolous. Yards and yards of the softest lace covered the under things. At least these were somewhat practical, the several pairs of gloves and all the fancy dresses were not. There were several fashionable yet serviceable morning dresses, a riding habit and …

Evening dresses. I had never seen—let alone thought about—wearing such dresses. One was burgundy chiffon, another dark blue velvet, and so on. Perhaps my favorite was a dress in ivory satin, simply cut yet very elegant. I noticed that the colors were colors I would have picked for myself—dark blues and greens, burgundy and ivory. There were very few items in pastel colors except for under things and nightgowns. That is what I would have wanted. With my hair and skin color, pastels didn't look right.

By the time the empty boxes were piled up around us and the new clothes had been admired and put away, I was exhausted. Sara smiled when I stifled a yawn and asked if I would like her to get my bed ready.

Suddenly, I thought of Mr. Fitzpatrick.

"Oh, dear," I said aloud.

"What's wrong, miss?"

"Oh, dear, I forgot," I stammered. I must go and thank him, I thought, as I ran out of the room. I rushed down the stairs, hoping I would find him in his study. I burst in on him, not bothering to knock. I was a little out of breath, so I just stood there gaping at him for a moment. He got up and came around from behind his desk.

He grinned at me, an impish, boyish grin, and I found myself smiling back at him—even though I was embarrassed and blushing.

"May I ask if there is something wrong?" he asked with a raised eyebrow.

"Where did it all come from?" I asked.

"London," was his quick reply.

"It must have cost a fortune!"

"Not as much as it could have. Because I was in a hurry, I had to settle for many ready-to- wear items and dresses that had been made up as samples. Your maid assures me that she can make any necessary alterations."

"I'm sure she can, but it still must have been very expensive. I hope you were able to get access to my accounts to help pay for it all."

"Not yet, but Mr. Cabot assured me that would be taken care of soon. I've put some money in the bank in town for you, and the shopkeepers there will send any charges you make here to me."

"Thank you." I paused for a moment. "You know, you didn't need to go to all that trouble. I've never had such extravagant, elegant clothing. Thank you, sir," I said, my voice quavering.

He brushed aside my thanks and gave me a strange look. The boyish grin disappeared, and he seemed to remember the mask he wore.

"I was simply doing my duty," he said brusquely, and went back to sit behind his desk.

I watched him in confusion. I didn't understand what had just happened. Had I done or said something to make him mad? I didn't think so. I said thank you again, told him goodnight and left without waiting for his reply.

CHAPTER 4

"What do you have planned today?" Mr. Fitzpatrick asked when I came down to breakfast the next morning.

"I'm going to walk to town."

"You're going to walk?" he asked. "It's almost 3 miles."

"That's fine," I told him. "I'm looking forward to the exercise and the fresh air."

"Suit yourself, but you'll find it's not much of a town."

I decided to ignore his pessimism. Perhaps he was just trying to goad me into an argument. Instead, I finished my breakfast, bade him good day, and left the house. It was a long walk, and by the time the houses started getting closer and closer together, I was ready for a rest. I was annoyed that I kept finding that my body was not as strong as I thought. I decided to take a quick look at the shops and then stop at the inn for tea. There was a beautiful old church, a post office, a blacksmith, and a few other places that I didn't have any interest in. There was also a small brick building that seemed to be the bank. Later, when I had rested, I would have to go examine the church, but for now I stopped at another shop that boasted on the sign out front that it had "a little of everything." It looked as though it had just about anything one would need, from sugar, flour and other food staples, to cloth, buttons, and household items. There were also a few expensive looking ladies' hats in the front window. I looked closely at these for a few moments, and then left to go get some tea.

As I was waiting to cross the street, Mr. Denson came driving through town in an open carriage. As soon as he saw me, he pulled up and stopped.

He tipped his hat. "Good morning, Kaitlin," he said amiably.

"Good morning."

"What brings you to town this morning?"

"I was curious as to what the town was like, so I decided to take a walk."

"You walked all the way here?" he asked, surprised.

"Yes. It's not that surprising, is it?" I asked, irritated that both he and Mr. Fitzpatrick seemed to think it so shocking that I should choose to walk to town.

"No, of course not," Mr. Denson said quickly. "But you must be a little tired. Please join me for some tea at the inn. They serve wonderful scones and clotted cream."

I would have rather had tea alone, but I found myself agreeing to join him.

"All right."

"Wonderful. Give me a moment and I'll be right there." He turned his carriage around and then parked it over in front of the inn. He tied the horses to a post there. While he was doing this, I walked across the street and waited outside the inn. Soon, he joined me, offering me his arm. We walked in together, and I was aware of the sudden silence when Mr. Denson and I entered and went over to a table by the window. I thought perhaps people were wondering who the young lady was that Mr. Denson was escorting.

"Is it just me, or did it get awfully quiet in here when we walked in?" I asked when he pulled a chair out for me.

"Oh, that's how it is in a small town. An eligible bachelor walks into the local inn with a beautiful young woman they've never seen before, and of course people are going to wonder about it. Now they're probably trying to decide whether or not I'm still an eligible bachelor." He gave me a meaningful look to accompany his words.

"They probably don't know who I am," I said quietly.

"I don't know. I'm sure the servants have spread the news that Fitzpatrick has a beautiful young woman living with him."

That was the second time in about ten seconds that he had called me a "beautiful young woman" and it made me a little uncomfortable. Mr. Denson's words weren't the only thing making me uncomfortable, however. It seemed that the silence that had greeted us when we came in had disappeared. Now, everywhere I looked, people were looking at me and whispering. I wondered what they were saying, but I determined not to let it bother me. If they thought that there was anything between Mr. Denson and me, let them think it.

After we had finished our tea, Mr. Denson and I rose to leave. Again, there was silence, and I found myself curiously tempted to laugh. Instead, I meekly allowed Mr. Denson to place my hand on his arm and walk me out of the inn.

"Thank you for the tea," I said sincerely. "I was rather in need of a rest and something to eat."

"If you're still tired, I could take you home in my carriage," he said quickly.

"Oh, I'm not really tired anymore," I said vaguely. I wasn't sure if I could politely refuse a ride from him or not.

"Please, Kaitlin, allow me to take you home. I'd really appreciate the chance to get to know you better."

"Thank you, that would be … nice."

He helped me into the carriage, and then we were off. During the ride, I worried over whether or not Mr. Denson was serious in his attentions. It almost seemed as though he were trying to court me, but I was definitely not interested in this man. I just hoped I would not have to come right out and tell him that.

Before long we arrived back at the house. Mr. Denson dropped me off at the front door, and I was surprised when the door opened and Mr. Fitzpatrick stepped out.

"Was the walk too much for you?" he asked, smiling sardonically.

"No. I met Mr. Denson in town. We had tea, and he offered me a ride home. I felt it would be rude not to accept."

Mr. Fitzpatrick didn't say anything as we paused to wave at Mr. Denson as he drove away.

"It's touching that you have no qualms about being rude to me, but you don't want to hurt Mr. Denson's feelings. Am I to suppose that that man will soon be coming to ask me if he can have your hand in marriage?"

I could only stare at him, shocked at his bluntness.

"Do you really suppose Mr. Denson means to marry me?"

"Of course he wants to marry you. How can you be so naive?"

"I am not naive."

"Fine, so you're not naive. Are you falling in love with him? I'm sure he's falling in love with you."

"No, I'm not falling in love with him, and I'm not so sure he's in love with me."

"After his gallant offer to drive you home, and the way his eyes follow your every move—come now Kaitlin, you must be blind if you don't see it."

"You really think he will ask me to marry him?" I asked, suddenly unsure of myself.

"I really do. Perhaps you should accept. It would make him a very happy man."

"I told you before that I have no intention of getting married anytime soon. Besides, I don't think Mr. Denson is my idea of a good husband. I don't trust him at all."

"Amazingly enough I agree with you about that."

With that enigmatic statement, he turned and walked inside. I really wasn't hungry for luncheon, so I went into the drawing room to work on my embroidery. I couldn't concentrate, however, so I soon flung it down in disgust and went to change into my new riding habit. Martin saddled up Spirit for me, and we went for a nice long ride.

I came back, refreshed, and ready for dinner. Sara helped me change into the burgundy chiffon dress Mr. Fitzpatrick had purchased in London. She fixed my hair for me, and then I finally went downstairs.

Mr. Fitzpatrick was already waiting in the drawing room, a drink in his hand. He offered me something, but I frowned at it. "How was your afternoon?" he asked politely.

"Good," I said. "But now I'm starving."

"That must mean your appetite is back."

"Yes, I feel better than I have since my father died."

Cook had produced a delightful dinner, starting with a creamy soup. The roast and potatoes tasted delicious, and the filled pastry we had for dessert was superb. I knew I was eating a lot, but I didn't care. I had only picked at my food for weeks, and I was eating to regain my strength. After the last course, I let out a loud sigh.

"That was delicious," I said contentedly.

"If only Mr. Cabot could see you now, he wouldn't worry about you wasting away," Mr. Fitzpatrick said, chuckling.

I smiled at his joking and rose to leave the table. After a fairly busy day, I was looking forward to a relaxing evening, working on my embroidery. I decided to put the handkerchiefs aside, so that Mr. Fitzpatrick would not see what I was working on. Instead, I started to plan out what design I wanted for the pillowcases. Soon, Mr. Fitzpatrick came in. He walked over to see what I was doing, but he stopped suddenly, his face pale.

"What are you doing?" he asked, quietly. He sounded calm, but I noticed that his voice was strained, and his jaw seemed unnaturally tight.

"I'm embroidering a pillowcase," I said, not knowing where the tension was coming from.

"My mother used to do that."

"I know, these were her things. I told Mrs. Parks I was

bored and I would like to do some sewing, so she took me to your mother's old room and helped me to find some things to work on."

He didn't say anything; he just walked over and looked out the window, his body rigid. Putting my pillowcase down, I walked over to him and put my hand on his arm.

"Is it all right with you if I use these things? If it's not all right, I'll put them back," I added quickly.

He looked down at me as if he were trying to figure out who I was and what I was doing there. Suddenly, he seemed to come back to himself. He shook my hand off his arm and turned away from me.

"I don't care what you do with those things. They have nothing to do with me."

With those strange words, he left the room. My peaceful mood was gone, and I no longer cared to sew. Instead, I took my own turn looking out the window. What was wrong with Mr. Fitzpatrick? What was it that seemed to haunt him, and what did it have to do with his mother? I knew these were not questions I could go and ask him, so I was left to wonder. Finally, I left my post by the window and went upstairs. I spent a little time brushing out my hair and talking to God, and then I went to bed.

A few days later, a couple came to visit. Mr. Fitzpatrick introduced them as Dr. Nathan and Amelia Fenton. I could tell right away that I was going to like Amelia. She was blond, with freckles on her nose and a smile on her lips. Although she was very petite—the top of her head only came to my chin, I could tell she was going to have a baby. Also, I could tell her husband loved her very much. He treated her like a china doll—and that's what she reminded me of.

"Would you like some tea?" I asked, not waiting for Mr. Fitzpatrick to offer.

Amelia, for I could not think of her as Mrs. Fenton, plopped in a chair.

"I would love some, my dear. And something to eat, too. I'm starved."

"You're always starved, honey," Dr. Fenton said laughingly, putting his arm around her shoulder. "You know, she woke me up at two o'clock in the morning last night wanting me to fix her bacon and eggs," he said, smiling.

"So did you?" Mr. Fitzpatrick asked helping himself to the cakes Mrs. Parks had brought.

"Of course," Dr. Fenton smiled amiably, "I didn't think it fair to ask our housekeeper to do it. Besides, I'm a pretty good cook, and I didn't complain a bit." His wife rolled her eyes.

I studied Dr. Fenton a little more closely. He was fairly young with sandy hair and boyish good looks. I felt that Amelia was a lucky woman.

"When is the baby due?" I asked and then wondered if I was prying.

But Amelia was pleased to answer. "About three and a half months. Sometime around the middle of February, according to the Doctor there."

I smiled. How nice it would be to have a baby. Then I remembered my views towards marriage and decided this would probably be as close as I would ever come to a baby of my own.

I asked impetuously, "Can I hold him when he's born? I mean if it's a him."

I blushed at the impertinence of the question. Dr. Fenton chuckled. Mr. Fitzpatrick grinned at my embarrassment. I realized then that Mr. Fitzpatrick was acting differently now than he did when he was with Mrs. Colton. He seemed more inclined to be good-natured.

"Of course it'll be a boy," Amelia said, "handsome just like his papa." Now it was Dr. Fenton's turn to blush. "And of course you may hold him, Kaitlin. I may call you Kaitlin, mightn't I?"

"Of course you may. May I call you Amelia?"

She smiled at me and patted my arm. She looked at Dr. Fenton and gave him a sort of "See, I told you so" glance. I didn't have time to speculate on it for Dr. Fenton's next question caught my attention.

"Well, Edmund, are you coming to church with us Sunday? We'll pick you up …" The statement hung in the air. I was surprised at the change in Mr. Fitzpatrick. His upper lip curled in a snarl.

"You know better than to invite me, Nathan. I've seen too much hypocrisy in my life to want to be a part of that lie."

"I understand how you feel, Edmund, but I will keep on asking you. I don't care so much that you don't belong to a church; I just want you to have a relationship with Jesus Christ."

These words were music to my ears. "I'd like to go," I said eagerly.

At the look on Dr. Fenton's face, I went on, "If that's all right, of course."

"Yes, yes, it's all right. It's just ... I didn't think you'd want to go."

Amelia coughed.

"Why would you think I wouldn't want to go to church?"

"No reason."

"But you seemed so surprised, Dr. Fenton, why?"

The doctor blushed.

"The reason is that my husband has a big mouth," Amelia calmly explained.

"I don't understand," I said.

"I do," Mr. Fitzpatrick growled and got up to pour himself a drink. "He means that the good Christian people of the town have jumped to the conclusion that your presence in my house is anything but innocent."

"That's hardly fair, Edmund," Amelia said.

"Isn't it?" he asked, glaring at her. She finally looked away. I was torn between a desire to defend Amelia and an urge to shout at the both of them that people couldn't possibly think there was anything wrong with my staying here.

Dr. Fenton came over and sat beside me. "I'm very sorry that such rumors have started. My wife and I did what we could to dissuade them, but people generally like to believe the worst. Besides, many of the worst gossipmongers saw you come into town the other day and have tea with Mr. Denson. When they asked him who you were, he told them, and so they know that Edmund has a beautiful young woman living with him. Apparently they feel that a lady of good moral conduct—especially one whose looks arouse jealousy in the hearts of others—would not stay alone in the house of an eligible bachelor." He turned to Mr. Fitzpatrick. "I tried to tell people that you are an honorable man, Edmund."

That honorable man grunted, finished his drink and poured another.

"I'm sure they believed you," he said cynically.

Nathan came over and took the glass away from him.

"How many times have I told you you don't need this stuff?"

Mr. Fitzpatrick smacked his lips. "I like the taste. Besides, I never get drunk."

I turned away from their conversation to look at Amelia. She had a sympathetic look on her face.

"Are they ... I mean are people really saying such things about me?"

Amelia nodded slowly.

"But I haven't been here very long!"

"I'm afraid you've been here long enough for talk to have started. Anyway, I'm sure people will stop talking as soon as they meet you."

"Then I will definitely go to church with you Sunday. I do believe in Jesus, and with His help, maybe my actions can set them straight."

"Bravo, my dear," Amelia said. "That's the spirit."

"Great," Mr. Fitzpatrick said, with a little less cynicism. "Now I'm really outnumbered. What's a man to do?"

"Give in," Dr. Fenton said, dumping the contents of Mr. Fitzpatrick's drink into the fire. As I watched the flames burst and then flicker, I was happy to know I had found real friends.

CHAPTER 5

When Sunday morning came, I dressed for church with great care. I put on a simple, light blue dress Mr. Fitzpatrick had sent from London. My eyes looked very blue this morning, and I was pleased when I looked at myself in the mirror. Sara had taken great pains with my hair. I wondered if she had heard the rumors and wanted me to look good when I faced the lions.

When I went down to breakfast, Mr. Fitzpatrick was already there.

"So, you're really going, are you?" he asked as I helped myself to some eggs.

"Yes, of course. I told you before that I'm a Christian. Christians go to church to worship God, and that's just what I will be doing."

"What you will be doing is feeding the gossip."

"That doesn't matter."

I sat down and poured some tea. He put his hand on my arm. I was displeased that it made my skin tingle.

"Look," he said, "I'm saying this as your 'guardian' for your own good. Just remember that just because people go to church, it doesn't make them good."

I knew exactly what he was saying. But, I also knew that regardless of the faults of people, the church was still the best thing we had. I would let God take care of the hypocrites.

As soon as I finished breakfast, I waited in the drawing room. I was feeling a little put out. Mr. Fitzpatrick had left the breakfast table without another word. Oh well, I decided I was not going to let his dark mood spoil my day. I hardly waited for the carriage to stop before I rushed out the door. The ride to church was very pleasant. Amelia complimented me on the way I looked.

"Fresh as a spring daisy," were her exact words. Dr. Fenton just smiled at us—mostly at Amelia. He looked like a man smitten.

"How long have the two of you been married?" I asked, then wondered what it was about the couple that made me speak so freely.

"We've been married two years," Dr. Fenton said.

"And he's still head over heels in love with me," Amelia said smiling.

We arrived at the church in a short time. Dr. Fenton helped us down from the carriage. Amelia, I could see, was starting to have a little difficulty getting out of the carriage. If she hadn't been so petite, though, you might not have even known she was pregnant.

As we walked to our seats, I was painfully aware of the stares I was receiving. I wondered if the whispers referred to me. I sat down and tried to focus on the service rather than the people. It bothered me more than I liked to admit that these people were jumping to conclusions about me. I heard the sermon, but I didn't really listen to it. Instead, I spent the time praying. I prayed for wisdom, for Dr. Fenton and Amelia, but especially for Mr. Fitzpatrick. I couldn't help but think that there was something eating away at his soul. In fact, I knew it. I just didn't know what it might be. I prayed that he might find peace in a relationship with Jesus Christ.

After church, we stood outside meeting people. Amelia introduced me by saying, "This is Kaitlin Howard. She is staying with Mr. Fitzpatrick, her father's great friend."

A few times Amelia added, "I'm so glad to have met her; she's such a fine young woman."

At least *she* made me feel welcome. I could see by the looks of some of the other ladies that they were not at all glad to have met me. One woman in particular was less than pleased. She was Lady Hermione Conrad, married to Sir Percival Conrad. She had two daughters with her, and from the looks she gave me, I gathered that she had set her sights on Mr. Fitzpatrick for one of her daughters. I didn't blame her; Mr. Fitzpatrick was a very handsome man, and wealthy, too. A fine catch he would be for one of her ladyship's daughters, but as far as I was concerned, they were welcome to him. Perhaps she wanted to catch Mr. Denson for the other daughter. No wonder she stared at me with such distaste. I wanted to tell her that I had no intentions of marrying Mr. Fitzpatrick or any other eligible bachelor in the neighborhood, but I kept silent. Besides, Mrs. Colton was the one she should be worried about.

"It is so good of Mr. Fitzpatrick to look after his good

friend's daughter," Lady Conrad said to Amelia. "He is such a gentleman, isn't he, my dears?" She glanced back at her daughters and they looked slyly at me. "It would be so unfortunate if he were ever to be entangled in any type of a scandalous affair."

Amelia's nostrils flared and I could see she had a bit of a temper, but she took a deep breath and said calmly, "We both know Mr. Fitzpatrick is too fine a man to be involved in anything scandalous."

Amelia grabbed my arm and pulled me away, but not before I heard Lady Conrad say, "But women are devious creatures and have ways …"

A rushing sound in my ears cut off the rest of her comment. I was stunned beyond belief, not just that this woman thought the worst of me, but that she would be so openly—and publicly—judgmental.

Why had my father given this man control of my affairs? Why had I allowed myself to get so depressed that I had been cajoled into coming to live here? Should I leave now and go back home to put an end to the gossip? These thoughts swirled through my head as Amelia led me to the carriage. For now I supposed I would have to accept my situation and be content. At least I had found a friend in Amelia.

"Kaitlin … Kaitlin!" Amelia was calling my name.

"I'm sorry, I was just thinking."

"Are you all right?"

I looked at Amelia and saw the worry in her eyes. Dr. Fenton looked concerned as well.

"I'm fine," I said.

"It was horrible the way that woman spoke to you, my

dear." Amelia said, patting my arm. "Of course, I believe she's been pushing her daughters at Edmund so hard that she's simply jealous. But she never should have acted that way at church!"

"I know," I said. "Mr. Fitzpatrick warned me this morning that just because people went to church it didn't make them good."

"He's right, unfortunately. Oh Kaitlin, I hope someday you'll understand the pain Edmund's been through and why he acts the way he does."

"Amelia." Dr. Fenton's tone was warning, and he shot his wife a stern look.

"I know," she said. "I wasn't going to say anymore. If he wants her to know about his past then it's up to him to tell her. But Kaitlin, please help us pray for him!"

"I will," I said quietly. I was very glad that Mr. Fitzpatrick had such good friends.

When we arrived back at the house, I asked Amelia if they would like to come in for luncheon. She declined, saying she was very tired. I was sorry to see them go.

I found Mr. Fitzpatrick in his study.

"Good afternoon," I said.

"So, the weary pilgrim is back from her treacherous journey," he said sarcastically.

I knew he was only joking, but it didn't seem very funny.

"I met Lady Conrad and her daughters—do you know them?"

"Ah, yes, how unfortunate for you. Lady Conrad really dislikes me, for many reasons, but she still insists on parading her daughters in front of me at every turn. As though I would really want her for a mother-in-law. Was she civil to you? She has a serpent's tongue at times. Shall I send for my aunt in London to come play chaperone?"

I was shocked at how close he had come to the truth of the matter. "No, I wouldn't want to put anyone to any trouble. If worse comes to worse, I'll just go back home. I really am feeling much like my old self."

At this Mr. Fitzpatrick shook his head sadly. "I'm afraid Mr. Cabot sent another letter. It seems that he had some workers take a look at the roof of your house and it is in imminent danger of falling in. He's having work done on it immediately. I'm afraid it won't be inhabitable for some time."

I stared at him. "You can't be serious. Why didn't Mr. Cabot inform me of this himself?!"

He only shrugged.

"Well, I suppose I could rent a house in London for a time …" I didn't know if this would be a proper thing for a lady to do—stay in London alone. I had walked over to a window, so I had my back to him when I said this, but I could hear him make a snorting sound.

"Absolutely not. Out of the question. Your father would roll over in his grave at the thought of your going off to London alone. If what people say bothers you then I'll just have to send for my aunt to come and visit me awhile. As for my part in it, I don't want to give in to a bunch of old gossips. Let them say what they will."

I absorbed this little speech in silence, and then Mr. Fitzpatrick offered me his arm.

"I told cook we'd be having luncheon shortly after you returned, so it should be ready."

We had a nice meal, though I was preoccupied. I couldn't help but keep remembering Lady Conrad's words and the way she made me feel. How dare she believe such a thing? I mean, did the entire town assume that I had come to stay with Mr. Fitzpatrick for the express purpose of being his mistress? Or did they think I was holding out, hoping to become his wife? My father had just died for goodness' sake!

Mr. Fitzpatrick seemed to notice that my mind was elsewhere, but he made no comment. We ate most of the meal in silence. When I finished I told him I was going to take a walk. I took a light jacket, for the air was cool. I went down the path that took me to the cliff's edge. I sat on some rocks there and watched the ocean for some time. It calmed me somewhat and I felt close to God in that place. I was amazed that finally I was no longer absorbed by the death of my father. The concerns I had now were much different. Now, I was faced with a situation unlike any other I had ever been in. What was I to do? What did God want me to do? I prayed, but I didn't feel like I was getting any answers. I spent a long time in that spot, thinking, praying, and watching the waves crash against the rocks below. Finally, I made my way back to the house. I decided that there was no reason to make any hasty decisions. Perhaps things weren't as bad as I imagined.

For the next few days, I was able to forget about what happened on Sunday. I settled into a pleasant rhythm. Taking rides with Spirit in the mornings, going for long walks in the afternoons. The weather had been glorious, and I loved the rugged countryside. It was only when I was with Mr. Fitzpatrick that life was not so peaceful. He seemed preoccupied, and our dinners together were strained. I longed to ask him more about his family, to find out what was eating away at him, but I dared not. Once, we played chess again in the evening. I almost beat him that time. Still, I wondered if part of the problem was that he felt obligated to be the dutiful host, when he longed for the company of Mrs. Colton.

On Thursday, I was reading in the library, when I heard agitated voices in the hall. I came out of the room to see Mr. Denson expostulating with Mr. Fitzpatrick.

"She didn't come home for luncheon," I heard Mr. Denson say. "She's been gone for several hours now and I'm worried that something has happened to her."

He looked up and saw me then and nodded his head in a sort of greeting.

"Of course I'll help you look. Where did she go?"

"She went out riding."

They started out the door and I walked after them.

"I'm going, too."

"What do you mean?" Mr. Fitzpatrick asked.

"I'm a good rider. I want to help you look for her."

Mr. Denson took my arm. "She can come with me. I'm going to go see if she went into town. You go check the south cliff path. I came down the road and didn't see her."

Mr. Fitzpatrick looked at Mr. Denson, and then he looked at me. He seemed to be struggling with some internal problem. Then he turned in my direction. "You'll go with me. You can help me search along the cliff path."

Mr. Denson opened his mouth as if to say something, but thought better of it.

Mr. Fitzpatrick and I mounted and rode out to the back of the house. He started on along the path where he assumed Mr. Denson had left it. We traveled along in silence until I gasped.

"There!" I said.

He saw it, too. As soon as we had rounded the outcrop of rocks, I had spotted the horse, lazily munching on some grass. Before I could point out the spot of color on the ground, Mr. Fitzpatrick had whipped his horse into a gallop. I dug in my heels and followed. By the time I pulled up, he had already jumped off his horse and was kneeling at Mrs. Colton's side.

"Is she ... okay?" I asked haltingly.

"She's alive," he said breathlessly. "I'm trying to check for any broken bones."

Suddenly, her eyelashes fluttered and she stared dazedly up at him. She gave him a look of soulful admiration, but when she glanced in my direction, I could tell she was none too pleased to see me.

"What happened?" she asked, holding her face close to his.

"You have had a fall." He looked over at the offending animal. "Do you remember how it happened?"

She put her hand to her head and winced. "No, I don't."

"Well, you may have a bruise on your head for a day or two, but I think you'll be all right."

"Yes," she said. "Thank you for interrupting your ride to help me."

"When it comes to helping such a lovely lady as yourself, the pleasure is all mine."

She batted her eyelashes at him and started to get up.

"I think I can get up now." She stood, with his assistance, but when she took a step toward her horse, her ankle wouldn't support her and she toppled into his arms.

"I'm sorry," she said with a slight laugh. "I guess I'm not quite as ready as I thought. Would you be so kind as to ride and send someone back to get me in the carriage?"

"There'll be no need," Mr. Fitzpatrick said. He steadied Mrs. Colton with one arm and then mounted his horse. He reached down and pulled her onto his lap. "There's no reason for you to wait out here in the cold for a carriage when there is such an agreeable alternate means of transportation."

She batted her eyelashes at him again and smiled at this pretty speech.

I almost gagged. I had a sneaking suspicion—one that had been growing by the minute—that her ankle didn't really hurt her. No wonder she was so sorry to see me here, I thought. I had spoiled her chances of "making the best of the situation."

But then, as I followed along behind the courageous victim and the gallant rescuer, I wondered if perhaps Mrs. Colton had had a fall at all. It was wrong of me to think so, but I could not help but believe her to be the type of person who would attempt such a charade just to improve her chances of making Mr. Fitzpatrick her husband.

I suddenly felt very sorry for him. I was amazed that he did not see through her scheme, but perhaps he knew what she was doing, but was too blinded by her beauty to care. I slowed my horse and let them pull ahead. Instead of following behind them, I rode back toward the cliff path. Whether they noticed or not, I don't know, but they didn't seem to care. Spirit and I had a nice long ride, and finally I came back to the house.

The evening passed quietly, except that Mr. Fitzpatrick informed me, "Tomorrow, we'll be going out. Melinda is planning a dinner party so that you can meet more people. She's invited several ladies and gentlemen that you might like to get to know."

"Do we have to go?" I asked without thinking. I really didn't want to see any more of Mrs. Colton than I had to.

Mr. Fitzpatrick frowned. "I would have thought you would like to get out of the house and do something interesting."

I felt a little ashamed of my poor attitude. "I suppose it might be fun."

Later that night, as I was getting ready for bed, I tried to reassure myself that I would enjoy myself at Mrs. Colton's dinner party, but it didn't work very well. I kept thinking that Mr. Fitzpatrick might be right when he said that Mr. Denson was falling in love with me. If we kept getting thrown together, he was bound to proclaim his affection for me sooner or later, and I wasn't ready for that. With all this on my mind, my sleep was troubled that night.

The next morning dawned bright and beautiful, but the day seemed to pass slowly. I was looking with dread towards this night. Finally, though, it was time to get ready.

I dressed with great care that evening. Sara helped me put on the dark blue dress that Mr. Fitzpatrick had sent from

London. He had exquisite taste. The sleeves were short and slightly puffed. The square neckline made my neck look graceful. Although the skirt and bodice were covered with intricate beadwork, the effect was a simple, rich elegance that only money could produce. The color of my dress set off the color of my eyes. Sara piled my hair in curls on top of my head and let a few tendrils fall and frame my face.

"Oh Miss Howard, you look ever so pretty," Sara cried.

"Thank you," I said smiling at her. I was touched by her compliment; it gave me an added boost of courage. Standing there, admiring my appearance in the mirror, I could almost believe I could compete with Mrs. Colton. Then, the illusion was shattered and it was just me staring back from the looking glass. The elegant, sophisticated woman was gone—replaced by a lonely, nervous, little girl. I shook myself and turned away from the mirror. I knew I was being vain, so I chided myself on being so concerned with my appearance.

I opened my Bible, trying to find something to calm my fears. My fumbling fingers came across Psalm 121:1 which said, "I will lift up mine eyes unto the hills, from whence cometh my help."

If you really believed that, I told myself, you would not be so worried about tonight. I repeated it aloud to myself, but when I started down to meet Mr. Fitzpatrick in the drawing room a few minutes later there was still a large knot in my stomach. During the carriage ride, Mr. Fitzpatrick tried to put me at ease. He seemed to sense my shyness and knew I was feeling uncomfortable.

"There's no need for you to be nervous," he said lightly.

I turned from the window and tried to smile at him. My

attempt failed. My bottom lip stuck out too far, and it was more of a pout.

"Miles will be on his best behavior, and I believe Melinda is inviting several young people. I'm sure that will be nice for you. She is really trying to help you adjust, I believe."

I wondered if he really did—believe that she was trying to be helpful, that is. Of course, he was not aware of our conversation that first night, and of her implied warning.

"I'll be fine," I told Mr. Fitzpatrick, trying to sound grateful. He had certainly done more for me than my father could have expected. I appreciated the fact that he was taking me to this dinner party. *He's going because Mrs. Colton will be there*, said a voice inside my head. I pushed the thought aside and tried to give him the benefit of the doubt.

When we arrived, Mrs. Colton's butler took the navy blue wrap I had worn and led us to the drawing room. He announced us, and Mrs. Colton put her glass down and came over to greet us.

Mr. Fitzpatrick bent down to receive the kiss she placed on his cheek. Then she clasped my hands warmly and pulled me into the room.

"My, you do look pretty tonight," she drawled. "Where did you get that beautiful dress?"

I could feel myself blushing, and I didn't know why. "My clothes were supposed to be sent from home on the train, but they never made it. Mr. Fitzpatrick was able to purchase some things for me while he was in London. He'll be reimbursed though—he is seeing to my finances until I'm twenty-one."

"I see," she said. "How very kind. But you mean to tell

me you're letting him control your money?" She smiled up at him, and he rolled his eyes.

"My father felt that he could trust him, so I believe I can trust him as well."

She smiled. "Perhaps your father was not a good judge of character."

I gritted my teeth to hold in an angry retort. The evening was starting out worse than I had imagined it would. A voice at my elbow caused me to start. Mr. Denson stood there looking blond and handsome. I wondered how much he had heard. "I'm sure your father was a wonderful man, Miss Howard. Melinda, dear, don't you think you should be introducing the young lady to your other guests."

He gave his cousin a strange look that I did not quite understand.

"Of course, Miles dear. Kaitlin, come with me and you can meet all the interesting people I've invited."

She took me over to a group of young men standing by the fire.

"Miss Howard, allow me to introduce you to Mr. George Kemp, Lord Henry Jacobson, Mr. Wilmont Tuttle, and Mr. Edward Carter."

I nodded to the gentlemen, and they echoed a chorus of "Pleased to meet you's."

"Her solicitor thought it would be a good idea for her to come and stay with Mr. Fitzpatrick who is a great friend of her family. He thought it would do her good to have a change of scenery after the sudden death of her father."

The gentlemen murmured polite phrases of sympathy, and Mrs. Colton led me over to a group of women. The ladies all seemed to possess a calm superiority that only years of breeding could have accomplished. I wondered if this was something they learned from their mothers; I had never learned anything like it from my father. Mrs. Colton introduced me to Miss Priscilla and Miss Matilda Conrad (whom I had seen at church on Sunday), Miss Harriet Spencer, and Miss Leona Birch—she alone seemed a little unsure of herself. They all wished me well and offered sympathy for my loss. When Mrs. Colton's butler came to announce that dinner was ready, she latched onto Mr. Fitzpatrick's arm and led the way to the dining room.

While she was directing everyone where to sit, I had time for a quickly whispered conversation with Mr. Fitzpatrick.

"Why aren't Nathan and Amelia here?" I asked.

"Melinda doesn't get along very well with Amelia. Besides, she wanted to introduce you to several 'eligible' men, and Nathan is hardly that."

"Well, why even invite the ladies then? Why not just invite the gentlemen and auction me off to the highest bidder?" I regretted my comment and my sarcastic tone almost immediately. I should have known he would resent criticism of his beautiful "Melinda."

"She is trying to do you a favor by having this party for you. The least you could do is act like you're enjoying yourself and be a little more appreciative," he said sternly. His tone was that of an adult to a spoiled child. Was I acting like a spoiled child, I wondered?

Mrs. Colton directed me to a chair between Mr. Denson and Mr. Wilmont Tuttle. The name itself would have been bad enough, but Mr. Tuttle had the appearance and personality to go with it. Mrs. Colton had informed me that he was a banker, and he definitely looked like one. He couldn't have been more than thirty, but the fair, reddish-gold hair on the top of his head was thinning. His round face was spattered with freckles.

After talking with Mr. Denson for a few minutes, I caught Mr. Fitzpatrick's eye. The look he gave me was mocking and speculative to say the least. Since I didn't want him to think he was right about that man supposedly being in love with me, I tried to turn my attention toward Mr. Tuttle. He was pleased, and he beamed at me from behind his thick spectacles.

The first course was a delicious soup. Mr. Tuttle sipped his soup for a couple of minutes and then turned to me again.

"I'm sorry about your father, Miss Howard," he said amiably.

"I appreciate your concern," I said, staring at my soup. I was worried that a man like Mr. Tuttle would feel it his duty to immediately propose matrimony to someone in "my state." I was pleasantly surprised when instead he remarked, "I'm glad that your father left you so well off. Your solicitor and Mr. Fitzpatrick have authorized three hundred pounds to be at your disposal at my bank in town."

"Such a large sum! Thank you, Mr. Tuttle, I am pleased to hear that."

He took his glasses off and polished them nervously. "I'm glad you are well off, my dear. You can afford to be much more careful with the choices you make—if you know what I mean."

"I suppose I do," I said vaguely. I was surprised at his almost grandfatherly advice.

I turned my attention back to my soup. Mrs. Colton had been eavesdropping on my conversation with Mr. Tuttle, though, and she spoke loudly to the table.

"Mr. Tuttle is right. Miss Howard is a very wealthy woman. She should be very careful in her choice of suitors." She looked pointedly at the gentlemen around the table then broke into jovial laughter.

"But dear Miss Howard doesn't need to worry about any of you, does she? I didn't invite any wolves to my table tonight, did I?" She smiled at each of the gentlemen, enjoying her little joke.

Mr. Tuttle blushed; Mr. Fitzpatrick looked uncomfortable—or maybe he was just bored. Mr. Denson lifted his glass in a mock toast to his cousin.

"You are indeed a jovial hostess, my dear Melinda, but there's no need to worry Miss Howard. I for one am very well off—she needn't fear that I'm after her money, only her heart."

He fixed me with such an angelic, soulful stare that I couldn't help but laugh out loud. Mr. Denson frowned. I'm sure he wasn't used to having his flirtations taken so lightly, but I just couldn't help it. I really didn't think he was serious. I giggled a little more then became serious when I feared Mr. Denson's pride might be hurt. Already the other gentlemen were hiding their smiles behind their napkins. Mr. Fitzpatrick had raised an eyebrow at my outburst then the corner of his mouth had twitched in what might have been the beginning of a smile—or a snarl.

After that, dinner conversation was scant. I ate in cha-
grined silence. I knew that it was my fault that there was
such a strained atmosphere. Mr. Fitzpatrick had specifically
asked me to attempt to be sociable and I had definitely let
him down. I would have to try and do better if given the
chance.

Finally, dinner was over and Mrs. Colton directed the
ladies to the drawing room. Once there, I sought out Leona
Birch. She struck me as someone who might need a friend,
and I thought she might be nice to visit with. I asked some
questions about her family, but she answered with so few
words and in such a quiet voice that I gave up after a while.

For the moment Mrs. Colton ignored me, and I was
glad. I did not want to be under her scrutiny. Instead, I sat
and listened to the other ladies discuss the gentlemen, the
fashions, and local gossip. Every once in awhile, they would
try to include me in the conversation, but I answered them
much the way Leona Birch had talked to me earlier.

Before long, the gentlemen joined us. Mr. Denson rushed
over and sat down in a chair near me. Would he never give
up? I wondered, agitated. Not surprisingly, Mr. Fitzpatrick
went over to sit near Mrs. Colton. Soon the maid brought
us coffee, and after the coffee had been poured and the maid
was gone, Mrs. Colton rose to address the company.

"You know," she said, looking conspiratorially at the
other ladies, "I think it's time we all get to know Miss Howard a little better. Would you like to tell us something about
yourself?" she asked.

"There's not much to tell," I said quietly.

"Oh, come now, dear. You're living quite a colorful life."

THESE *Rugged* CLIFFS

She chuckled and looked at Mr. Fitzpatrick. "I mean, she's staying there with Edmund all alone in that great big house," she said with an expressive look at the other ladies. I could feel my cheeks turn red. I wanted to slap her across the face and storm out of the room, but I could do no such thing. The ladies all twittered with laughter and I wondered why they were so spiteful. Perhaps they saw me as some sort of competition for a husband, and they were trying to turn me into a laughing stock.

Some of the gentlemen had the grace to look uncomfortable, and Mr. Denson gave his cousin a look of mild reproach. I didn't want to look at Mr. Fitzpatrick. I didn't want to know if he was uncomfortable, or enjoying my discomfort—laughing along with them. Finally, I decided to hazard a look at him, but that didn't help. His face was inscrutable. The mask was firmly in place.

I thought she was done tormenting me. Instead, she picked up her fan, pointed it at my dress and said with mock sincerity, "What a beautiful dress, my dear. Do you know where she got it?" she asked the group of ladies. "I had to squeeze it out of her earlier. She blushed most prettily and told me that Mr. Fitzpatrick had picked it out in London— along with the rest of her wardrobe. I didn't know he had such good taste. My dear, whatever have you done to deserve such clothes? And she calls herself a Christian," she added as an afterthought. A couple of the gentlemen had the decency to look shocked. Whether at her impertinence or at what they thought me to be, I didn't know.

For a moment I was stunned into silence. I didn't know what to say. Finally, I calmly replied, "Mrs. Colton, you know that all my clothes were supposed to be sent here by train, but they never made it. Mr. Fitzpatrick was nice enough to buy me some things to wear. He will certainly be repaid when my finances are settled."

She didn't say anything more to me. Instead, she turned to the lady sitting next to her, Priscilla Conrad, and whispered something. Miss Conrad laughed and then whispered it to her sister.

Mr. Fitzpatrick stood up. "I believe my guest and I have had enough fun and gaiety for one night. Miss Howard, are you ready to go home?"

"Leaving so soon, Edmund?" Mrs. Colton asked, rising and going over to place her hand on his arm.

"Yes, I'm afraid we must," he said, coming over to take my arm.

"Well, then. Perhaps you can come back later after my guests have all gone," she whispered for only him and me to hear. The look she gave him implied that this was a common occurrence. He gave her a long look, but didn't say anything.

He took my arm and led me out of the room and toward the carriage. His grip on my arm was painful, and when I tripped getting into the carriage and his hand tightened, I cried out. He looked down at me almost absently, and loosened his grip.

"How foolish of me. Are you hurt?"

"No, I'll be fine," I said rubbing my arm, tears springing to my eyes.

He helped me into the carriage much more gently and then got in himself. We rode on in silence for awhile.

Finally, he spoke. "You shouldn't take Melinda's teasing too seriously."

"You mean the part about *my* being your mistress or *her* being your mistress?" I asked boldly.

He looked at me with distaste. "She was just being catty. Consequently," he said, as if it somehow mattered, "what she implied about my visiting her after her guests leave was part of her little joke. We, uh, do not have that kind of relationship."

"I'm glad to hear it," I said rather snappishly. I would have been more pleased if I felt I could really believe him. We rode along in silence for a few minutes, he sitting in cold silence, I looking out the window on the moonlit scene. Suddenly I noticed an old barn I had seen during my travels. It was situated about a quarter of a mile from the house at the top of a small knoll. It was a large old building, and it looked in the moonlight, both grotesque and picturesque.

"What's that old barn used for?" I asked, pointing out the window.

Mr. Fitzpatrick leaned forward and looked out. "Nothing, now. It's pretty run down."

"Well, I can see that. What did it used to be used for?"

"It used to be used for the farmers to store grain, feed, tools, and other things. Now, there are several smaller barns around the estate that serve the same purpose."

I found it uncomfortable even to talk about such a mundane subject as a barn, so I didn't bother to make conversation. Instead, we rode on in silence. We arrived home very shortly, and I was glad to be able to get away from him.

CHAPTER 6

When Nathan and Amelia picked me up for church on Sunday, I could tell something was wrong. From the moment I climbed into the doctor's carriage, I could sense the tension.

"Is something wrong?" I asked bluntly.

Amelia looked away. Nathan concentrated on the reigns.

"Not really," Amelia said quietly.

I saw Nathan's quick glance at her and I knew she wasn't telling me everything.

"Amelia was shopping in town yesterday and ..." Nathan said through clenched teeth. "Tell her what you told me. She has a right to know."

Amelia glanced at me then looked down. "There were some ladies talking while I was there. I think one of them might have been one of Lady Conrad's servants. They were discussing your wardrobe—the clothes Edmund bought you in London. It seems that gossip keeps spreading that the reasons for his interest in you are anything but innocent."

Amelia looked up at me, and for a moment I feared that she was being swayed by the gossip.

"My clothes never made it here. They were to be sent on the train, but they were lost somehow. When Mr. Fitzpatrick went to London, he bought some clothes for me. He will be reimbursed though. It was a very nice gesture, but I assure you not payment for services rendered."

Amelia flinched at the sarcasm in my voice. She looked up at me with tears in her eyes.

"Oh, Kaitlin! I didn't really believe them!"

She flung her arms around me and I hugged her tightly. I had never had a close female friend, and I was thankful that I had one now.

If I had thought the whispers were bad last week, the icy stares I received when I entered the church today were much worse. We sat down and a few bold women continued to stare. Lady Conrad was one of them. One of her daughters looked pointedly at my dress, whispered to her sister, and they both started snickering. What was worse—Lady Conrad glared at Amelia. My dear friend simply ignored her.

Before the service started, I whispered, "I'm glad you're brave enough to sit by me. I seem to be something of a social pariah."

Amelia reached down and grasped my hand. "As far as I'm concerned, gossip is one of the deadliest sins," she whispered back.

I tried to listen to the Pastor's words, but I was too distracted. After the service, Mrs. Stevens, the Pastor's wife, made a point of coming over to talk to me.

"We would love to have you over for dinner some Sunday, Miss Howard,"

"Thank you," I said graciously. I was grateful that this woman, at least, was untouched by the rumors that were flying about. Out of the corner of my eye, I saw Lady Conrad and a group of ladies approaching.

"Before long, we'll be decorating the church for the Christmas season. We'd love to have you help us," Mrs. Stevens said kindly.

Lady Conrad stopped in front of us. "Are you sure that would be wise, Millie?" she said.

"What do you mean?" Mrs. Stevens asked innocently.

"Would you let loose a viper amongst our innocent lambs? Can you be sure what influence this harlot would have on the young ladies of this church? Do you really think it wise that you should associate with her? I, for one, will not. In fact," she said in a low growling voice, "I could make it very bad for you if you do."

With that, she turned her back on us, as did the women with her. Mrs. Stevens gave me a baffled look—unsure how to handle the situation. I didn't want her to be stuck in the middle of something like this.

"Please tell Amelia I'm going to walk home," I said quietly.

I didn't stay and defend myself or stand up to them; I just walked away. A few moments later, Amelia called after me. I ignored her and kept walking. In her condition, I didn't expect her to run to catch up with me, and I was glad. I wanted to be alone.

I tried to sort out in my mind what had happened.

Simply because my clothes had been lost and Mr. Fitzpatrick had chivalrously provided for me people assumed the worst. My reputation was shattered. As far as these people were concerned, my presence in church was a horrible act of hypocrisy.

Tears began streaming down my face as I relived the morning's events. What was I going to do? I obviously couldn't stay here any longer. I didn't relish the idea of telling Mr. Fitzpatrick about this. What would he say? It would be terribly embarrassing just to discuss it with him.

My head hurt by the time I was getting closer to the house. As I came over a hill, and I could just see the house, I noticed Nathan and Amelia's carriage parked out front. I froze. I didn't want to face them right now. Just then, they came outside and got into the carriage. Off they went without looking in my direction. I was thankful. Mr. Fitzpatrick stood and watched them leave. Then I thought he turned and looked right at me. When he turned and went back inside without acting like he saw me, I assumed I had been mistaken.

When I went into the house, my plan was to slip upstairs unnoticed. My dress was dirty, my hair windblown, my eyes puffy from crying. As soon as I started up the stairs, Mr. Fitzpatrick came out of the dining room.

"Kaitlin," he called to me.

I kept going up the steps as though I hadn't heard him.

"Kaitlin!" he called again.

This time I picked up my skirts and ran the rest of the way up the stairs and to my room. It was a childish gesture, I knew. Once inside my room, I tried to compose myself. A few minutes later there was a knock on the door and Sara called, "It's me, Miss."

When I let her in she said, "Mr. Fitzpatrick said cook's been holding luncheon for you. He said you was to come right away!"

She was certainly overexcited. I wondered if he had been angry when he sent her up to get me.

"Very well," I told her, "I'll be right down."

No time to change my dress, I thought, so I did my best to pat my hair into place. It still looked very much like I had been crying. When I came downstairs, he was waiting in the hall. I scanned his features to see if he looked angry, but I couldn't tell. My stomach was churning when he led the way to the dining room. I tried to eat, but I truly wasn't hungry. Mr. Fitzpatrick seemed preoccupied, as well. Perhaps he was as uncomfortable as I with the thought of discussing the rumors. Not once did he mention Nathan and Amelia's visit or my walk home. And, as far as I was concerned, if he wasn't going to bring up the subject, neither was I.

As we finished eating, I said, "I'm not feeling very well. I think I'll go up to my room and lie down."

"Kaitlin," he said, as I was leaving the room. I turned, sure that he would say something about Nathan and Amelia's visit, dreading the conversation. Instead, he shook his head. "Never mind. It can wait until you are feeling better."

I went upstairs then, wondering if I would ever feel better.

Although I would have liked to spend the afternoon resting, I found myself pacing around the room instead. Finally, my energy felt sapped from the crying and the worrying and I lay down and slept fitfully for a time. Sara came to fix my hair before I went down to dinner, and even though she didn't say much, I was grateful for the company.

As I came down the stairs, I caught sight of Mr. Denson and Mrs. Colton going out the front door. What could they have come over for? Perhaps I didn't want to know.

I found Mr. Fitzpatrick in the drawing room. He was refilling a glass of brandy and I felt a pang of sadness at the fact that he should want to.

"Good evening, Kaitlin—I haven't called you 'Miss Howard' for a while now. You don't mind, do you?"

"Kaitlin is fine," I said, wondering what kind of mood he was in.

"And you must call me Edmund," he said.

"I'll try."

"Good. Tonight I thought we'd dine in the morning room, if you don't mind. It's not so formal."

"That would be fine," I said, as Jeffries came in to announce dinner. He led us to a lovely room toward the back of the house. It lay on the adjacent side from the dining room, with the kitchen lying between the two rooms for easy access to either. The room was decorated in soft cream colors with light blue accents.

"It's lovely," I breathed, as Mr. Fitzpatrick—I must try to think of him as Edmund—seated me in a chair at the small table.

Edmund did his best to put aside his tendencies towards cynicism and sarcasm. He was jovial and flippant; his manner much changed from this afternoon at luncheon.

"Did something happen this afternoon to affect your mood?" I asked abruptly.

He set down his knife and fork and looked at me keenly.

"As a matter of fact, as you 'rested' this afternoon, I had the pleasure of a visit from Melinda and Miles."

"I saw them leave," I said dully.

"You're not particularly fond of young Miles, huh? Well then, I won't tell you of our conversation until after we eat. You might lose your appetite."

It was too late. Something in the tone of his voice told me I was not going to like what he had to say. I no longer wanted my food.

"I'm not hungry anymore. I'd like to know what went on this afternoon."

"You will permit me, at least, to finish *my* dinner, won't you?" he said and grinned at me.

I couldn't understand this vexing delight he took in teasing me. I suppose it was only human for him to try and get some enjoyment out of a situation that must be very tiresome to him. I sat and tried to wait patiently. While I fidgeted, I remembered Amelia's words to me in the carriage. "Help us pray for him," she had said. I tried to do that while I waited for him to finish eating.

However, it wasn't easy. I think he savored every bite just to try to annoy me.

Finally he stood up and asked me to follow him to his study. I had a nervous, fluttery feeling in the pit of my stomach, but I didn't know why. I followed him into his study and sat down in the chair he pointed to. He sat behind his desk. I was struck suddenly by the feeling that this had all happened before. I had already undergone one interrogation, and I didn't like to think I was in for another. Uneasy, I wondered why I felt like a lazy maid about to be dismissed.

He got up and came to lean against the corner of his desk. I had to tilt my head back to see his face. I waited while he poured a drink from the decanter on the table. It was a gesture of habit, for when he looked at the glass, he frowned and set it back down.

Still, I waited—finally, he spoke.

"Perhaps you are wondering why Nathan and Amelia stopped by after church. They stopped to tell me that you had walked home. They said Lady Conrad had been rude to you again, and Mrs. Colton and Mr. Denson came by to let me know that Lady Conrad had visited them, spreading rumors. Nathan apologized that you had been treated so rudely today, but I guess no one expects my 'mistress' to come to church."

I was startled by this concise, and blunt, rendition of events.

"I see," I said quietly, my face crimson.

"Nathan feels that the situation is forcing you to compromise your Christian values, and he and Amelia feel that this bothers you very much. Do the rumors bother you? Are you upset that your reputation is ruined?" He asked, looking closely at me.

"I don't know." He stared at me until, embarrassed, I looked away.

"Melinda and Miles were also concerned about your reputation."

"They were?" I asked.

"They came by to express their deepest sympathy for the intolerable way that people have been slandering your name, and to offer their wish to be of any possible service. It's funny, you know, that no one says much about me. *My* name, apparently, is not being slandered, but then, I guess it's only natural for a man to behave any way he wants to.

"Anyway," he continued, "they informed me that the only way to salvage your reputation would be for me to see to it that you were married."

I made an unladylike snort. It was so nice of Mrs. Colton to want to help me when the rumors had probably started because of her, I thought sarcastically.

"So, Miles has consented to be your savior and has asked for your hand in marriage."

I made an even more unladylike sound and stood up.

"What did you tell him?" I choked as I began to pace back and forth.

"I told him that I agreed that you should get married and that I would ask you about it."

I stopped and stared at him. I felt my control slipping a little.

"You said what?! I told you that I have no intention of marrying anyone, let alone a worm like Mr. Denson."

"I see. Well, you have quite ruined their plans. I think what they would have liked was a double wedding. You and Mr. Denson. Melinda and me."

"You've got to be kidding," I said in disgust. "I don't care what you do, but I will not marry Mr. Denson."

"That's fine with me. As for my part, I have no intention

of marrying Melinda. She may be nice to look at, but I don't believe she's at all the sort of woman for me. You see, it's not that she loves *me*, it's my money she finds so attractive. And, I have a pretty good idea that that's how Mr. Denson feels about you."

"I can believe that," I said. "But why then did you agree with him that I should get married?"

Edmund smiled. "I agreed that you should get married, but not necessarily that you should marry *him*. I already have in mind the perfect man."

"Who?" I asked cautiously.

"Me."

The word hung in the air. I found it hard to breathe. This man knew how I felt about marriage, and yet he still proposed such an outrageous idea.

"But why?"

"Because, my dear, even if you haven't realized it yet, it would be a perfect solution to both our problems. You would no longer be considered a social outcast, and you could have all the freedom and independence you want in the marriage. I, on the other hand, would be free from fortune hunters and the Lady Conrad's of the world. I could finally go out in public without the fear of having to sit and listen to hordes of doting mamas proclaiming the virtues of their daughters.

"So you see the arrangement would benefit us both. We could go on as companionably as we are now."

I sat in stunned silence. There were a million questions that flooded my mind, but I blurted out, "What will you do for an heir? Children, I mean."

He grinned impishly when I blushed. "I can assure you

that I am in no hurry to have a child, unless you wish to provide me with an heir right away?" At the look on my face, he went on, "Who knows what the future may hold. If I have to, I'll leave everything to my cousin's son. He's a nice little chap."

He poured a bit of brandy into a glass and offered it to me. I shook my head no.

"Kaitlin, I know this must be a shock to you. You haven't refused me outright, though, so you must be considering it. Are you sure you're all right? You do look pale."

"I'm fine," I said and tried to convince myself of it. I was shocked that I was even considering the idea. It would solve a lot of my problems. No one would ever bother me about getting married. I would be more independent and have more freedom as Mrs. Fitzpatrick than I would ever have as Miss Howard. And I wouldn't have to worry what people were saying.

"What shall I do when my house is fit to live in again?"

"That will be up to you, though I believe Amelia would sorely miss you."

"But why would you agree to such an outrageous thing?" I asked him.

"I told you before that my motives are purely selfish. I've never wanted to be a family man in the conventional sense of the word, and I have no doubt that I would make a poor husband to any woman who loved me—I did not have a very good role model. This plan would let me be married without having to worry about either of those points."

"I'd like some time to … pray about it."

"Certainly. You can tell me in the morning. I'll have to get a special license, but I think we can be married soon."

When I was silent, he said, "I've thought a lot about this, and I think it's the best thing for you to do. It's what your father would have wanted."

At the mention of my father, I knew I was going to cry.

"I'll let you know my decision in the morning," I said as I hurried out of the room. The tears were flowing quite heavily by the time I reached my door. I shut and locked it and threw myself on my bed.

I couldn't believe everything that had happened in the past weeks. I cried for my father's loss and because I didn't know what to do now. I tried to pray, but it was hard. My mind seemed too confused to listen for that still small voice. What did God want me to do?

CHAPTER 7

When I tried to go to bed that night, I could not. Mr. Fitzpatrick's proposal was still fresh in my mind. It was late, but I
knew I would not sleep. So, I lit a lamp and went in search of
a book in the library—anything to keep from having to make
a decision—for I had not yet decided what I should do.

Earlier, Sara had come to tell me that Mr. Fitzpatrick
had gone out and would not be back until late. I wondered
where he had gone. And, as I made my way through the dark
house, I wished he had not left. I determined not to think
of where he might be. It made me uneasy to imagine he was
visiting Mrs. Colton.

I found the library with no problem. It was right next to
the study. Curiosity caused me to check and see if perhaps
Mr. Fitzpatrick (I *must* try and think of him as Edmund) was
in his study. He was not. Having been courageous thus far,
I remembered there had been a room next to the study that
Mrs. Parks had not shown me.

Tonight, I decided, I would visit the room, alone.

I held the candle close to the wall as I looked for the door. It was not hard to find, and it was not locked. Turning the handle cautiously, I slowly entered the room. What I first noticed was the smell. I didn't think the room had been properly aired for some time. Next, I lit a few of the candles that were still in place around the room.

As soon as my eyes became accustomed to the dim light, I noticed the picture hanging above the mantelpiece. The woman was beautiful, even more so than Mrs. Colton. I knew from the blue eyes and the set of the jaw that this must be Edmund's mother. She had creamy white skin, and the black hair piled high on her head accented her high cheekbones and aquiline nose.

I wondered what such a beautiful picture was doing shut away in an unused room.

Then, I saw it—a large ivory colored piano set in one corner of the room. It matched perfectly with the pale yellows, blues, and greens that were everywhere. I pulled back the pale yellow curtains that covered one of the windows and tried to lift up the sash. It slid up with a little effort.

A gust of wind and rain billowed in and I breathed in the salty scent of the sea. A crash of thunder startled me, and I closed the window until there was just a breeze and then went to sit at the piano. I had always played for my father when he was alive, but I hadn't played since his death. He had been my audience—I didn't want any other one. My fingers ached to play this beautiful instrument and I cautiously tapped out a tune.

When Mrs. Colton had asked if I could play and sing, I had said "a little." That was only half true. I could sing only a little, but I loved to play. Perhaps I was not as good as she, but my father used to say there was no one whom he would rather listen to.

Soon I was lost in the haunting melody that my father loved. I kept playing it over and over again. It was as if as long as I kept playing the tune, my father would be close by. Tears were streaming down my face, and my fingers had begun to hurt, but I could not stop.

"Kaitlin."

The name was spoken softly, but it startled me and I swung around.

Edmund was standing next to me, his face a cloudy mixture of emotion. I quickly tried to get hold of myself. I wiped my eyes with the back of my hand, but it did not help, the tears were still flowing. I was unreasonably angry with him for being a witness to my pain.

Edmund took my face in his hands and gently wiped away the tears that were rolling down my face.

"I didn't know you could play," he said softly.

"I used to play for my father."

"I see." I looked up at his face. The emotion I had seen was gone. The mask was back in place. He stood up and walked over to look at the picture on the wall. His body tensed and he turned around.

"Why did you come in here?" he asked. The emotion missing from his face was there in his voice.

"I ... couldn't sleep. I was looking for a book."

"This is not the library," he said sarcastically. He made a sweeping gesture with his arm. "This was my mother's favorite room. She decorated it herself. That's a picture of her on the wall."

"She's beautiful."

"You mean she *was* beautiful." He paused for a minute, gazing at the picture, his head cocked to one side. "Yes, she was, wasn't she. She was a wonderful woman."

He looked at me suddenly, a piercing stare that went right through me.

"You know, Christianity is not a new concept for me. My mother claimed to be a Christian, though I'll never know for sure if she was a horrible hypocrite or the victim of an unspeakable act of violence."

He came back over and sat on the edge of the piano bench and looked into my face.

"I don't like this room. It's beautiful, but it holds too many ugly memories."

"What do you mean?"

He didn't answer.

"Tell me, Edmund. Why do you have such a hatred of Christianity?"

He looked down at me with cold dislike.

"I learned very early that people can say one thing and do another. And even in the midst of the teachings of God, there can be pure evil. You wouldn't understand that. You've lived a sheltered life. You've learned to trust people and that's good. But I haven't." He took a deep breath, "And I don't know if I ever will. Yes, I'm cynical, but that's what your Christianity has done for me."

"How do you feel about God?"

His eyes sparkled with some strange emotion and he

lifted his lip in a grimace. "God? I learned a long time ago that if there was a God, He didn't care about my mother and He didn't care about me. It's much easier to believe that He doesn't exist than to believe that He doesn't care—or worse, that He has enjoyed my pain."

I didn't know what to say. I realized now that something horrible must have happened in his past to give him such an outlook. My heart ached for him and it must have shown in my face.

He stood up quickly and glared down at me.

"Don't look at me like that! I don't need or want your pity." I stood up and put my hand on his arm.

"Edmund, how can you propose to marry me when you don't even like me?" And why am I even considering accepting, I added silently to myself?

When I had spoken the words, the anger went out of him. He ran his fingers through his hair.

"I'm sorry, Kaitlin. You're not the one I'm mad at. I shouldn't be taking it out on you. It's just … the people I'd like to take it out on are dead."

"It's all right," I said.

"No, it's not, but that just shows you why I wouldn't make a good family man." He paused. "I suppose when we're married you'll want to use this room." He walked over and pulled a dust cloth off a chair. I gave a slightly hysterical little laugh at the incongruity of his last two sentences.

"You would let me use this room?" I asked, trying to stay focused on the conversation.

He shrugged. "Why not? The memories are going to haunt me no matter where I am."

"Please tell me."

"No. I'm afraid I can't do that. Some things are better left unsaid. Just be glad your father died an innocent death."

With that he turned and left the room. I was puzzled by the entire conversation. He surely did not act like a man trying to woo a bride. I could hardly even remember his reasons as to why it would be a good idea.

How could I possibly marry a man like this? How could I even think about it? I went upstairs and knelt by my bed.

Dear God, I prayed, *help me to know your will in this situation. Part of me feels that this man needs me—that he's drowning and that the love of Jesus is the only thing that can save him. With your help I could show him that love, but I'm scared. I don't know what kind of a man he really is. While part of me wants to run as far and as fast as I can, another part wants to go through with this irrational, illogical scheme. But how can I go through with this when I have so much doubt?*

Suddenly and inexplicably I heard the words—*give it to God.* At that point, I came to a decision. I got into bed, and amazingly, quickly fell fast asleep.

When I awoke the next morning, it was with a clear sense of determination. I prayed for wisdom and guidance, but found no answer other than the one already in mind. Though it may have been ludicrous, I couldn't help but think that Edmund needed me, that he needed to see what being a Christian meant. I would try my best, with God's help, to show him.

I found him in the dining room. At the sight of him bent over his eggs, my heart started pounding wildly. My brain told my feet to walk into the room, but they would not obey. In fact, they wanted to run the other way. Finally, he looked up.

"Good morning, Kaitlin. Come have breakfast with me."

My feet reluctantly carried me to the table. There was toast and tea set out, but my stomach was repulsed at the sight of food. I poured a cup of tea, but didn't drink it.

"Have you reached a decision?"

The question startled me, even though I had known it was coming. I paused for a moment and gathered my courage.

"I will marry you," I said, "on one condition ..."

"And that is?" he asked, smiling.

"That you will go to church and face those hypocrites with me."

I remembered what he had said last night, and I half expected him to pound the table with his fist and tell me not to be so presumptuous. From the little he had said about his mother, he apparently held Christianity—and the church— in great contempt.

Instead of an outburst, I got a calm, even stare. I held his gaze at first, but then turned away.

"I don't know why it should matter to you, but I'll go with you."

I smiled.

"Although I must warn you that my motives are none too pure. I just want to see the look on Lady Conrad's face when she finds out that her daughters have no chance of catching me."

I didn't let his motives worry me. I just hoped that they

would soon change. I drank my tea and even managed a slice of toast.

"I'll contact the pastor and see how soon we can be married. Amelia and Nathan will act as witnesses."

Something was bothering me. "What will Mrs. Colton say when she finds out?" I asked. She had had such plans.

"I wouldn't worry about her. I'm sure things will go on much the same between us."

Whatever that meant. He got up to leave the room, but turned when he got to the door. "Don't be too alarmed—after the wedding, I'll have Mrs. Parks move your things into your new room." I was startled by this proclamation because I hadn't thought I would have to change rooms. At the look on my face he chuckled. "There is a room with a sitting room that is connected to mine by a dressing room. That's where you will be staying. The servants will have less to talk about that way," he said with a smile and walked out of the room.

I wondered what I would say to Amelia. What would she think? She would know we were not in love. Would she disapprove of my motives? I began to feel very worried that I might displease her.

I took a quick walk down the path to the cliffs. Everything seemed fresh and wild this morning. The dew seemed to sparkle. The sun was shining, reflecting off the water in what seemed like millions of directions. I stood breathing in the glorious sea air. I looked back up to the house. The slope was covered with grass, though it was starting to turn brown. It would be Christmas before too long. I looked up at the great house. What fun it would be to decorate—to put candles in the windows.

THESE *Rugged* CLIFFS

I finally realized what I was doing. I was trying to forget that in a few days time I would be getting married to a man I didn't know, a man with a troubled past. And why? Because of a vague feeling that this was "God's will." Was I really sure that this was not just a trap set by Satan to destroy my life? Or was that a little too melodramatic? But how did I really know this was "God's will"? Did God want me to introduce Edmund to Jesus? Could I do it?

Over the next couple of days, I was plagued by doubts, but I was determined not to back out now. I had told Edmund I would marry him, and so I would. I longed to go talk with Amelia, but I was afraid of what she would say. On the day that I was to become Edmund's wife, I had Sara bring up a tray to my room for luncheon. I couldn't bear the thought of trying to carry on a conversation with him. I was still having doubts, and I didn't trust myself not to tell him that I had changed my mind and that the wedding was off.

I didn't have a proper wedding dress, so I wore a beautiful ivory colored dress from the selection Edmund had bought. When I had picked my own wardrobe, it was much more conservative. I could tell Edmund had slightly more flamboyant tastes—or at least he thought *I* did. Sara did not talk while she fixed my hair, like she usually did, and I wondered what the servants knew about all that was happening.

When I came downstairs, it was almost five o'clock and Dr. Fenton and Amelia were already there, as were Edmund and Pastor Stevens and his wife. When Amelia saw me, she came and took both of my hands in hers.

"He may be cynical, Kaitlin," she whispered in my ear, "and he may not always be the most sensitive man alive, but I do believe he will treat you well. He is a good man, and if we keep praying for him, he may become an even better one." She smiled at me then and looked deep into my eyes. "You'll be good for him."

I was so relieved that she understood a little of why I was going through with this that tears formed in my eyes. I smiled back at her.

"Are we all ready?" Edmund asked as he came and offered me his arm. I nodded, not trusting myself to speak.

"You didn't invite Melinda and Miles?" asked Nathan.

"No," Edmund said grinning. "I didn't want to embarrass my bride-to-be." I wished he hadn't said that. It only made me wonder even more what their relationship really was.

He looked very handsome, and I knew I should have been proud to have acquired such a husband, but I knew I had nothing to be proud of. He was gaining freedom with this marriage, too. Not to mention the fact that I would let him have all the control he wanted over my finances.

The ceremony was brief. I said what I needed to say without embarrassing myself or swooning. When it came time for the groom to kiss the bride, I expected him to peck me on the cheek. Instead, he kissed me full on the lips. I felt a warm tingle in the pit of my stomach which I pushed aside as more nervousness. Then it was over, and Edmund was taking a deep breath and offering me his arm. We went into the dining room where cook had provided a delicious dinner. I barely ate. My mind was too full of troubling thoughts. What would the future hold for me now that I was a married woman?

After dinner Amelia began to feel sick. Dr. Fenton took

her home, and the Pastor and his wife left. Edmund excused himself also and went to work on something in his study. I had nothing to do, so I went back to my room. The room was empty. I felt a pang of alarm until I remembered that Edmund had planned to move my things to a new room. I went back out into the hallway, trying to figure out where this new room might be. Just then, Sara came down the hall and I asked her if she would show me.

"Of course, Madam," she said. She led me to a room at the back of the house.

She left me then to let me explore my new room alone. It was breathtaking. It had tall windows on two sides, and I was pleased to see that the room overlooked the cliffs and ocean in the distance. At least it would in the daytime. Right now, I could see a sliver of moon reflecting off the sea. A fire had been lit, as well as several oil lamps.

The carpet was a soft cream color. The bed and matching furniture were an ivory color. I could tell Edmund's mother had had a hand in decorating it. Just like the room downstairs, the rest of the bedroom was decorated in yellows, pale blues and greens, with gold accents.

"Do you like it?"

I turned around. Edmund stood with his hands in his pockets.

"It's beautiful."

"You can change it if you want to."

"I wouldn't change a thing."

Edmund went over to a door in the back corner of the room. He opened it, "This leads to the bath and wardrobe we share."

Inside the room was a large tub, ample closet space and a screen, behind which one could change. He went in and opened the other door. I caught a glimpse of a large bed and a lot of dark blue.

"This is my room. This door will be unlocked in case you ever need something—or in case you're afraid of the dark." He added jokingly.

I let myself smile at his teasing.

"Good night," he said.

"Good night," I repeated and retreated back to my room.

Once there, I found my Bible and did some reading. I found a small amount of comfort in rereading the stories of Isaac and Rebekah and Ruth and Boaz. Those ladies had not known their husbands before marriage and yet everything had worked out well. I wondered what the future would hold for me.

CHAPTER 8

In the first days after the wedding I noticed a definite change in Edmund's manner towards me. He was very distant and almost never at home. No longer would I find him breakfasting when I came down. He was off riding, visiting his tenants, or shut away in his study with a stack of papers. I knew he was avoiding me. I worried that he had decided it had been a grievous mistake to have married me. I knew that some men felt trapped by marriage. Perhaps that was how Edmund felt.

All I knew was that the days were long and boring. I visited Amelia several times, taking the path along the cliffs, but I didn't stay too long. I didn't want to tire or bore her.

Since Edmund had seemed to bury himself in his estate, I decided I might as well find out more about these people that lived here. I didn't want to ask Edmund to take the time to introduce me to everyone, however, so I asked Martin if he would go for a ride with me. He seemed a little surprised, but

I was determined. I took along some paper so I could make a list of the tenants and their wives.

When we passed by the cottage of Mr. and Mrs. Singer, Martin said gruffly, "Well, you know who lives there." I put a star next to Mrs. Singer's name. I would have to go and visit her soon—under better circumstances than the last time.

The next morning I awoke to find rain pouring down, and I was very disappointed. I wanted to go visit Mrs. Singer. I prepared myself for a dreary day spent indoors, but by late morning, the sun was shining brightly. I ate an early, light luncheon, then packed up some bread and cheese to take with me.

When I came riding up to the Singer's cottage, I saw Mrs. Singer standing in her yard, her head in her hands. I dismounted and rushed over to see what was the matter. Her two small children peeked around a corner of the cottage at me. The girl went to her mother and began pulling on her dress.

"What's wrong, Mama? What's wrong?" she cried.

"Mrs. Singer?" I asked tentatively.

She looked up slowly, her eyes red from crying. It was then that I noticed the once clean laundry littering the ground, covered with dirt and grime. I saw where the pegs that had held the line taut against the house had pulled loose.

"Yesterday's washing," she sobbed. "And bread to bake today. What'll I tell Jake? He'll want to know what I've been doin' all day. He'll kill me!"

"Is there something I can do for you, Mrs. Singer?"

She finally looked at me. "Oh! It's Mrs. Fitzpatrick now, right?" she asked breathlessly. I nodded and she swallowed several times. "Oh, ma'am, I'm sorry about this mess," she cried. She tried to curtsy, but she was hampered by the dirty laundry she was holding.

"There's nothing to be sorry about," I said briskly. "Now what can I do to help?"

She gaped at me. "You can't do anything, ma'am. I shouldn't have been so clumsy as to …" She broke off and a gurgled sound escaped her lips.

"What are you doing Mrs. Fitzpatrick?" she asked in a loud whisper.

"I'm helping you get your laundry done."

She followed me around while I picked up soiled linen, taking things from me as soon as I picked them up.

"But you *can't* ma'am!!"

"I can and I will, Mrs. Singer. You show me what I can do to help wash these clothes while you bake your bread. We'll get a lot more done if you help me instead of stand there staring at me." I smiled at her then, to soften my words, and she seemed to get the idea that I was serious—if rather eccentric.

She set up a washtub near the house, filled it with water and gave me a bar of lye soap. She filled a second bucket with clean water for rinsing and told Laura to bring me the dirty laundry. She gave me a strange look and then went inside.

"Here, you'll need this," she said, coming back to hand me an apron.

I rolled up my sleeves, grateful that I was wearing the gray flannel dress that was perhaps the plainest I owned. I put the apron on and got busy. I was inexperienced but I figured two pairs of hands were better than one. Dear God, I prayed,

I hope I did the right thing. I knew I tended to act first and think later. I had always been a little impetuous. Now I realized that I may have put Mrs. Singer in a very embarrassing—even humiliating—situation. I hoped she would understand that my offer to help was based on kindness. Perhaps I would even be able to share God's love with her.

The Singer's had a short fence in front of their cottage, and Laura and I placed the clean clothes on there. When there was no more room, I folded the items and she took them inside. Several times Mrs. Singer poked her head outside and asked if I was okay.

While I worked, I let my thoughts run free. What concerned me the most was that when Mrs. Singer had said that her husband would kill her, she had sounded frighteningly serious.

After a time, Mrs. Singer came outside. Her hands and face were covered with flour. "Well, the bread's almost done!" She sounded almost cheerful. I smiled at her.

"Mrs. Fitzpatrick, can I ask you something?"

"Of course."

"Why are you doing this?"

I chose my words carefully. "Well, I'm a Christian, Mrs. Singer. And I know God loves me very much. I feel that the least I can do for Him is to show other people His love."

"Oh."

"Do you go to church?" I asked quietly.

"Well, usually," came the hurried reply. "But I don't get much out of it. Jake—my husband—doesn't go. Maybe it'll be different this week."

"Maybe it will," I said with a grin.

I looked up and the grin left my face. Sitting on his horse, not twenty yards away, was my husband. Why hadn't I heard him approaching? He looked very tall and silent and— I couldn't quite tell what other emotion showed in his face. Was he furious that his "wife" was doing servant's work? Was he angry with me for sharing my faith with one of his tenants? Or was I jumping to the conclusion that he was upset? Perhaps the look he was giving me was just a variation of his normal arrogant, cynical stare.

At some point during my musing, Mrs. Singer had turned to see Edmund staring at us. She had gasped, and for a moment I had thought she might faint. She pulled herself together admirably, however, and when Edmund dismounted and walked over to us, she managed a quick curtsy.

"I must go check the bread," she said in a strangled voice. She gave one last quick look at both of us and then fled into the house.

I doubted whether Edmund had heard what she had said or even noticed that she had gone. From the moment I had seen him, his eyes had not left my face. I still could not tell what he was thinking, but I began to feel a dull ache in my stomach, and I knew I was uneasy.

He leaned over and looked into the wash bucket. For the first time I noticed my hands. My skin was rather sensitive, and my hands were beet red. I noticed a stinging sensation in the palms. I hid them in my apron and looked up at him, biting my lip. His own lip curled in a grimace. He reached out and grabbed my wrist before I could step away from him. He held my hand up and examined it with a cynical smirk. I was helpless to do anything but stand there meekly while he examined my red skin.

Finally he let my hand fall. "You don't do things by the half, do you, my dear?" he said quietly. At first I thought it was a compliment and I started to smile. Then he went on in a much harsher tone.

"But if you think your little display of 'witnessing' is going to do anything more than embarrass Mrs. Singer and make you susceptible to any number of snide remarks, you are sadly mistaken."

I bit my lip again. Furious with myself because I had to try and hold back tears, I held his gaze for a second longer, then turned and walked to the door of the cottage. I didn't trust myself to say anything. It wasn't that I thought I would say something unkind, I just didn't think I could say anything without tears of frustration interfering with my words.

I handed Mrs. Singer my apron and gave her a weak smile. She just stood staring at me, open-mouthed. I turned and walked out the door. Edmund still stood in the same spot, and I knew he was watching me, but I walked over to where I had tied Spirit without looking at him. I held my head high and tried to look as though I did not regret my impetuous behavior. My proud exit was spoiled by the fact that I could not mount my horse. My fingers were cramped and my shoulders ached. I tried to use the fence to aid my ascent. I pushed off the fencing, trying to jump and pull myself up at the same time. My muscles didn't work right and I fell backwards.

"Allow me."

I turned quickly and came face-to-face—face-to-chest, rather—with my husband. I put my hand on his shoulder and

I stepped on his cupped hands. He lifted me effortlessly and settled me on the horse.

"Thank you," I said stiffly.

He turned and walked away from me, and tears stung my eyes. When I showed up on Amelia's doorstep, I was sure I looked like a disheveled mess. Amelia's housekeeper answered the door. She uttered a cry of dismay when she saw me. "Are you all right, ma'am?" she asked.

"I'm fine. I would just like to see Mrs. Fenton."

"Of course, of course," she said and quickly ushered me into Amelia's sitting room.

At the sight of my red face and mussed hair, Amelia rose and came toward me.

"Kaitlin! Whatever is the matter?"

I waited until the housekeeper had left and Amelia and I had set down on the settee to pour out my story. She listened in silence as I shared what had happened and how I felt. I was so upset with myself for acting without thinking. How would I ever show Edmund what God meant to me if I kept doing things to annoy him?

For some reason, after I had finished talking, Amelia started to laugh.

"Oh Kaitlin, I know it's not funny, but can you imagine the picture you must have made—bent over that washbasin, a determined look on your face, your hair flying."

"I must admit, I probably did look pretty funny," I said sheepishly. Then I looked down at my hands. I held them up for Amelia to see. She gasped and then rang for her housekeeper. "Mrs. Evans, will you please go tell Dr. Fenton to bring me some of his special ointment, right away." Mrs.

Evans hurried away and Amelia clasped my hands in hers and looked closely at them.

"You poor dear, I didn't know you had battle scars. I'm sorry I laughed. We'll take care of you in just a minute."

"It's just because my skin is so sensitive. I'm sure it will go away in no time. Amelia—it's not my hands that I'm worried about. It's Edmund. He was so angry. Do you think he'll ever forgive me? I'm not sure I even understand why he was so upset."

Amelia was silent for a moment. "You know, maybe Edmund was upset because you showed him a glimpse of God's love that he doesn't want to know exists. I still think if you keep working on him, he'll come around."

"I hope you're right. It's just—I'm afraid I may have embarrassed him."

Amelia smiled compassionately at me, but before we could speak any more Dr. Fenton came in.

"What do you need the ointment for, my dear?" he asked, smiling fondly at his wife. "Good day, Kaitlin."

"For this," she said, holding up my red hands for him to see.

"My goodness, Kaitlin," he said, "What have you been doing?"

"Washing," Amelia answered for me. Dr. Fenton looked like he was going to speak, but his wife silenced him with a look. I had no doubt that she would tell him what had happened later, but she had at least saved me some embarrassment.

After Dr. Fenton had liberally smeared ointment over my irritated skin, Amelia gave me a couple of her gloves to wear "to hold the ointment in," and I took my leave. I told

Amelia I would visit her again soon and let her know how things were going.

I was feeling much better when I left Amelia. I chose to walk my horse, though, because my shoulders were still very sore. For some reason, I thought of my father then, and I wondered what he would think of all this if he were alive.

I didn't want to go down to dinner that night and face Edmund. I was afraid he would make some biting comment about the afternoon. I kept thinking about what Amelia had said and I hoped I could still reach him. No matter what he says, I told myself, I won't be upset.

When I came into the drawing room, Edmund was pouring himself a drink.

"Good evening," he said, appearing to be sociable.

"Good evening."

"Shall we go in to dinner?" he asked amiably.

"Of course."

He offered me his arm. My hand felt strange resting on the folds of his dinner jacket. Perhaps what was so strange was that while I was this man's wife, and while my arm was intimately entwined with his, I knew so little about him. I didn't know or understand his moods and I knew nothing of his past. I glanced up at him, struck once again by how handsome he was. But what did it matter if he was the most beautiful man alive when he wanted nothing to do with God?

Edmund looked down at me, one side of his mouth lifting in a smirk. "Are you admiring my profile?"

"Actually, I was trying to build up the courage to apologize."

"Apologize?"

"Yes, I'm sorry for my impetuous behavior this afternoon."

Edmund pulled my chair out and I sat down.

"I wanted to talk to you about that," he said.

I felt my stomach do a little flip, and I felt a lump in my throat.

"Oh?" I said, a question in my voice.

Edmund waited until the food had been served. He dismissed the servant and then turned to me.

"After you made your grand exit, I talked to Mrs. Singer."

"You did?"

"Actually, Mrs. Singer talked to me."

"She did?"

"As soon as you were riding away, she came over and started singing your praises. I think she was afraid that I was so angry that I would beat you or something. Anyway, although she was trembling the whole time, she let me know in no uncertain terms that I should not be upset with you—that you were the nicest person she had ever known and she implied that she would be devoted to you for the rest of her life. She even told me I should thank God every day that I was married to you."

I listened in stunned silence.

"She said all that to you?" I finally asked in a whisper. He nodded. I couldn't believe that meek Ellie Singer would stand up to her landlord like that. She must have felt the need to protect me.

"What did you do?" I asked, fearing his answer.

"I laughed."

"Edmund, you didn't!" Oh, how that must have crushed Mrs. Singer to have him laugh in her face.

"Don't worry, I'm not that heartless. I laughed and told her—kindly—that she was absolutely right. I was too hard on you. Her words reminded me that I will have much more success as a landlord if my tenants respect me and are devoted to my wife. So, I thanked Mrs. Singer for showing me the error of my ways and I left her blushing prettily to go back to her children."

He leaned back in his chair and fixed me with a mischievous grin.

"So there you are. I see that I overreacted a bit. I had no business playing the tyrant husband. I'll try not to control your every action. Besides, I realized that as long as you are preaching at Mrs. Singer and the other tenants' wives, you are not preaching at me, so I'm content to leave it at that."

Tears stung my eyes at his mocking tone. *What are you so upset about?* I chided myself. At least he had been kind to Mrs. Singer and given me somewhat of an apology. I remembered the prayer I had prayed earlier, though, and forced myself to smile.

"I'm sure I'll have plenty of time to preach at you too, Edmund, so you needn't feel left out."

He made a production of groaning.

"Perhaps someday I can do something for you that will show you how much God loves you."

The playful tone of the conversation was gone when he got serious and said to me in low tones, "I'm afraid, my dear, that it would take a very great deal for me to see God's love. I found out a long time ago that if there really is a God, He is anything but loving."

We ate the rest of our dinner in silence, but afterward, Edmund challenged me to a game of chess. We hadn't played since we had gotten married, and perhaps Edmund felt he had been ignoring me (I certainly felt that way). By the time the game was set up, the tension seemed to have gone, and if Edmund tried to bait me any, it was in a much more playful way. He won both of the games—I was still rusty, since I hadn't played in a while, but I knew I was getting close to beating him. When we had finished playing and we were putting the game away, Edmund reached over and took hold of my wrist, turning it over to look at the palm of my hand.

"Does it hurt?" he asked, looking at the redness.

"Not really," I told him, "Dr. Fenton put some cream on my hands and that helped."

"So Nathan and Amelia know of your little escapade."

"I'm afraid so."

Silence hung in the air, and I rose to go upstairs.

"Edmund," I paused to say, "I'm sorry about today. I'm sorry if it was embarrassing for you to have me washing your tenants' clothes. Sometimes I do things without thinking. I'll try and do better."

Edmund smiled, almost fondly, at me and shook his head sadly. "I have a feeling you will do a lot of things without thinking. It seems to be your nature." After a pause, he went on. "However, I think you will definitely make life interesting."

For some reason, I blushed. I quickly mumbled "Good night" and went upstairs. It had been a very strange day.

CHAPTER 9

Sunday finally came, and I wondered if Edmund remembered his promise to go with me to church. He was not in the breakfast room when I came down, but when the carriage pulled up in front of the house, Edmund emerged from his study.

"I told Nathan that I would be bringing you to church this Sunday," he said, chuckling. "You should have seen the look on his face."

He helped me into the carriage, and we were off. We said little during the ride. I was wondering how I was ever going to share Jesus with him when we talked so little.

When we arrived at the church, I noticed he seemed to be holding his emotions in check. As we walked inside, we were greeted by many smiles. Amelia and Dr. Fenton grinned warmly at us. Mrs. Singer was there with her two children. She gave me a weak smile. She seemed happy to see me, but I also thought she was a little preoccupied. I wondered if I had judged these people too harshly. Then I realized that most of those who were welcoming us were Edmund's tenants—women and children that I had visited over the week.

There were also a few gasps and murmurs here and there. I caught Lady Conrad's eye, and the look she gave me was hateful. I gripped Edmund's arm a little more tightly as we walked to our seats. I wondered what had happened to make these people so surprised to see him—us—here. I felt that I needed to know more about his past.

I thought the service was quite good, but Edmund seemed uncomfortable, embarrassed. When it was over, he grabbed my arm and led me out. He nodded to the Pastor, but that was all. We didn't talk to anyone. Instead, we made our way straight back to the carriage. Once inside, Edmund leaned back, crossed his long legs and grinned at me.

"Well, that was a small price to pay for your hand in marriage," he said cynically.

"What do you mean?" I asked.

"You said I had to go to church with you. I just did." He gave me a lopsided grin that told me he was mocking me; yet he was serious, too.

"I meant every week."

"That may have been what you meant, but that's not what you said."

All of a sudden I was angry. I was upset that he was treating me like this, making light of my belief. Perhaps it had been wrong of me to make him promise to go to church with me the way I had, but I felt so helpless. I didn't know how else to try and get him interested in a relationship with God. I knew I probably had no right to be angry, but my pride was hurt by his mocking. I balled up my fists and glared at him.

I sat on the edge of my seat, leaning towards him. "Why are you being so pig-headed and stubborn?" I yelled. "You make judgments about hypocrisy, and how horrible Christianity is, and I don't even know why. You talk evasively about your mother, and use your past as an excuse for your abominable behavior. Well, I think that's ridiculous!"

At this point the carriage bounced over a rough spot and I landed in his lap. My face was red, and I was breathing heavily after my outburst. Edmund stared down at me for a moment. His face was calm, but his jaw was clenched. He set me back on my seat with a slight thump.

He held my glance for what seemed like an eternity, and I was proud that I did not turn away. I thought we would go on forever like that, and my willpower was flagging, when the carriage stopped in front of the house. He silently got out and helped me down. We walked into the house in silence, and Edmund headed for his study.

"Don't wait for me for luncheon. I'm not hungry."

"Edmund!" I called to his back, following after him. "Edmund, talk to me. Tell me what is wrong!"

He turned suddenly and brought his face close to mine.

"There are some things—my naive little wife—that you don't need to know."

With that, he turned and entered the study, shutting the door in my face. I stared at the door for a minute, then turned and ran up to my room. I lay on my bed for awhile, staring at the ceiling. I was mad at myself for my outburst. How did I ever expect Edmund to respect or even want to share my beliefs when I acted like a spoiled child? Soon there was a knock on the door. Sara came in.

"Are you feeling well?" she asked.

"I'm fine."

"Cook was fretting when no one came to dinner."

I sat up. "I'm sorry, Sara, Edmund and I didn't feel like eating."

Sara looked sympathetic.

"Is there anything you need?"

"No, thank you. I was just getting ready to go for a walk."

Inevitably my feet took me down to the cliff's edge. I felt I needed to go see Amelia. I hoped she would tell me some of the details of Edmund's past. I walked down the path heading in the opposite direction from Mrs. Colton's. After following the cliff's edge for a couple hundred yards, the path curved back inland into a large stand of trees. Dr. Fenton and Amelia's house was just a little way further, once you passed through the wood. It was a very pleasant walk. Generally, it would take 10 or 15 minutes or so. Today, I was upset and walking fast. Once in awhile I would jog a few steps, such was my sense of urgency. I believe it was this sense of urgency that kept me alive. I had just passed through a spot where the underbrush was dense when I came to a clearing. Just as I began to race through the opening, a shot broke out. I gasped when a bullet hit a tree just behind me.

I didn't know where the shot came from, but I didn't wait to find out. I spun around to head the other way. I heard another shot and felt a bullet whiz by my ear. I think I screamed.

Frantically, I retraced my steps and ran for the dense underbrush. I didn't stop there. I flew through the woods, my hair flying behind me, checking over my shoulder every few seconds. For some reason, I felt I needed to make it out of the woods. At that moment I thought I was running for my life. I had almost reached the edge of the woods when I tripped over a fallen branch. Tears were streaming down my face as I struggled to get up and keep going. Then I was up and running again. I turned back to see if there was anything behind me, and suddenly I collided with something hard. It grabbed me and held me tightly, but I fought against it.

Finally, I realized it was calling my name.

"Kaitlin! Kaitlin!" Edmund yelled.

I stopped struggling and went limp with relief. Then I started crying.

"What's wrong? What's happened?" he shouted at me.

I was still a little hysterical, not quite coherent.

"In there … in the woods … shots … at me …" I told him between gasps.

"What are you talking about? Kaitlin! Calm down and tell me what happened."

I took a few deep breaths and wiped my eyes on the handkerchief Edmund gave me.

"I was going over to see Amelia. I was in a hurry, and I started to run, and the next second a shot rang out and struck a tree right behind me. For some reason, I panicked. Another shot whizzed by and I began to run. I … I was so scared."

Edmund held me close for a minute. I was thankful for his comfort.

"Come with me," he said releasing me and taking my hand. I had no choice but to follow him back into the woods. I showed him where I had been when I heard the shots and tried to determine where they had come from. We walked in that direction for a minute or so, until Edmund gave an exclamation.

"Look here!"

There were a couple rabbits lying on the ground. Each had been shot recently.

"Poachers," he said quietly. "Someone must have been shooting these when you happened along. When he realized he had come close to shooting you, he must have rushed off without his prey."

I shuddered. I didn't understand it, but I knew that I had felt like prey. I could see the evidence right there before my eyes, but my mind could not believe it.

"But … it seemed as though they were shooting at me!" I argued.

"Of course it did," Edmund said in a patronizing way. "I can understand that you were afraid, but you needn't worry anymore. If someone is poaching in these woods, he'll be much more careful from now on."

"I hope so."

"Do you still want to go see Amelia? Or should I walk you back to the house?"

"I'd like to go back now," I said.

We didn't say much on the walk back. I was deep in thought. Edmund had seemed so calm about the whole situation. I did not feel so. I think it was at that moment, walking back up to the house with this man who was my husband, this man I didn't know, that I began to have serious doubts about my wisdom in marrying him. I wondered if I had been a fool. I had thought that I was doing the right thing, but now I was not so sure.

I realized that in all my musings, I was forgetting to thank my Heavenly Father for keeping me safe. I knew that He was with me, but I was still plagued by doubts. I needed time alone to seek God and pray—for myself and for my husband.

When we finally reached the house, Edmund turned to me and said, "Melinda and Miles will be dining with us tonight."

"They will?" I asked, disappointed.

"Yes. I figure after thwarting their plans the way we did, the least we can do is to keep up our friendship."

"Why don't we have Dr. Fenton and Amelia over?"

"We will, but not tonight. You know they don't get along very well. I'm not up to that sort of evening. Now, please stop arguing and get ready. They'll be here soon."

And stop wasting my time with your wild imagination, I could almost hear him say. I was not looking forward to this evening. It would be the first time I would see Mrs. Colton since Edmund and I were married. I thought Edmund had been over to visit them a couple times this week, but he hadn't told me.

Once back in my room, I sat down in the chair by the window and began to cry. What was I going to do? Why had I allowed myself to marry a man I didn't love and didn't even know?

When my thoughts started taking a dangerous turn toward supposition, I was ashamed of it, but I couldn't stop it. *Why had Edmund been walking in the woods? How did I just happen to run into him after I heard those shots, and how did he find those rabbits so fast?*

I felt myself trembling with fear and cold. What if *he* had fired those shots? What if he had thought to make it look as though I had had an accident in the woods? I knew Edmund didn't love me. It bothered me that he seemed to be so smitten with Mrs. Colton at times. I wondered if he would have married her if he had not been afraid she was only after his money. Perhaps his pride had gotten in the way of his feelings for her. I didn't like the idea of Edmund's marrying me as a way of getting back at Mrs. Colton—as retaliation for a bruised ego. I was sickened at the thought. Was he now regretting his decision to be saddled with a woman he did not love in order to punish the woman he did love? Perhaps it would solve his problems if I were to "accidentally" die. But that was crazy, I kept trying to tell myself. He wasn't the sort of man who would kill an innocent young woman—was he? I realized with sadness that I did not know.

If I were gone, he would be free to marry Mrs. Colton, and he would have all of my money as well. With that thought, I began trembling uncontrollably, and I had to shake myself to gain some composure. I went and splashed cold water on my face. I had always had a habit of letting my imagination run away with me, but this was real life. People don't go around killing their wives in real life, I told myself.

After I gave myself a good talking to about the dangers of flights of fancy, I said a quick prayer that seemed to sum up all I was feeling.

Oh, God, I prayed, *I may have made the biggest mistake of my life. Please forgive me if I have and help me be content with the consequences.*

Soon after, there was a knock on my door. Sara came in to see if I needed help dressing for dinner. I decided to wear a striking gown of burgundy velvet. Sara helped me put it on and then fixed my hair. Finally I was dressed for dinner. I gave Sara a weak smile and then headed downstairs.

I remembered plainly that first evening when I had come down these same stairs to have dinner with these same people. I couldn't believe I was a married woman, and yet I didn't feel all that different. I was still extremely nervous.

When I came into the drawing room, Mrs. Colton came over and kissed me on the cheek.

"I'm so happy for you," she purred.

Surprised by her congratulations, I thought to smile and respond warmly, but she went on.

"You know, I couldn't believe it when I heard that Edmund had married his young ward." She glanced up at Edmund who had come to stand near us. "But then, who can explain love?" She laughed. "I mean, you are in love, are you not?"

I didn't know what to say. My mouth gaped and I stared blankly at Edmund. He smiled a strange smile, and said, "Shall we go in to dinner?" He offered his arm to Mrs. Colton, and she smiled slyly at me as they left the drawing room.

Mr. Denson appeared from out of nowhere to offer me his arm. "I guess we'll have to go in together."

I tried to give him a kind smile; then we followed the other two. During the first course, Melinda dominated the conversation. I said very little until she forced me into the conversation.

"Edmund, I hope now that you are married you won't forget poor Miles and me. We would still like to have you come by and see us. I'm sure your new wife won't mind sharing you a little, will you Kaitlin?"

I could feel Edmund's eyes on me. I glanced at him and saw him looking at me expectantly.

"I'm sure he should go and visit someone he regards as such a *friend*."

Edmund's expression was unreadable, but when I glanced at Mrs. Colton, she smiled an evil smile. "Whatever you say, dear," she said.

Something about the way she said those words gave me to believe she was mocking me. Soon dinner was over, though, and Mrs. Colton and I went back into the drawing room.

"Well, my dear, it seems we have had an interesting turn of events. I must say I was disappointed to hear Edmund had married you. It was a wise move on his part, though. You do bring him much more wealth than I would have. I am afraid I would have been a burden to him."

At first I didn't know what to say, but I gathered my thoughts and remarked, "I had heard Edmund was such a wealthy man that he wouldn't have to worry about his wife's income when he married her. He married me for other reasons—not because of the money I would bring him."

"You go ahead and think that, my dear, but there is a certain type of man—and Edmund is the type—that is never satisfied with the amount of money he has. He will always do *whatever* it takes to get more."

I was saved from having to comment by the gentlemen's entrance.

"Why don't you play for us, Kaitlin," Edmund said as he came and sat down by the fire.

"All right," I said softly. I didn't really want to play in front of our visitors, but I didn't want to refuse, either. I started by playing the same haunting melody I had played so many times for my father. This gave me a chance to relax and forget about my audience. After that first song, I played several others my father had loved, and I felt somewhat comforted by the familiar music. When my fingers began to get tired, I played the first song once more, and then I rose and went back to my seat on the settee.

"Well," Mrs. Colton said when I came back over and sat down, "That was very interesting. A trifle 'dark' perhaps, but good."

"When I play, I can't help but think of my father, and I feel as though I am playing for him. Those were his favorite songs," I told her.

"My goodness," she exclaimed to the gentlemen, "Miss How—excuse me—Mrs. Fitzpatrick's father must have been a rather depressed gentleman."

My jaw tightened as I tried to hold in a biting comment. It didn't matter, I couldn't think of a biting comment, anyway. My face grew a bit red, but I sat quietly.

Distraction came when Mr. Fitzpatrick remarked, "I took Kaitlin to church this morning. It was quite a service.

I'm afraid many people were too busy staring at me to get much out of the Pastor's sermon."

"Edmund! You can't be serious. You—at church? I don't believe it," Mrs. Colton gave him a look of shocked reproach. "Is this going to be a habit?"

"Ah, no. As a matter of fact—" He looked over at me. I don't know what my face must have looked like, but I was surprised at his next words. "It probably won't be a habit, but I wanted to go with Kaitlin in order to see the look on Lady Conrad's face when she found out that the marriage had indeed taken place."

Suddenly, the tension I had felt was gone, and I realized I had been holding my breath. I looked over at Edmund, surprised that he had not taken such a wonderful opportunity to make fun of me. He could have told Mrs. Colton and Mr. Denson about the silly promise I had made him make—how I had 'forced' him to go to church, and how he had gotten the better of me. But he didn't. I looked over at him to try and see what he was thinking, but the look he gave me was inscrutable.

Nothing more of consequence happened. Before too long, Melinda and Miles took their leave. Edmund walked them out into the hall, then came back into the drawing room and fixed me with a mocking grin. "There now, that wasn't so bad, was it?"

I rolled my eyes at him. I was so tired. It had been a very long day. I wanted nothing more than to go to my room and quietly cry myself to sleep. I didn't know what to think of Edmund. I had been so upset after church at the way he had made light of my beliefs and twisted my words, and this afternoon I had been almost terrified of him, and yet, this evening he had spared me more humiliation. While sometimes he seemed to try and treat me kindly, at times I wondered if he even liked me at all. I didn't know what to think of this strange man I had agreed to marry. I was afraid I had made the biggest mistake of my life, and I couldn't believe I had been such a fool.

Edmund poured himself a drink. I was just getting ready to say good night and excuse myself to the solace of my room, where I could try and sort out my thoughts, when he spoke.

"On Christmas Day, we'll have Melinda and Miles and Nathan and Amelia over for dinner. That way you can see how they get along."

"All right." I got up from my chair by the fire and headed for the door. "Good night," I said, looking back at him. Apparently, he hadn't heard me. He stood staring into the fire. I noticed the way the firelight accented the hard set of his jaw. He was scowling, and I could feel his pain. I had been so angry with him after church, but now tears of pity pricked my eyes. He had been lighthearted this evening, flirting with Mrs. Colton, baiting me—as usual—but now it seemed as though his own tormenting thoughts had come back to haunt him.

CHAPTER 10

After the incident with the poacher the day before, I was a little nervous about going through the woods to talk to Amelia. I went anyway. The walk was uneventful, and I felt a little foolish over my squeamishness. Amelia was glad to see me. When I entered her parlor, she rose, put down the knitting she was working on, and came over to greet me with a hug.

"I was so glad to see you and Edmund at church yesterday."

I grimaced.

"Well, it was not really a great accomplishment. I told Edmund I would marry him on the condition that he come to church with me."

"Oh."

"I meant every week, but he said he fulfilled his obligation by going with me—once—and so he doesn't think he'll set foot in church again."

"I'm so sorry, Kaitlin," Amelia said, her eyes moist.

"I take it that something terrible must have happened in his past …" I said, hoping Amelia would open up to me.

She frowned and looked uncomfortable.

"What has Edmund told you?" she asked evasively.

"He hasn't told me much of anything. He told me a little about his mother, then he told me to mind my own business," I said angrily, "but I think I have a right to know."

"You do have a right to know," Amelia said soothingly, "but I'm afraid I owe it to Edmund not to speak about it if he doesn't wish it."

I knew she was right, but I felt petulant. "I know something terrible must have happened to his mother," I said.

Amelia nodded but didn't say any more.

"How am I supposed to help him if I don't know what's bothering him?"

Amelia gave me a sympathetic look and then changed the subject. We talked for awhile about neutral topics and I took my leave before long.

When I rose to leave, Amelia reached out and put her hand on my arm. "Be patient with him. Talk to him. It would be much better for you to hear it from him."

She gave my arm a squeeze and I left the room.

A few days later, I decided to take Spirit out for a ride. I rode down the path toward the cliffs. For a time, I sat admiring the view then led the horse along the path to my left. I wound along the path, sometimes near the cliff's edge, sometimes inland.

When I came across the tumbledown shack that I had visited once before, I left the path and moved closer to the cliff's edge to try and stay as far as possible from the hut.

Since that time during the storm, I had passed by here several times and had never seen him. Suddenly, the small, wiry man came running outside towards me.

"Get away from there!" he was screaming, brandishing his walking stick.

I was struck dumb with bewilderment and simply sat on Spirit and stared at him. He came over, grabbed the horse's saddle and pulled him toward his shack.

"There! You be safe now," he cackled. "Old Jim'll keep ya safe."

I knew that this man was not quite in his right mind, and I felt a surge of pity.

"Don't go near the edge, Missie, it ain't safe! Them are ... them are rugged cliffs!"

"Okay. I'll be careful." I slid off my horse.

"Why did you try and scare me that one day?" I asked.

He smiled sheepishly. "Old Jim don't like strangers."

"I'm sorry I went inside your ... house, but I was trying to get out of the rain."

"Old Jim is sorry he scared you," he said, but he eyed me suspiciously for a minute.

"Who are ye?" he asked peering into my face.

"Kaitlin ... Fitzpatrick." The name sounded unfamiliar on my tongue. I had not gotten used to the idea.

He looked at me strangely for a minute, then he smiled. "Ah. You be married to her son, eh?"

"Yes, Jim."

"That poor, pretty lady. Old Jim knows things." He tapped his head with a gnarled finger.

"What do you know?" I asked, curious.

He ignored my question and walked back toward the shack, then stopped and turned around.

"Come back again, Missie. Come back for tea," he said and disappeared into the house.

I wondered what Jim knew. I wondered why he had called Edmund's mother "that poor, pretty lady." I decided I needed to find out more about Edmund's past, but I wasn't sure how to do it. I knew there was some secret, but I didn't know what it was.

When I came down for dinner that evening, I found Edmund to be in a jovial mood. Perhaps tonight I could get him to tell me more about himself. During the main course, after the servants had left us, I decided to be bold.

"Edmund, I have a confession to make."

He raised an eyebrow. "Oh?"

"Yes. The other day I rode over to visit Amelia with the express purpose of trying to get her to tell me about your past. However, she wouldn't do it. She said she owed it to you not to tell your 'secrets.' She told me I should find out from you. I know I've asked you before why you don't share my Christian beliefs and what happened to make you so bitter about your mother, and if you refuse to tell me now, I'll try to never ask again. But, I am your wife now, and if it doesn't bother you that Amelia knows, well ..." My voice trailed off, unsure how to go on.

I sat back and waited patiently for my speech to sink in. I wasn't sure if I was prepared to never find out what his past was like if he refused to tell me now. I could only pray that he would trust me enough to tell me.

For a long time he said nothing. He held my gaze for

awhile; it almost seemed as though he stared through me. Then he bowed his head and closed his eyes.

Finally, he spoke, and I realized I had been holding my breath.

"Perhaps I was wrong to keep this from you. I had my reasons, but I can't argue with your logic. If I trust Amelia enough to know my tragic past, I should trust my wife that much. Very well, be prepared for a sad tale of tragedy and woe."

He gave me an impish grin then, as though he somehow enjoyed the pain he felt, as though he nurtured his bitterness.

"My father died when I was very young—tuberculosis or something like it, I think. When I was around eight or so, my mother remarried Mr. Stephen Beville. My stepfather—on the surface—was a righteous and holy man. He went to church every week and my mother and I went, too. My mother went to church out of devotion to God, for Mr. Beville it was all for show. He liked to be looked on favorably by the community.

"At home, he was a tyrant. I think my mother lived in mortal terror of him. I know I did. At church I heard all this talk about trust and love, and at home I learned fear and hate. I felt humiliated because I couldn't stand up to him. I couldn't scream at him and put the 'fear of God' in *him*. He treated my mother very badly, and I watched her go from a grand, confident, laughing woman to a timid, fearful, mouse—afraid of her own shadow.

"It was all because of him, and I could do nothing about it. I told the pastor one day, but he ignored me, saying that

Mr. Beville was a model citizen and an upstanding member of the church. But I knew he was a hypocrite, and my dear 'Christian' mother was slipping further away.

"Finally, she left me altogether. I had been spending some time at my aunt and uncle's home, and it was at their house that I first met your father. My mother sent me there often, and I feel now that there was a certain tension in the air at that time.

"Anyway, according to a servant, my mother and stepfather had an argument one afternoon and he slapped her. She ran out of the house—to go for a walk, so it seemed.

"Later, when she didn't come home for dinner, my stepfather went out to look for her. Apparently she had found living with him too much. Her body was found at the bottom of the cliff. Everyone assumed, of course, that it was suicide. But I knew my stepfather drove her to it. Instead of getting justice, though, he gained the sympathy of the town. When they found out that he no longer had any claim on the estate and would have to leave, the townspeople—especially the church—were aghast. They thought I should let him stay. I was only 14 years old, so my opinion didn't matter.

"Luckily, my uncle knew a little of my stepfather's real character and he promptly kicked him out of my home. Then we closed up and left for London. But not before I accused the church people one Sunday morning of murdering my mother with their apathy and hypocrisy. I told them I didn't want anything to do with their church or their God. I said a few more colorful things and then left.

"That was 14 years ago, but I think many of those people still remember. That's why we got some strange looks the day we went together. I had vowed never to go there again. Of course, I think I once made a vow never to get married, but I guess I broke that one, too."

"Wasn't there an inquest or something?" I asked finally. I was shocked and appalled at the story. I understood a little more why he was so bitter toward the church.

"Surprisingly enough, no. There was no inquest," he said flatly.

"But how do you know that your stepfather didn't push her off that cliff. Maybe it wasn't suicide at all," I was grasping at optimistic possibilities. I was surprised at Edmund's anger at my suggestion.

"While it would be nice to think that my mother didn't kill herself, it's not as though I can just go out and find proof. My stepfather died several years ago, and so I will never know. I might rather accept the worst possible scenario than walk around assuming life is a bed of roses. You might as well face facts like I did. My mother jumped off that cliff rather than have to live with that man. I can't forgive him for that. In fact, I think I hate him more for pushing her to suicide than I would have hated him for pushing her off himself."

"But wouldn't it be better to find out the truth."

"No, it wouldn't." He gave me a severe look. "And I don't want you speculating about what might have happened that day. Understood? I just want to forget about it."

I couldn't quite believe that. It must be a horrible burden for him to bear—feeling that his mother didn't love him enough to stick around and help him. I knew he felt that she had deserted him, and I felt that he had never forgiven *her*. Suddenly I thought about old Jim and the conversation we had had along the cliff. It hadn't really been a conversation. Rather, Jim had cautioned me not to go near the cliff because bad things happened there. He acted as though he knew something. I wondered if he had seen what had happened the day Mrs. Fitzpatrick died.

Maybe the best Christmas present I could give Edmund would be to find out what really happened to his mother.

⚜

The next morning, I awoke to find a beautiful day dawning. It was cold, but the sun was shining. Instead of satisfying my desire to find out about Edmund's past, I got the idea that I should go visit Mrs. Singer. I wasn't sure why I should have that thought. Perhaps I was pleased that I had seen her in church last Sunday, and I wanted to see if she had enjoyed herself. I had noticed that her husband was not with her. She had commented that he didn't come to church, and I remembered how frightened she had seemed of him when I had "helped" her with her washing. I was a little concerned with the type of man he was.

It was almost luncheon when I finally decided I would go, so I told Jeffries that I would probably be late. I took along some cakes for the children. I hadn't counted on Mr. Singer being home. Something seemed to have put him in a foul mood. I could hear him yelling and cursing as I rode up. I jumped down from my horse just in time to hear a loud crash and see Mrs. Singer shuffle her children out the door. The little girl took her young brother by the hand and led him around the side of the house. Mrs. Singer hadn't noticed

I was there. Apparently she was too preoccupied with her enraged husband. I had no idea what had upset him.

A moment later, she came rushing out of the small house. She almost ran me over, and at the sight of me, a gurgling sound escaped her lips.

"Hello," I said calmly.

She gave me a look filled with despair then her eyes flew back to the door her husband had just come through.

"I told you to get away from here!" Mr. Singer shouted.

I instinctively stepped in front of her to act as a barrier between them. He looked like he wanted to kill her.

"What's the matter, Mr. Singer?" I asked, still calm.

"She's been cheatin' on me that's what. Ain't nobody gonna cheat on Jake Singer!"

He took a step toward us and Mrs. Singer pushed in front of me.

"I told you Jake, I've never been unfaithful to you," she pleaded.

He grabbed her by the shoulders and shook her. "You're lying!"

I could see he was about to strike her. I grabbed onto his arm and pulled. He glared at me, annoyed, and flung me away from him. I hit the ground hard.

The next few minutes were a jumble of confusion. All of a sudden, Mr. Singer began hitting Mrs. Singer. I heard myself yell and then I jumped on his back. I got my arms around his neck and tried to pull him away from his wife. Again I found myself being flung away and landing on the ground. I heard Mrs. Singer call my name, and I could tell she was sobbing. My interference just seemed to make him madder. When he grabbed her around the neck, I felt a surge of adrenaline. This time when I jumped on him, I was vicious. I pulled his hair with one hand and tried to gouge his eyes with the other. I felt a surge of satisfaction when he grunted with pain and let her go. I heard her scramble away, but I still held on. I was sure his face must be bloody where my nails had dug in.

Finally, it was too much for him. He summoned some inner strength of his own, reached back with one hand and threw me down again—hard. After that, however, he stalked off.

I lay on the ground for a minute with my eyes closed. I told myself I just wanted to rest for a minute, but the truth was my head hurt something awful. Slowly, I opened my eyes to see Mrs. Singer's face—anxious and worried— and another. My mouth dropped open when I recognized Edmund kneeling beside me.

"Mrs. Fitzpatrick! Oh, Mrs. Fitzpatrick, are you okay?"

"I'm fine," I told the distraught Mrs. Singer. "I just need to sit up."

I tried to do just that, but it made my head hurt even more. I leaned heavily against Edmund while I fought the dizziness.

"Oh, Mrs. Fitzpatrick!" Mrs. Singer said, clutching my arm. "You were so brave!" She added in tones of great admiration.

"Oh yeah, real brave," said my husband sarcastically, "just not very bright. What were you thinking—taking on a man twice your size?"

At the mention of her husband, Mrs. Singer burst into tears.

"I'm so sorry," she cried.

I patted her on the shoulder and told her it was okay. I looked pleadingly at Edmund. I didn't know what could be done. Edmund gave me a look with just a little compassion.

"I'll talk to your husband, Mrs. Singer. I'll see to it that this never happens again. And if it does, let me know. I will tell Jake what will happen if he ever lays a hand on another woman—especially my wife!"

Edmund glared at me then as though this was all my fault. Mrs. Singer simply bowed her head, said "Yes, sir," and went to collect her children, who were hiding behind the woodpile.

I looked up at Edmund. "Can you really make sure he doesn't hurt her?"

He gave me an arrogant look.

"Do you doubt my authority? I have it in mind to give him a good thrashing myself for what he did to you."

I gave him a worried look. He had almost sounded serious.

"You mustn't do that," I said quickly, "He is a very big man."

"I wouldn't let his size deter me from punishing him. He knew you were my wife, yet he still treated you the way he did. I mean, he had no regard for your honor or dignity."

I frowned. Now I knew he was not serious. "You're mocking me," I said.

"Yes, you're right," he said getting to his feet and pulling me up. "But you must permit me that indiscretion. After all, you're not the one who came upon the sight of your wife attacking a huge beast of a man in a fit of furious righteous indignation, only to see her hurled to the ground, skirts flying. It makes my blood run cold and my hair stand on end just thinking about it."

I smiled sheepishly at the picture of myself his words evoked.

"I am sorry if I embarrassed you," I said seriously, realizing that that was a possibility.

"Of course you didn't embarrass me," he said offhandedly. "But at least now I know not to do anything to put you into a fit of temper. You do fight dirty, my dear."

I knew he was trying to goad me into getting angry, but at least it helped me to focus on something other than the situation at hand.

"Can you ride?" he asked, when I reached my horse. I nodded, and he helped me up.

"Can you make it back to the house okay?"

I nodded, but with a certain sense of foreboding. He jumped onto his horse, then reached over and grabbed my reins. He pulled my horse close to his and looked down at me. There was a strange intensity in his eyes.

"I'm going to go talk to Mr. Singer now. He won't be bothering you again, but I want you to promise me that you won't be getting into any fights with any other big hulking brutes. I don't really want to have to spend all of my time fighting men bigger than I am."

I thrust my chin up defiantly. "I can't promise that, sir. If I feel the need to defend someone, I will. I don't really need you to protect me, either. I can rely on God to do that."

He gave me a long look, sighed heavily, then galloped off in the direction Mr. Singer had gone.

I turned my horse and headed back to the house. When I got to my room, I rang for Sara and asked her to bring me a tray of food. I was suddenly very hungry. Sara took one look at my disheveled appearance and wondered what had happened. I decided to give her a bland rendition of the truth. She said she would fix a bath for me as soon as I had eaten. She seemed to be of the opinion that there was no problem that a hot bath and a good meal couldn't fix.

When I finally went back downstairs, I checked to see if Edmund was in his study. Surprisingly enough, he was.

"Did you find Mr. Singer," I asked shyly.

"Yes, I did."

"And what happened?" I asked.

"I merely explained that if he wanted to live and work on my estate he would never hit his wife again. And I told him that if he ever touched *my* wife again, I would break every bone in his body."

"I see," I said doubtfully. I cocked my head to one side and gave Edmund a long look.

"Is something wrong?"

I paused. "I was just trying to decide if you really *could* get the better of him. I have firsthand knowledge of his strength. But, I suppose you *might* be just as strong."

He smiled. "Ah, so now *you're* mocking *me*! Well, I'll take it as a compliment that I might be *almost* as strong as that monstrous man."

CHAPTER 11

While I was trying very hard to follow Edmund's orders and not think about what had happened to his mother, no matter how hard I tried, I found myself doing things to try and get closer to the past. I would stand in the late Mrs. Fitzpatrick's sitting room (my sitting room now) and stare up at her portrait. She was such a grand lady—full of life, with a glint in her eye. I couldn't imagine such a vibrant woman throwing herself from a cliff. What kind of a change had taken place after she had married Mr. Beville?

When my neck would begin to ache from staring up at her, I would go over to the beautiful ivory piano in the room and play haunting melodies. No longer did I play only for my father, I felt closer to Mrs. Fitzpatrick when I played, as well. Sometimes I would find my way to her bedroom, with the excuse that I was looking for some embroidery thread, but instead, I would sit on her bed, or stare out her window at the cliffs in the distance.

I tried to get close to her—to understand her. One morning, I happened to be looking—snooping, actually—through her dresser drawers and I came upon her Bible. Amazed, I flipped through the dog-eared pages. Mrs. Fitzpatrick had truly studied God's Word. All through the book, passages were outlined and sometimes there was a short notation written in the margin. I sat down on her bed and read the passages she had outlined and her own interpretations of what different verses meant to her. I couldn't believe that a woman who would study her Bible so faithfully would ever doubt God enough to throw herself from some cliff. I had lost track of time completely, and I was startled when I heard someone calling my name.

"I'm in here," I called absently.

Edmund stepped inside the room, just barely, as if he could not bear the thought of coming all the way in.

"What are you doing in here?" he asked, more harshly than I thought necessary.

"I came to look for some embroidery thread—no, that's not entirely true. I came to see if I could feel closer to your mother. I found her old Bible."

Edmund looked at me for a long moment. Finally he said, "You missed luncheon. Don't miss dinner," and he turned and walked away.

What was I to think about that? Had it bothered him so much that I was in his mother's room, looking at her Bible that he could hardly trust himself to speak to me? I hoped I hadn't upset him too much. That night at dinner, I would apologize. For now, with my stomach growling as accompaniment, I continued to sift through the wonderful things in

Mrs. Fitzpatrick's Bible. When I finally left her room, I took the Bible with me. I hoped no one would mind.

When I came into the drawing room later that night, Edmund was pouring himself a large drink. I went right over to him.

"Edmund, I am sorry if it bothered you that I was in your mother's room, reading her Bible. But, I couldn't help it. Once I found it, I couldn't put it down. She had underlined passages, and made notes about them—it's amazing. You should read it some time."

Edmund's jaw was clenched so tightly I thought his teeth would crack.

"Kaitlin, this obsession you have with my mother has got to stop. I told you before that I don't want to think about the past. I want to forget it. I don't want to read my mother's Bible—I don't even want to be reminded that she had one. Please don't make me sorry that I told you about my past. Please respect my wishes to leave well enough alone."

"I'll try," I said meekly.

After dinner, we played a few games of chess, and Edmund seemed to be back to his old self—baiting me and finding all kinds of things to bicker about. It didn't bother me as much anymore that he would want to engage in these verbal battles. I knew the only reason he did it was to keep his mind off more painful thoughts.

As we were putting the game away, Edmund remarked, "I've invited guests for dinner tomorrow night."

"You have," I said dully. I didn't want to spend another evening with Mrs. Colton and Mr. Denson.

"Yes, Nathan and his pregnant wife will be dining with us."

"That's great!" I said, not bothering to take exception to the fact that Edmund referred to Amelia as "Nathan's pregnant wife." I couldn't wait till tomorrow. I couldn't wait to show Mrs. Fitzpatrick's Bible to Amelia. Since it was getting late, I told Edmund good night and went upstairs. I spent a little more time reading, then my eyes got heavy and I drifted off to sleep.

I awoke early the next morning, feeling restless. I was out of bed and staring out of my window when Sara brought in my water for washing up.

"Oh, Mrs. Fitzpatrick, you're up early!"

"I know, but I couldn't sleep. I decided I might as well get up and start getting dressed."

After I ate breakfast, I went out to the stables to have Spirit saddled. I was going to ride into town and do some Christmas shopping. Nathan, Amelia, Melinda, and Miles would be coming for Christmas dinner, and I wanted to get a small gift for each of them. I was also going to get something for Sara.

At first I thought to ride into town, but then I decided I would walk. It was a little cool, but the crisp air was refreshing. Once in town, I couldn't decide what to buy. Finally, I settled on some jewelry for the ladies. I had done some embroidering, and I would be giving some of those things to them as well. I got Nathan a small Bible that I thought he could give as a gift to his new son or daughter, and I purchased a fancy pair of "cheap" cufflinks for Mr. Denson. As I was coming out of the store with my sack full of packages, I met Mr. Denson on the street.

"Can I help you with that?" he asked, taking the sack from me before I had a chance to argue. "How did you get to town? Did you ride or did you walk?"

"I walked."

"You can't possibly walk home carrying this heavy sack," he said with a wink. "I'll take you home in my carriage. But first, let's get some tea at the inn."

"I really should be getting back," I said evasively.

"Nonsense," he said, brushing my protestations aside. "I'm sure you are in need of some refreshment."

"All right, but I can't stay long."

He put my packages in his carriage, and we went into the inn. I did not feel comfortable spending time in this man's company, but I supposed it wouldn't hurt anything.

Once we had settled ourselves at a table, Mr. Denson said, "How have you and Mr. Fitzpatrick been doing? I hope married life is treating you well."

"Oh yes, I am enjoying married life quite well, thank you," I bit my lip after I said the words. Was I enjoying married life? Considering all of the strange and embarrassing things that had happened, I didn't know if I could say that with all truthfulness. Something in my manner must have struck him as odd, for he gave me a strange look.

"Are you sure nothing's wrong? You seem different somehow, Kaitlin."

"I can assure you that I haven't changed a bit."

This time I tried to sound more believable. I wanted to

put an end to his interrogation. Something in *his* manner was making me nervous.

"Then why do you seem colder, more aloof? I thought we were friends, Kaitlin." He fixed me with a gaze of soulful admiration.

"I don't want to give the town gossips anything to talk about. As a married woman, I can't be too familiar—even with old friends." I didn't particularly regard Mr. Denson as a *friend*, and I was glad to have the excuse of propriety to keep him from paying too much attention to me.

"If this is too public a place for our meeting, I could arrange for us to go and talk somewhere more private." As he said this, he reached over and grasped my fingers in his hand—an action I was sure was witnessed by half a dozen ladies having tea.

I was annoyed, rather than shocked, at his veiled intentions. Apparently he thought he was so attractive to women that even my marriage to Edmund would not keep me from falling for him.

I tried to keep my voice low, as I said, "Mr. Denson, if I didn't care whether or not I made a scene, rest assured you would be wearing my tea and my tea cup as well. I will not sit here and listen to your veiled insinuations. Do not follow me out of here, or I may make a scene anyway."

I stood gracefully and left before he had a chance to say anything. He did not follow me. I retrieved my sack of packages from his carriage and began walking home. By the time I reached the house, I felt rather worn out. I had forgotten Nathan and Amelia were coming for dinner. That afternoon, I worked on finishing my Christmas presents. I had learned to do my embroidering alone, in my room, for whenever Edmund found me sewing, he would scowl and quickly walk away. I didn't want to keep making him angry, not when my goal was to share God's love with him.

The afternoon passed quickly, and soon I was dressing for dinner. I remembered that I was going to show Mrs. Fitzpatrick's Bible to Amelia, so I took it downstairs with me. I must have taken longer getting ready than I thought—Nathan and Amelia were already there when I came down.

"Amelia, look what I found," I said, as soon as I saw her. I brought the Bible over to her. "It's Mrs. Fitzpatrick's Bible. I found it in her room."

Amelia gave me a strange look. "Did Edmund tell you about his mother?"

"Yes, he told me about his horrid stepfather and his mother's apparent suicide." I looked over to where he was, deep in conversation with Nathan. "Edmund is convinced that his mother jumped off that cliff, but I'm not so sure. He doesn't want to believe that she may have been murdered."

"But we don't really know what happened—I don't really think you should jump to conclusions."

"Oh, I know, but after reading what she wrote in her Bible, I think she was a wonderful Christian woman. I don't know what her husband did to her, but I can't believe he could have driven her to suicide." I spoke passionately, willing Amelia to understand my point of view.

"We may never know," Amelia said wistfully. "But I am curious about her Bible. Would it be all right if I took it and looked at it for awhile?"

"Sure," I said smiling, "After you've looked it over, you may agree with me."

During dinner, Nathan and Edmund discussed politics, and Amelia and I discussed the baby she was carrying.

"Have you picked out any names?" I asked her.

"Anna if it's a girl, and Nathan if it's a boy."

We continued to make small talk until dinner was over, then we left the gentlemen and went back into the drawing room.

"So, Kaitlin," Amelia said, when we were seated, "How is married life treating you?"

When I broke into a fit of laughter, Amelia looked shocked and concerned.

"I'm okay," I told her, and then I recounted what had happened this afternoon when I had had tea with Mr. Denson, and how he had asked me much the same question.

"Edmund still seems to enjoy baiting me, but I can't say that he mistreats me in any way." I paused. "It's just that—sometimes I wonder if he even likes me at all. I seem to annoy him no matter how much I try to be a witness to him. I just don't know what to do."

Amelia patted my hand. "I think you're being too hard on yourself. Edmund is not always an easy person to understand, but I think I know him well enough to know that if he disliked you, he would never have married you. It may take time, but I think you will have a good influence on him."

Tears stung my eyes at Amelia's words. I only hoped I could be as optimistic as she was. When Nathan and Edmund came into the drawing room, I quickly wiped my eyes so I could see well enough to pour the coffee. Edmund's eyes locked with mine as I handed him his coffee cup. There was a question in his gaze, and I quickly looked away. I was once again surprised at how observant this man was. He always seemed to know what I was thinking.

We talked for a while, but Nathan kept looking at the clock on the wall and asking Amelia how she was. He seemed worried that she was overtiring herself. Finally, he convinced her that they had better go home. I thought how nice it would be to have someone who was that concerned about me.

After we had seen them to the door, Edmund asked me to come back into the drawing room with him.

"Is something the matter?" I asked, wondering what he wanted.

For a moment, he seemed at a loss for words. Then he asked bluntly, "What were you and Amelia talking about earlier that made you cry?"

Now it was my turn to be speechless. "I—I don't know what you mean," I said evasively, turning away from him as I spoke and going over to the window.

I could hear him walking over to me. He stood behind me, waiting.

"Oh, bother!" I cried, turning around to face him. "I can't lie very well, can I?"

"No, and that's a good thing," he remarked. "Now, tell me what was bothering you."

I paused, trying to decide just how truthful to be. Finally, I decided to hit him right between the eyes with the truth.

"Well, Amelia asked me how married life was treating me. I told her I was doing fine except that," here I stumbled.

This was harder than I thought. "I told her I was doing fine except that I sometimes wondered if you even liked me, since I always seem to be doing things to annoy you."

I turned back toward the window—I didn't want to see the look on his face. I tried to shut my ears to any shout of laughter. Surprisingly, none came. I waited for what seemed like an eternity for something to happen. Then, finally, his hand on my arm gently turned me around to face him.

"And this concern about whether or not I like you made you cry?"

I nodded, fighting back tears once again.

He shook his head. "How stupid of me not to consider your feelings in all this! You must know that I bicker with you and tease you because I enjoy your company. I don't dislike you. In fact, I very much enjoy the intelligent conversations we have—and our games of chess. And, Kaitlin, there has not been a moment when I have regretted my decision to marry you." He gave me a look with such fierce intensity that I knew he was telling the truth. Without thinking, I threw myself into his arms and held him tightly. After a moment, he put his arms around me and held me, as well. With my cheek on his chest, and his hands absentmindedly caressing my back, I wanted this moment to go on forever. Instead, he gave me a final squeeze and then stepped back.

"Do you feel better now?" he asked.

"Yes. Uh, good night," I said walking toward the door. "And thank you."

Very quietly, almost so that I could not hear it, he said, "You're welcome."

For a time, it was easy to keep my mind off Mrs. Fitzpatrick. Edmund and I seemed to have settled into a more friendly relationship, and for that I was grateful. Christmas was only about a month away, and I had a lot to do if I wanted to finish the handkerchiefs for Edmund and the other gifts I was working on. I had more fun than I could remember decorating the house. It wasn't until the decorating was all done, my presents were all finished and wrapped, and the plans were all made for the dinner, that my mind turned back to the problem of Mrs. Fitzpatrick. I just had to know what exactly had happened to her.

I couldn't shake the feeling that something was not right. I really couldn't believe—after reading what Edmund's mother had written in her Bible—that she would have committed suicide. I was sure she had too much faith for that. The question remained—what had happened that day?

That question that had so plagued me was pushed to the back of my mind during holiday preparations, but then two days before Christmas, I suddenly remembered the strange little man I had seen by the cliff. Jim. Did he know something about what had happened, and how could I get him to tell me? Perhaps the answer to the past could be found in the slightly twisted mind of that old man. Curiosity was starting to get the better of me, and I knew I would have to go find Jim. I decided to go for a ride right then, and I took some bread, cheese, and cakes along. I hoped that would make him more willing to talk.

I rode Spirit down the path, but when I got close to Jim's

shack, I dismounted. I pushed some wisps of hair out of my eyes and looked around. The wind had picked up and it was getting cloudy. I wondered if we were in for a storm. I had a slight feeling of uneasiness, as though God were warning me not to meddle in the past. I didn't listen to that still small voice, though if I had, it might have saved me much pain. I was too curious, though. I did not want to leave well enough alone—I wanted to find out things.

When Jim didn't appear right away, I started walking toward the shack.

"Jim! Jim! It's me, Kaitlin Fitzpatrick!"

Finally, I saw a grimy little face peer through the doorway.

"Hello, Ma'am," he said seriously. "So you've come to see ol' Jim, have ye?"

"Yes, Jim, I have come to see you. You see, I need your help."

"You need ol' Jim?" he said, not quite believing me.

"Yes, I need you. I've brought some food. Would you like to eat while we talk?"

He took a few steps out the door and looked greedily at the basket I had in my hand. I felt guilty trading food for information, but I brushed that aside and dove right in. Jim looked back at the shack, and then gazed around. When he spied the large pile of rocks where I had seen him before, he said, "Come over here, ma'am."

We sat down on the rocks and I opened the basket. I took out the bread, cheese, and cakes and Jim's eyes grew wide.

"You brought all this for ol' Jim?"

THESE *Rugged* CLIFFS

"Yes. But Jim, I have some questions for you. Can you please tell me about Mrs. Fitzpatrick?"

He eyed me suspiciously.

I tried again. "Did you see her much?"

"Sometimes her'd walk along here. Sometimes her'd ride."

"She was pretty, wasn't she?"

Jim took his hat off and gave me a reverent, tearful look.

"Her was beautiful. It was so sad."

"Do you remember the day she died?"

He gave me a terrified sort of look and acted as though he would run away.

"Don't be afraid, Jim. No one's going to hurt you. What happened that day?"

"I was sitting by the rocks. Her came. I wasn't hurting nobody. I just liked to watch her. Her was pretty. Then that man came and they yelled at each other. He grabbed her. Then—I shut my eyes. Her screamed and then her was gone."

"Did that man push her over the edge?"

"I don't know."

"Jim, would you tell my husband what you just told me?"

He shook his head violently, "No, ma'am, no. I don't want to talk to no police."

"My husband won't hurt you, Jim. He's not the police. I'll make sure he doesn't hurt you. Please, Jim. Please say you'll talk to him."

"Ok, ma'am. I guess so, if you say so."

When I left Jim, I told him Edmund and I would be back tomorrow at the same time. He nodded his head sadly, then ran into his shack. I hoped he wouldn't get scared off. I was so proud of myself for finding out what really happened. I couldn't wait to tell Edmund.

CHAPTER 12

By the time Edmund and I had luncheon the next day, I was a bundle of nerves. The night before, time had seemed to drag ever so slowly, but now it was revelation time.

While we were eating, I told Edmund, "We have to go for a walk after luncheon so I can give you your Christmas present a little early."

"What do you have in mind?" he asked with a raised eyebrow.

"I have to show you something."

We walked down to the cliff and I led the way to the large rock pile. Jim was waiting there.

"Edmund, this is Jim. Jim, this is Mr. Fitzpatrick." Edmund gave me a strange look and said, "I know him."

"Good. Now, Edmund, Jim has something he'd like to tell you about the day your mother died. Go ahead, Jim," I encouraged.

Jim had slunk around to the other side of me, apparently terrified by this man I had brought to talk to him.

"Go ahead, Jim. Tell him what you told me."

"Well," Jim said nervously. "I told her how ma'am used to come down here when her was sad. Her was sad that day, too. I liked to just look at her. Her was so pretty. That day, the man came. They was both really mad. I mean, they really yelled. Then he grabbed her and I was so scared I closed my eyes. Then I heard her scream and when I looked up her was gone."

I had been concentrating on watching Jim tell his tale, but now I looked over at Edmund. He had turned a terrible shade of white.

"Did you tell the constable?" he asked quietly.

"No, sir. I didn't want to tell the constable. I was scared."

"Did you tell the constable?" Edmund said more loudly, as though he hadn't heard Jim. The look on Edmund's face was making me uneasy.

"No," Jim said, backing away. "I was scared."

Edmund pushed me out of the way and leapt at Jim. It happened so fast, I could hardly take it in. Jim couldn't either. A look of shock passed over his face, then it turned to fear.

"Why didn't you tell the constable?" Edmund screamed into the man's face. He had picked him up and was shaking him like a rag doll. "You fool! Why didn't you tell the constable?" Edmund shouted again. Jim's eyes were closed, and I didn't know if Edmund would ever stop shaking him.

"STOP IT!" I screamed, grabbing Edmund's arm. He tried to fling me away, but I hung on. "You're hurting him! Stop hurting him!" I pulled up the sleeve of his coat and dug my nails into the side of his arm. He yelped and let go of Jim. The old man collapsed in a pile on the ground and I quickly bent to see if he was okay.

"Jim, are you okay? I'm sorry, Jim. I'm so sorry," I said.

I stood up and faced Edmund then, angrier than I had ever been in my life.

"You Monster! What do you think you're doing? I told him you wouldn't hurt him!" I pounded my fists into his chest, but he caught my wrists and held them still. I looked up into his face then, and my knees almost buckled. For a moment, I thought he was going to strike me, or shake me like he did Jim, or even toss *me* over the cliff.

"Don't you see what he did? He let that man get away with murder! He was the only one who could do something about it and he didn't!" He screamed the words into my face.

"He couldn't help it. He was scared," I said weakly.

"Because of that old fool's stupidity, my mother was killed and her murderer went free!"

I turned around to look for Jim, but he had already run off.

"I thought you would be happy!" I screamed back at him.

"What?"

"I thought you would like to know that your mother didn't commit suicide. I thought you would like to know that she didn't leave you. She didn't turn her back on God and jump over that cliff. I thought you'd like to know that!"

"You think I should be happy about this?" he flung the words at me, and I could almost feel them pierce my skin.

"You want me to rejoice at the cruelty of a God who would allow this to happen to my mother. She loved God. She went to church. And He let that man come into her life and kill her."

"It wasn't God's fault! You can't blame Him for the evil in the world!"

"Yes I can and I will! Not only did He let that man kill her, but all the *good* people in town who could have stopped it or brought that man to justice stood by and honored him as the suffering victim of his wife's selfish suicide. And all along, there was a witness to my mother's death. But the witness was a scared half-wit who never told anyone. Was that part of God's plan? And I should be happy? Am I supposed to be happy that the man that I would love to seek my revenge on is already dead?"

He stopped and raked his fingers through his hair.

"You Christians say God is love. I don't see it. Where is this loving and compassionate God that you serve? He stood by and watched my mother die." At this point he gave me such a look of pure hatred that I sucked in my breath.

"Edmund," I said, putting my hand on his arm. He flung my hand away. I tried again. "Edmund, I—" but he would let me get no further. He waved me away from him as he dropped to his knees and held his head in his hands.

At that moment I knew what it meant for your heart to break. The tears were flowing down my face, but I stood rooted to the spot. I kept reliving the awful scene that had just passed, and each time it felt as though a knife were being thrust deeper and deeper into my chest. I saw that Edmund's shoulders were shaking, and I knew he was overcome by a new kind of grief. I longed to go comfort him, to stop this aching of his, but I knew that I had already meddled far too much. I had caused him pain that I could not undo.

The wind had picked up, and it looked like we were in for a storm. I stood staring out over the sea, watching the gray clouds piling on top of each other. My teeth were chattering, and I couldn't seem to stop shaking. Edmund had stood up and walked over to look down over the edge of the cliff. I left him like that, staring out into the rising storm. I started back up to the house, surprised that my legs would even carry me.

⚉

Much later, I went into Edmund's study to see how he was doing. He sat at his desk, looking out the window, an almost empty bottle next to his elbow.

"Bring me another bottle of brandy, Jeffries, it's going to be a long night," he said without turning around.

"Edmund." I said his name softly and he slowly turned to face me.

I walked over and stood in front of his desk. I could tell by the odor that he had been drinking—a lot.

"I thought you said once that you would never drink so much that you would get drunk—now look at you."

"Yes, go ahead, look at me. Pity me all you want, despise me all you want, but it's not going to change me. I told you once that I wouldn't make a good husband." He smiled sweetly, "I guess I was right."

All of a sudden I was angry. "Go ahead," I said, "Wallow

in your brandy until you make yourself sick. And I'm not pitying you one bit. You're doing just fine pitying yourself. You're not the only one who has ever had to face tragedy, Edmund Fitzpatrick. I know what it's like to lose someone you love. I know what it's like to question God, but I didn't let it get the best of me. You assume you have ample justification to do anything you want to do, but you still have to behave like a gentleman!"

I was breathing heavily at the end of my tirade. At first, the only indication he gave that he had heard me was a few quick blinks of his eyelashes. But then a cynical grin replaced his blank look.

"Aren't you Christians supposed to be meek and mild?" he asked mockingly.

I tried to think of something to say, but couldn't come up with anything that would do me credit. So I simply gave him a long stare and silently left the room. I stood outside the study door for a minute willing myself not to cry.

Supper was a lonely affair. Not surprisingly, Edmund did not come to dinner. After eating, I went to find a book in the library. That room seemed too dreary, so I took my book to his mother's old sitting room. I could understand now why Edmund had kept it shut up. The past seemed stiflingly close. I tried to read, but my mind kept returning to the man in the study.

Finally, I felt a stab of shame. I realized that I had gone too long without prayer. I had been acting on my own with no thought of my Heavenly Father, and I regretted it. In fact, I realized now that my conscience had been pricking me all along, telling me not to meddle, but I had pushed the still small voice aside. The stab of shame grew until I began to feel very guilty. What worried me the most was the fear that I had done irreparable damage to our relationship. The friend-ship that had been growing between us seemed doomed to die an early death. I knew I must apologize to Edmund and ask his forgiveness. I also knew that I had to go back to the study, not to lecture or to preach this time, but to pray.

I stopped when I reached the study door, though, afraid to go any further. My eyes closed in prayer, and I leaned my forehead against the cool door. I asked the Lord if this was a good idea.

Deep down, I knew I must. I swallowed my pride and knocked. When he made no reply, I went in anyway. It was dark in the room, except for the firelight and the light from the full moon, but I could just make out the features of his face. He was staring out into the night, his jaw clenched. I walked silently over to the large settee to the right of the doorway. It faced the windows, so I sat and looked out at what he was looking at. Or, at least, I appeared to. Instead, I focused every atom of my being into a simple prayer for Edmund.

God, be real to him. God, show him your love.

"It's a beautiful night tonight," Edmund said idly, swiv-eling around to face me.

"Yes, it is," I said, looking out at the moonlit sea.

"I love the way the moon reflects off the water."

"Are you drunk?" I asked him.

"You're thinking I sound rather normal for a person who should be intoxicated?"

"Yes."

"Well, I don't feel too bad right at the moment."

"Oh."

"Why are you here?"

I took a deep breath. "I felt like I needed to pray for you."

At my words he started as though I had struck him. He got up and made his way over and sat heavily beside me. I think he couldn't stand.

"What did you say?" he asked angrily, shaking me till my teeth rattled. He had gripped my arms so tightly that I wondered if I would have bruises tomorrow.

"You're hurting me," I said quietly.

He quickly let go of me, but repeated his question. "What did you say?"

"I'm praying for you."

"I don't need your prayers!" he said vehemently. For a moment I feared he would strike me, so great was his barely controlled rage. Then he seemed to rein in his emotions and look closely at my face.

"You're crying," he said, putting his hand on my cheek.

"Sometimes I cry when I pray," I said quietly.

He reached up and gently wiped his thumbs along my cheekbones as if to erase my tears. He gave me one long last look—I felt I could almost reach out and touch his soul. Then he collapsed. He ended up passed out with his head in my lap and most of his body on the settee. It couldn't have been comfortable, but he didn't seem to care.

I looked down at his face—troubled even in his sleep. I knew it would be a long night, but I was ready to pray hard.

CHAPTER 13

When I awoke, I was stretched out on the settee with a blanket spread over me and a pillow tucked under my head. I felt stiff and sore from sleeping in such an awkward position. Edmund was gone; I had no idea when I had finally fallen asleep. I got up, stretched, and then went upstairs to wash up and change. I was a little worried about seeing Edmund, but I decided I couldn't avoid him forever.

"Good morning," he said when I entered the dining room.

He didn't look like he was any worse for yesterday's debauchery.

"How are you?" I asked, helping myself to some eggs and toast.

"Never better." He grinned at me. "Did you sleep well last night?"

"Not exactly."

"I'm sorry to have put you in such a compromising position, but I must say I was comfortable. I slept better than I have in ages."

I gave him my best scathing look. I was hurt that he was making light of the situation.

"You know," he said, smiling at my rising anger, "if you would sit on my bed and let me fall asleep on your lap every night, I'm sure I would have perfect dreams."

I threw my toast at him and walked out without saying anything. What right had he to bait me so? I could not believe he would mock my Christianity so blatantly. Didn't he know I had come back to his study to pray for him because I cared about him?

I walked blindly out the back door and onto the veranda. I was already regretting my fit of temper. Would I *never* be able to act like a Christian around that man? After all my prayers and my resolve to behave differently toward him, I had failed miserably. I had almost made it to the edge of the gardens when I felt a hand on my arm. I tried to fling it away, but Edmund's grip was too strong. He swung me around.

"Where do you think you're going?" he asked. "You haven't finished your breakfast."

I didn't know what to say, so I wisely kept my mouth shut. He finally looked closely at me and must have seen the hurt in my eyes.

"I was only teasing you," he said, chastened.

"Well, it wasn't very funny. Do you remember how you treated me yesterday? Do you think I can take it all as a joke? I mean—" I stopped then, unable to go on. I thought about what I had prayed so fervently for last night. Now, because I was embarrassed and my pride was hurt, I was going to go right on and say whatever I wanted to. I turned away from him for a moment, trying to collect my thoughts.

"Edmund," I said quietly, turning back to face him. It took a lot of courage, but I looked him in the eye. "I'm very sorry for the way I went behind your back to find out what happened to your mother. I'm sorry I made you talk to Jim and dredge up the past. I'm sorry I meddled. I—I don't always do things the way I should, and sometimes I'm not a very good example of what it means to be a Christian. If I could, I would go back and change everything I did yesterday. We were actually starting to get along, and I want us to be friends again, though I wouldn't blame you if you can't stand the sight of me. But, if you can, please … forgive me."

Tears stung my eyes as I tried to share from my heart, and I looked away then, not wanting to see the look on his face.

"You … are apologizing to me?" he asked quietly after a moment of tense silence.

"Yes."

He reached over and turned my face up to look at him. It was hard not to look away. There was uncertainty, confusion, in his eyes, as though he didn't understand something.

"Why?"

"Because, as I was trying to say, I was wrong. I shouldn't have tried to find out about your mother, and I shouldn't have spoken to you the way I did."

"That's not exactly what I meant by 'why.' Never mind— perhaps I have misjudged you a little."

At his words, I embarrassed myself even more by start-ing to cry. Great sobs shook my shoulders, and I couldn't hold back the tears. I was still upset with myself, and I still felt horrible about what had happened yesterday.

"I'm sorry," I said, trying to choke back the tears. "I just can't help myself."

Edmund didn't mock me. He simply put his arms around me and let me cry all over his chest. If I hadn't felt so humiliated, I might have been grateful.

When Mrs. Parks came to check the menu with me, I realized it was Christmas Day. We would be having guests for dinner! So much had happened yesterday that I had forgotten. My first Christmas Eve as a married woman had been a disaster; I could only hope that today would turn out to be better.

That afternoon, I lay down for awhile to take a rest. I began dressing for dinner early. Sara was excited about doing my hair for this special occasion. I was just getting ready to ring for Sara, when I heard a knock on the door that led to Edmund's room. It startled me, and for a second I couldn't figure out what the sound was.

"Yes," I called out.

"Can you come in here?" Edmund asked.

"I'll be right there."

I finished dressing, and then walked into Edmund's room. He was not finished dressing. His hair was slightly damp. He stood there in his trousers, his shirt unbuttoned. I couldn't help it; my eyes were drawn to his bare chest.

"Hello, madam," he said politely.

"Did you need something?"

"Yes. I have something for you—a Christmas present. I didn't really want to give it to you when our guests were here."

He handed me a box. I took it from him and held it gingerly in my hands. I looked at it as though it were some strange creature. Slowly, I opened it. A gasp escaped my lips when I saw the necklace. It was silver, simply set with several small diamonds, with one large diamond in the center.

"Edmund, it's beautiful." I had the strangest urge to kiss him on the cheek. I smiled up at him but his gaze made me uncomfortable. I looked away.

"I don't know what to say," I said quietly.

"Then don't say anything."

My eyes flew to his face. Was this simply because he felt guilty about last night?

"You can't be serious. It's too much!"

"It suits you and I want you to wear it. It was my mother's, and I can't help but think she would have wanted you to have it. In fact, I have a feeling she would have liked you very much. Please don't argue with me."

"All right," I said slowly, tears pricking my eyelids, "I'll wear it."

He walked up behind me and fastened it in place. I looked at my reflection in the mirror. The necklace was breathtaking, and I couldn't believe how elegant it made me look.

"Thank you," I said. "I … need to finish getting ready."

"You look beautiful already."

I started toward the door.

"Kaitlin."

I stopped and turned around.

"I have another Christmas present for you," Edmund said quietly.

"You don't need to give me anything else," I said fingering the necklace. "This is so beautiful."

"I'm not *giving* you anything else, exactly. It's just—" he paused, and then went on slowly, looking me straight in the eye. "I'm sorry about the way I treated you last night. I never would have believed that I could drink myself into such a state that I would behave so ungentlemanly. It will never happen again."

"I'm sure it won't," I said, astonished at his apology.

"I *know* it won't," Edmund said firmly. "I've decided I'll not drink anymore."

"Are you serious?"

"Very," he said solemnly.

"I don't know what to say, except I'm glad."

"I thought you would be."

I left then, bewildered, and shortly after, Sara came in to fix my hair.

"You look beautiful, madam," she said with awe when she finished. The necklace looked beautiful set against the rich dark blue velvet of the dress Edmund had sent from London. I didn't know if I *felt* beautiful, but I was very pleased with my appearance. I could hardly believe Edmund would give up drinking because of what had happened. I wouldn't have blamed him if he had never forgiven me, but instead he seemed to have had some sort of change of heart.

I said a prayer of thanks to God for working in Edmund's life. I prayed that I might be a better witness from now on.

By the time Sara had finished my hair, I was feeling very nervous. I wondered how this evening would go. It would be the first time Nathan and Amelia and Melinda and Miles would be dining together. Perhaps they would all be more likely to get along because it was Christmas. I said yet another quick prayer, asking that God would help things go well this evening, and then I went downstairs to play hostess.

Edmund was in the drawing room when I came down. For my benefit, he smirked and looked longingly at the decanter of brandy that was still there.

"Ah, Kaitlin, you look quite beautiful this evening," he said generously.

"And Edmund, you look quite—thirsty, let me get you a glass of water," I said playfully.

He flung his head back and laughed at my attempt at humor. Just then, Mrs. Colton and Mr. Denson were announced, and they came into the drawing room.

"Why, Edmund, you do sound happy this evening. May I ask what has put you in such good humor?" Mrs. Colton asked.

"Of course, you may ask. The very funny thing that just happened is that my beautiful wife offered to get me a glass of water."

He looked over at me and winked, then he broke out into another fit of laughter at the look on Mrs. Colton's face.

"You do have such an interesting sense of humor, dear Edmund," she said.

Mrs. Colton moved out of the way as Nathan and Amelia blustered in.

"Sorry we're late," Nathan said amiably, "but it seems to take Amelia so much longer now that she's getting dressed for two!"

Nathan laughed at his joke and Edmund roared with laughter—he appreciated Nathan's attempt at humor more than the rest of us did. I giggled at the sight of the two of them laughing hysterically, and Amelia simply shook her head. Mr. Denson looked uncomfortable and out of place, and for the moment, Mrs. Colton did not seem her usual confident self. I was glad when Jeffries came and told us dinner was ready. When Edmund came over and took my arm to lead me into the dining room, I was a little surprised, and very pleased. I even felt a little sorry for Melinda. However, I figured she would find some way to get the upper hand again—she always seemed to.

Dinner was lovely. Although I had my doubts as to how the group would get along, I needn't have worried. Edmund did a good job of choosing topics of conversation that both gentlemen felt free to join in, and amazingly enough, Amelia did a wonderful job of drawing Mrs. Colton into conversation. While there seemed to be little in common between them, Melinda actually seemed to enjoy talking with Amelia. Before long, the meal was over. Amelia, Melinda, and I started to excuse ourselves.

"Just a minute ladies," Edmund said, causing us to pause. "The gentlemen and I will come with you. Since I no longer wish to have my after dinner drink, we might as well escort you to the drawing room."

At his words, everyone gaped at him but me. He smiled in my direction, came over and took my arm, and left everyone to stare in shock at his back as we walked away.

When we got into the drawing room, Nathan had recovered enough to ask, "Do you mean, Edmund, that you don't drink anymore?"

"Nope, I decided it wasn't good for me."

"It was as simple as that?" Mrs. Colton asked.

"Yes. Now my dear," he addressed Mrs. Colton, "I would be pleased if you would delight us by playing a few Christmas carols. I must say I am in quite a festive mood."

As we all walked over to the piano, Amelia grabbed my arm and whispered in my ear. "Wonders never cease, Kaitlin. I don't know what has gotten into Edmund tonight, but I'm guessing you must have had something to do with it. Well done, my dear."

I blushed at her compliment. If she only knew the mess I had made of things. It was only by the grace of God that things had turned out as well as they had!

We sang along as Mrs. Colton played a few Christmas carols. Then Edmund brought out a bag and passed out some gifts. He gave Nathan a new pocket watch and Amelia an ornately embroidered shawl. He gave Mr. Denson a pair of riding gloves, and he gave Mrs. Colton a pair of satin gloves.

Mrs. Colton looked a little put out at this impersonal gift. Then she gave me a sweet smile.

"Why, Edmund, didn't you get your new wife a gift?"

Edmund grinned at her and reached over to put his arm around me. His fingertips lightly brushed my skin and

I caught my breath as he lifted the necklace to display it for Mrs. Colton to see.

"This was her Christmas present," he said. He let the necklace fall back onto my skin. He gave my neck a gentle caress and then let his hand rest on my shoulder. My cheeks felt hot, and I knew I was blushing. I looked up at Edmund, but he wasn't looking at me; he was looking at Mrs. Colton. The smug look on his face annoyed me. It seemed as though he was only acting like a loving husband to make her jealous.

Soon Mr. Denson brought out some gifts from him and his cousin. He had to leave the room to get my gift. He came back with a wriggling form in his arms. The puppy was a spaniel type and there was a bow around his neck. He presented me with the puppy and a rhinestone collar with a leash attached.

I had never had a dog before, and I wasn't too sure what to do with it. But when Mr. Denson set him in my lap, the puppy stood on his hind legs and licked my nose. I giggled. I looked over at Edmund. He did not seem to be terribly amused. Oh well, I thought, I needed something to keep me company. For awhile we sat and chatted then the puppy began to whine.

"He probably needs to go out," Miles said. "I'll take him."

Miles was gone for a few minutes. When he came back, he set the pup down and we watched as he nosed around the room and finally curled up by the fireplace to take a nap.

Suddenly, there was a disturbance outside. A group of carolers had come. Mrs. Parks was ready with hot cocoa and tea. Apparently, this was a Christmas tradition. Edmund acted the true country squire—jovial and generous—and it was obvious that his tenants respected and admired him. When the families finally left, our other guests took their leave as well. When everyone was gone, Edmund wished me a Merry Christmas and went on upstairs. Suddenly I remembered my Christmas present. When all the carolers had invaded the house, I had quite forgotten my puppy.

I searched the drawing room, but the dog was nowhere to be seen. I checked the hall, but he wasn't there either. I wondered if he could have slipped outside when all the carolers were coming in or out. I felt guilty for having lost him so soon. I decided to go out and look for him.

I grabbed a coat from the coat closet. I didn't take a lantern because the moon was shining brightly. I looked around outside for a moment and then I heard a faint sound in the distance. It sounded a little like a dog whining. I headed in the direction of the cliffs. As I walked, I could hear the sound more clearly. It couldn't be far now.

Suddenly, the wind picked up and the moon went under the clouds. I stumbled along in the dark, listening for the sound of the puppy's yelps. The sound was clearer now, and I knew I was getting close. The ground was uneven and I still couldn't see very well. The dog must have heard me because he began to whine and cry.

Suddenly, I came to a standstill. I started to go on, but I couldn't take another step. It was as if a wall had suddenly blocked my way. Almost audibly, a voice said "Stop!"

I stood there, uncertain what to do, then the clouds shifted and the moon shone brightly. When I saw where I was, I started to shake. I stood rooted to the spot, right on the edge of the cliff. I looked out over the dark angry sea and now I could feel a breeze coming up from the ocean. If I had put my foot out in even one more uncertain step, I knew I would have fallen to my death.

I heard someone screaming, and it scared me. I covered my ears to try and block out the sound, but it went on and on. The pup was silent. He was stuck several feet down on a ledge in some brush.

The air went out of my lungs in a loud whoosh when hands grabbed me and swung me around. It was then that I realized that *I* was the source of the screams. I looked up at Edmund and blinked a few times. I was confused.

"What is going on?" Edmund yelled, shaking me a little.

"The puppy ..." I said weakly.

All of a sudden, Martin appeared and climbed down to get the dog. I watched as he untangled the dog's leash and lifted him back to safety. As Edmund pulled me away from the ledge, I felt a sharp stab of pain in my chest. Fear and shock mingled, and I couldn't quite catch my breath. I had a feeling that someone had purposely put that dog on that ledge and tied his leash so he couldn't get away. I let Edmund lead me back to the house. He called for Mrs. Parks to bring some tea to the drawing room. He set me in a chair in front of the fire and pulled a chair up across from me. For a moment he didn't say anything. I rubbed my hands together and stared at the fire. My teeth were chattering.

Mrs. Parks brought the tea in and gave us both a strange

look before leaving the room. I hadn't seen the puppy come in, but when I looked down, I saw the dog lying at my feet.

"Tell me what happened," Edmund said after I drank some tea.

I explained how I had worried that the dog might have gotten outside when the carolers came. He listened intently as I told him what happened, but his look turned incredulous when I said, "Why would someone do this to me?"

"What do you mean?"

"Didn't you see that the dog was tied to the brush? I would have fallen over the edge if something hadn't compelled me to stop! Who would do that?"

"Who indeed?" Edmund said.

I had the feeling he wasn't taking me seriously. I felt the tears well up in my eyes.

"Don't just sit there. Say something!" I yelled when he continued to just sit and stare at me as though I were hysterical.

"I think you're jumping to conclusions. I can't see why anyone would want to do you any harm."

"I know, but then how did the puppy get outside—with his leash on?" I asked, my voice catching. When Mr. Denson had brought him in, he certainly hadn't left his leash on.

"Perhaps one of the children was playing with him tonight and thought to take him outside and then forgot."

In spite of myself, I was a little annoyed at his pat answer. Then he went on.

"Besides, how would they know that you would go looking for the dog in the dark, without a lantern?" he said nonchalantly, crossing his ankles and leaning back in his chair.

"I don't know," I said, deflated.

For another moment I sat staring at him. Then I stood up and started to leave the room.

"Kaitlin."

"Yes?" I said, coming back.

He stood up and looked down at me. "I'm sorry you had such a scare. I know it might look to you like someone purposely put the dog down there to lure you over the cliff," he said softly, his manner no longer mocking. "But I just can't imagine anyone would do that to you."

"I know," I said. "I can't believe anyone would do anything like that, either, but that doesn't change what I saw."

He put his arm around my shoulders and led me toward the door. "What you need is a good night's rest. Things will be better in the morning. By the way, I think we did a good job of making Melinda very jealous tonight. I could tell by the look on her face she was a little put out."

"So that was your goal tonight—making Melinda jealous," I said, opening the door.

"Of course, didn't you think it was fun?"

"I don't know," I said quietly, then I went upstairs without another word.

CHAPTER 14

Edmund had said things would look better in the morning. How wrong he was! I awoke with a terrible headache, and I couldn't get Edmund's words out of my mind. All last night, when I thought he was truly being jovial, when I really thought he was being nice to me, it was all just for show, to make Melinda Colton jealous. I had been so happy last night, and then the evening had turned sour. My thoughts were so consumed by Edmund and Melinda that I had forgotten all about the incident with the dog. Now that I remembered what had happened out on that cliff, I shivered. Could someone have really tried to lure me to my death? That sounded so fanciful as to be ridiculous. And yet, I had thought so last night.

All of a sudden, I realized that I should thank God for keeping me safe. I had no doubt that the voice I heard—causing me to freeze on the edge of the cliff—came from Him. My heart full of gratitude, I noticed that my head felt better, and I was suddenly hungry. Edmund was gone when

I came down for breakfast, and I was somewhat relieved. I didn't really want to face him this morning. After I ate, I decided that I wanted to go out and see the ledge where the dog had been. While it seemed impossible that someone was trying to harm me, I figured it wouldn't hurt to examine the scene.

Taking a cloak to ward off the chill that was in the air, I tried to retrace the path I had taken the night before. Finally, I came to a spot where the ledge below it looked about right. The grass and brush looked somewhat trampled. I thought about trying to find a way to get down to the ledge to get a closer look, but I was still shaken from my ordeal the night before, and I really had no desire to climb down there. I wondered what I would have done last night if I had had a lantern and would have seen the puppy. Would I have tried to climb down to get him, or would I have gone for help? Knowing that I like to take care of things myself, I figured I would probably have stupidly tried to climb down and get him. Would I have ever made it back up? I wondered.

Standing there, wondering what might have been, I began to shiver. Enough of this, I told myself sternly. There is no reason to believe anyone intended anything malicious. Who would want anything to happen to me? Suddenly, my thoughts went back to that day in the woods when I had thought shots were being fired at me. What if those shots really *were* aimed at me? That would mean that twice now my life had been threatened. I didn't like the direction my thoughts took from this point on. The only person who gained by my death was Edmund. If I were out of the way, he would have my money—and he would be free. Free to marry Melinda if he wanted.

At some point, I had stopped shivering and started shaking. I could not let my thoughts run away with themselves. I had absolutely no reason to believe any of that. I stamped my foot, willing my imagination back under control. *I will not believe it, I will not believe it,* I kept repeating. I decided that a little exercise would do me good. I followed the path along the cliffs towards Jim's shack. Perhaps I would see him and have a chance to apologize.

When I got to the large pile of rocks near his house, I sat down and stared out at the sea. I was trying to determine whether or not to go and knock on Jim's door and disturb him. I really felt I needed to talk to him, but I was afraid I would scare him more.

Finally, I decided it wouldn't hurt to just go over and call his name and see if he came out to talk to me. If he didn't show his face, I would know I was not welcome. As I was walking around the pile of rocks, I stumbled over something and fell down. Frustrated, I got up and turned to see what had made me fall.

It was Jim. I gasped and fell to my knees beside his body. He was lying facedown behind the rock pile. His one foot had stuck out just enough for me to trip over it. At first I thought he was sick, or hurt, but when I felt his arm, I knew he was dead. When I rolled him over to get a better look, I shuddered. One side of his forehead was a mass of bruised and bloodied skin. He had been hit by something large and sharp. I turned away quickly, hoping my breakfast would stay down. It didn't. After I was finished being sick, I stood on wobbly legs. The world seemed to be spinning, and I was terrified that I was going to pass out. After a few big gulps of cold air, though, I felt much better.

I walked back toward the house. It would have been faster if I could have run, but my legs felt too weak. In the distance, I saw a horse and rider. I thought I recognized it as Edmund, but I wasn't sure yet. When I began calling his name, the rider came galloping toward me. He seemed to know something was wrong as soon as he saw me. Jumping off his horse, he grabbed me by the arms.

"What is it, Kaitlin? What's the matter?"

"It's—Jim. He's—dead." At that point tears began rolling down my cheeks, but I ignored them and concentrated on leading Edmund back to Jim's body. I turned away as Edmund rolled the body back over and examined the wound.

"His face is a mess," Edmund said. "Did you see this, Kaitlin?"

The choking, gagging sounds I was making behind the rock seemed to answer the question.

"I'm sorry you had to see that," he said, coming over and putting his arm around me.

"We'll have to go back to the house and have someone fetch the constable."

"Come on, you can ride with me." He mounted his horse and then reached down and helped me up in front of him. We were both silent on the ride home. Edmund sent Martin to fetch Constable Hardy and Nathan (though his medical expertise was hardly needed) and then we went into the drawing room to wait.

I just couldn't believe Jim had been murdered. At least, I assumed he didn't get that gash on his face by tripping and falling on a rock. Someone had hit him very hard. I thought of the few times I had spoken to him. He had been a harmless sort of man. Why had this happened to him?

"Why did this happen to him?" I muttered, aloud. I found myself staring at Edmund. I knew how enraged he had been the day before yesterday. Would he have been mad enough to kill?

All of a sudden I realized that he was staring back at me. "When did he die?" I asked quietly.

He didn't answer for a moment, and I looked away. I was worried that he might read my thoughts.

"You don't think I killed him in a fit of rage, do you?"

"I don't know."

"I shouldn't think you would have any doubts, but to put your mind at ease, no, I had nothing to do with the old man's death."

"I'm glad."

He snorted. Clearing his throat, he said, "There'll be an inquest, you know. You and I may be called to testify since we found the body and were probably the last to see him alive."

"Except for the person who killed him," I said.

"We don't know that it wasn't an accident," he said unconvincingly. He looked at me closely, then, and he must have seen how upset I was, though I tried to hide it.

"I'm sorry about Jim, Kaitlin. I know this has upset you, and as soon as the inquest is done, I'd like to take you away from here for awhile."

"What do you mean?"

"My aunt lives in London, and she keeps writing to tell me to visit. She'd love to see you—if that's all right with you."

"I would love to visit your aunt," I said with conviction.

Soon, the constable came and asked us some questions, but we weren't able to tell him much. When Nathan arrived, Edmund took them to the spot where I had found Jim. I stayed at the house. I didn't think I could handle watching as they examined the body more closely.

While they were gone, I sat in the drawing room and stared out the window. I couldn't believe all that had happened in the last few days. What a wretched time it had been! A small sound caused me to look down. My puppy whined, wanting me to pick him up. I scooped him onto my lap and absentmindedly petted him. As soon as all this was over, Edmund and I would go visit his aunt, and hopefully things would be better. I knew his aunt was a Christian, and I very much looked forward to meeting her.

By the time the men got back, it was time for luncheon. Edmund invited the men to stay and eat with us, but they both excused themselves, saying they had things to do. Edmund and I did our best to eat, but neither of us had much appetite. There was an uncomfortable silence between us, and as soon as I could, I left the table.

After searching all over the house, I finally found the puppy. I grabbed his leash and headed over to see Mrs. Singer and her children. I had thought it over, and I was going to give Laura and Johnny the puppy—if it was okay with their parents. I didn't know what I would do with him in London, and I couldn't help it—after what had happened last night (and this morning), I wasn't too eager to have the dog around reminding me of it all.

When the children saw the puppy, they came running to meet me.

"Can we play with him?" Laura asked shyly.

"Go ahead," I said handing her the leash. The puppy jumped around, barking and licking the children's fingers as they tried to pet him. I could tell he was a happy little dog to have someone to play with. I would have to try and convince Mrs. Singer to let them keep him.

"Hi, Mrs. Singer," I said when she came out to see what the noise was all about.

"Hi, madam," she said shyly.

"I came to ask you a big favor."

"Whatever I can do, Ma'am," she said.

"Well, you see, I got that puppy as a Christmas present. But, Mr. Fitzpatrick and I will be going to London soon, and I don't know what to do with him. I was wondering if it would be all right with you if I made a present of him to your children. As you can see, they love him already. If you'll keep him, I'd like to send over some food for him to help repay your kindness."

Mrs. Singer wiped her hands on her apron and looked around.

"I don't know. I think I better ask my husband."

"That would be fine. Would it be all right if the children watch the dog for me today? If Mr. Singer doesn't want them to keep him, maybe he could bring him over tonight?"

"I'm sure that would be fine," Mrs. Singer said. "Thank you."

"No, thank you. I was really worrying about what to do with the poor dog. I'll just go and tell the children that they can keep watch of him today. Good-bye, Mrs. Singer."

"Good-bye, Mrs. Fitzpatrick."

The children were very pleased to take on such a great responsibility as watching a dog. I left them looking very sober. Laura was explaining to her brother that they must take *very* good care of the doggie. I smiled and hoped that Mr. Singer would let them keep the dog.

When I was going into the house, I met Edmund coming out.

"Edmund, will you be seeing Mr. Singer today?"

"Why?" he asked quickly.

"Oh, nothing really. It's just that I went over there to see if they would let the children keep the dog Mr. Denson gave me. It would be a bother to have it in London, and I know the children would just love him. Mrs. Singer said she'd ask her husband, but if you could just talk to him, maybe you could convince him that it would be a good idea."

"Madam," Edmund said in a mocking voice as he bowed at the waist, "I shall do my best."

Thankfully, Mr. Singer did let them keep the dog, and when I walked by their house a couple days later, I was pleased to see the children playing happily with him. However, I was not so pleased when the day of the inquest came. I was going to have to give testimony, and even though there was not much I could tell, I was still very nervous.

When they called my name, I practically jumped out of

my skin, but once I began answering questions, I relaxed and the anxiety went away. It was no surprise when the judge gave the verdict, "Murder by person or persons unknown." Then they adjourned, and we were free to go. It seemed that if any more evidence turned up, there would be a second inquiry into the matter.

Before we left for London, Edmund asked the constable if it would be all right if we went away for a few weeks, or if we should stay in case he needed to ask us any questions. He said it was fine if we left, but he had Edmund leave the address where we could be reached.

"Just in case," the constable said, "though I can't really see us finding anything more to go on. It surely is a puzzle."

I agreed with him wholeheartedly. There was absolutely no reason why anyone should kill Jim. Edmund probably had the best motive, and it was simply ridiculous to think of him as a murderer.

On our way home, Edmund said, "I can't wait to get away from here for a bit. Have your maid begin packing immediately. If I get my way, we'll leave for London in the morning."

I nodded. I wasn't going to argue with him. I would be just as happy as he was to get away.

CHAPTER 15

Edmund got his wish, and we were ready to leave the next morning. It felt so good to be able to put all of the problems of the past week behind me. When we arrived at his aunt's home, she came right out to the carriage to meet us. She kissed Edmund and he picked her right up off her feet in a big bear hug. She gave a little shriek and said, "Put me down," rather sternly, but there was a twinkle in her eye.

When her feet finally touched the ground, she turned to me.

"Aunt Mary, let me introduce you to my wife, Kaitlin."

"My dear," she said hugging me, "I'm so glad Edmund had the good sense to marry you." She stepped back but held my hands tightly.

"You look like your father. Edmund said you favored him and he was right. He also said you were a Christian, and I can't tell you how happy it makes me."

"Edmund told you ... ?" I said, surprised. I couldn't

believe Edmund would have thought it important enough to mention.

"Yes, he wrote and told me all about you. He knew I would want to know." She smiled up at him.

I gave him a questioning look, but he just turned and reached our bags down from the carriage. Aunt Mary led us upstairs to a suite of rooms that she had specially prepared for us. They consisted of a bath, sitting room, and a large bedroom with one large bed. I glanced uneasily around, but said nothing. Edmund could tell I was uncomfortable; he grinned wickedly the entire time his aunt was showing us the rooms.

Finally she said, "I'll leave you two to unpack and get settled. We'll have tea in the drawing room as soon as you're done."

The footman left our bags by the door and he and Aunt Mary walked out together. I went over and began unpacking my dresses. Edmund stood at the window and looked out.

"How long are we planning to stay?" I asked after a short time.

"I don't know. A couple weeks, perhaps," he said without turning around.

"Oh."

After a tense silence, Edmund took his bags and set them in the sitting room.

"I'll sleep in there if it'll make you stop acting like a scared kitten," he said peevishly.

I stared at him, taken aback. "I'm not acting like a scared kitten," I said.

"Hmmph," he grunted.

I looked in the sitting room. It was a nicely decorated

room; there were several high backed chairs and a couple small tables scattered about. Also, there was a small divan in front of the fireplace.

"You can't possibly sleep on that sofa. You'll never be comfortable. Why don't you just ask your aunt for a different room?"

"I'll be fine," he said. "As far as my aunt is concerned, we are a conventional married couple. She thinks we are madly in love. I'll not spoil that for her." He came over and took my arm to lead me down to tea.

"So, don't be alarmed if I give you an affectionate kiss or a warm smile. It would make my aunt happy if you would do the same."

I stared at him with my mouth open. He gave me a quick kiss on the forehead and then led me toward the door.

"There now," he said mockingly, "don't look so shocked. You should know a wicked sinner such as myself would not hesitate to lie to his aunt." He flashed me an impish grin as we started down the stairs.

He kept on talking about something—I don't know what. I was trying to keep my footing without leaning heavily on his arm. I had the strangest feeling in my arms and legs—as though they had turned to cotton, and I had a strange feeling in my stomach—as though I were nervous about something.

I was not really looking forward to dinner that night, but surprisingly, Edmund was a delightful dinner companion. He seemed relaxed and at ease in his aunt's company. He was kind and courteous to me and loving to his aunt.

After dinner Edmund asked if I might play for them. I did so. His aunt's pianoforte was a delight to play. When my fingers began to ache, I went and sat on the divan. Aunt Mary sat in a nearby chair, crocheting. Edmund came and sat beside me and put his arm around me. Aunt Mary smiled fondly at the quaint picture of marital bliss we made. Even though I knew it was just an act on Edmund's part, I let myself believe he was fond of me, too, and I relaxed in the circle of his arm. I woke up to see Edmund looking down at me with a teasing grin on his face. My cheeks grew warm when I realized I had snuggled up against him as I dozed off. His aunt saw my discomfort and chuckled.

"Young love is so refreshing. You don't have to be embarrassed, my dear. It just shows how much you trust and have come to rely on my nephew," she said.

I blushed more and would have set her straight, but I knew it meant a lot to her to see Edmund "happily" married. So, I just smiled at her and ignored Edmund's raised eyebrow and irritating smirk.

Finally it was time to retire. Edmund took me by the arm and led me up the stairs. Once inside the room he began to laugh. He collapsed on the bed and chortled till there were tears in his eyes and he was short of breath.

"You should have seen the look on your face when you woke up," he said between gasps.

I made myself busy taking off my jewelry and removing the pins from my hair.

"I'm sorry, Kaitlin, but when Aunt Mary was spouting that stuff about 'young love' and you learning to 'rely on me,' I didn't think I could take it."

He finally stopped laughing, seemingly exhausted. "Well," he said, breathless, "It's been a long day. I think I'll go try and make myself comfortable on that tiny couch in the sitting room and leave you to get some more beauty sleep." He smiled at me impishly and left the room. I changed into my nightclothes and fell asleep almost as soon as my head hit the pillow.

※

We had been in London for about a week. There had been a whirlwind of parties and visits. Edmund had been kind and courteous towards me when his Aunt Mary was around, but when we were alone he was rather quiet.

After breakfast, I was walking through the hall on my way upstairs when I heard Aunt Mary call to me from her drawing room, "Kaitlin, dear, can you come in here for a minute?"

I walked in and she motioned for me to come sit by her on the sofa. When I sat down, she stared at me for a moment and then clasped my hands in hers.

"Edmund is not here right now. I sent him on some errands because I wanted to have you all to myself for awhile. I didn't want him to interrupt."

I felt a little uncomfortable with her intense gaze.

"My dear, am I right in assuming that things are not quite as they seem between you and Edmund?"

I looked at her in amazement. I was surprised that she was so observant. I shifted uncomfortably.

"What do you mean?" I asked quietly.

"I mean that whatever your reasons were for marrying

each other, it wasn't because you were madly in love. Am I right?"

I looked down at my hands clasped in my lap.

"Yes, I'm afraid you're right. How could you tell?"

"Oh, my dear, I've been around for a long time. I know my nephew well, but that's not really it. You see, Edmund has done a pretty good job of acting his part. However, you haven't fooled me a bit. When you look at my nephew, there is longing in your eyes, not love."

My eyes grew wide at her words. "What do you mean, longing?" I asked her.

She smiled, silent for a moment. "You look at him in much the same way I do. You want him to become a Christian?"

"Yes, I do."

"Well, that is also my fondest wish."

"I've tried to do what I can to show him God's love, but I've done a horrible job of it. I've done some stupid things, Aunt Mary. I don't know if he'll ever want anything to do with God after what I've done."

I felt tears stinging my eyes as I told her that. All the guilt and shame that I had felt came back in a flood, and I wanted to tell her all about it.

"Tell me what you did, child. I'm sure it can't be as horrible as you think."

"It is," I said, and then I poured my heart out to her. I told her everything, about how I always seemed to say or do the wrong thing to annoy Edmund, about my stubbornness, and about my wish to help Edmund find out what happened to his mother, but the clumsy way in which I had gone about it. I told her about trying to apologize. I even told her about

Jim and how I felt that it was somehow my fault that he was dead. By the time I had finished, tears were streaming down my face. Aunt Mary surprised me then by hugging me. She held me tightly while I cried. When I heard a sound behind me, my heart sank. I didn't want him to see me like this.

"What's this, Aunt Mary?" Edmund asked. "I leave my bride alone with you for a few hours and you reduce her to tears."

"Oh, Edmund," she said, exasperated.

I drew away from her and dried my eyes.

"We were just chatting about God," she said. "I was just going to tell Kaitlin that I think she's a wonderful Christian. She's a good example for you, Edmund."

He was suddenly serious. "You're right, you know," he said.

"Kaitlin, you look like you could use a rest. Why don't you go upstairs and lay down for awhile? I would like to speak to my nephew alone."

I glanced at him, but he wouldn't look at me.

"All right, Aunt Mary," I said rising. I bent down on impulse and pecked her on the cheek. I knew Edmund was watching me as I left, but this time I didn't look at him.

I shut the door behind me, wondering what she wanted to talk to him about. I took her advice and went upstairs to lie down. I found that crying always made me tired. I fell asleep almost immediately. When I woke up, Edmund was walking around the room. "Hello," he said when he turned and saw that I was awake.

"Are you feeling better?" he asked.

"Yes."

"I'm sorry if my aunt upset you."

"Actually, we had a good talk. I really like your aunt."

"She's a dear. And a sharp old lady, too."

"Yes, I know."

"Do you have anything planned today?"

"Yes. Aunt Mary wanted to take me window shopping this afternoon."

"I'm sure you two won't mind if I tag along?" he asked with a raised eyebrow.

"That would be nice," I commented. I couldn't really believe he wanted to go with us. I wondered if he had some ulterior motive in mind.

After we finished our luncheon, Aunt Mary asked me if I was ready to go do some shopping. I told her I couldn't wait, and Edmund chimed in to say that he was going to go, too. Aunt Mary looked at him in surprise. We walked along a beautiful tree-lined street full of shops. After awhile, Aunt Mary coaxed me into a hat shop. Edmund came in and tried to watch patiently as we tried on hats, but he soon began to look bored.

Finally he said, "I'm going to wait outside."

Aunt Mary tried on a couple more hats, then decided on one. She handed me a pair of gloves that she said would be perfect with my ivory dress. We made our purchases and then left the shop. Edmund had walked a little farther along, so we hurried toward him. The streets were crowded with people and hackney cabs hurrying by. We caught up with Edmund, and Aunt Mary saw a chocolate shop across the street that she wanted to visit. We were waiting for a carriage drawn by two large horses to pass when I felt a hand on my back.

I assumed it was Edmund, but suddenly I was given a sharp push. I fell to my knees in the street, the carriage bearing down on me. I lifted my head to see the driver struggling to stop the horses. They reared and bucked, and I put my arms up to try and ward off the thrashing hooves.

In the same instant, I was snatched out of harm's way, but not quite soon enough. One of the hooves struck me. Edmund spun me around in his arms to face him. He looked up at the carriage driver and apologized for our being in the way. I ignored the pain in my arm for the moment and scanned the audience. The hand I had felt on my back must not have been Edmund's, but whose? I looked back at Edmund. He was brushing hair out of my face and looking to see if I had been hurt.

"Someone pushed me!" I cried. He seemed to ignore me; he was staring at my arm. There was a tear in the sleeve of my dress, and I could see blood trickling from a gash on my upper arm. The skin had already begun to turn purple. As soon as I saw the wound, my arm began to throb. Aunt Mary hovered in the background making soothing comments and patting me on my other shoulder. I tried to forget the pain in my arm and focus on the problem of who had tried to kill me.

"Edmund," I said, gripping his arm. "Someone pushed me in front of the carriage."

He was still scowling at my arm, trying to tear the material away so he could get a better look, but he finally seemed to hear me. "What do you mean someone pushed you?"

I sighed loudly. "I felt a hand on my back and then it pushed me."

He looked at me incredulously. "Why would anyone want to do that? You must have been mistaken. No doubt someone in the crowd bumped you. Now, if you are done jumping to conclusions—which seems to be a favorite pastime of yours—we'd better get you home and have that arm looked at."

Aunt Mary had been standing close beside me, her hand around my waist to steady me. "Edmund's right, dear," she said. "We must get you home. We've all had quite a scare."

I let them lead me home. During our walk back to the house, the throbbing pain became almost unbearable. I gritted my teeth and tried not to let it show. I just hoped I wouldn't pass out. Finally, we were back inside the drawing room, and Aunt Mary was helping me sit down on the sofa. Edmund sent for a doctor and then sent a servant to fetch cold cloths and tea. I leaned back and Aunt Mary propped my arm up on some pillows.

Edmund tore off the sleeve of my dress and wrapped some of the cold cloths around my swelling arm. Aunt Mary used the other cloth to wipe my forehead.

"Does it hurt much?" she asked.

"Unfortunately."

The doctor soon arrived. Aunt Mary introduced us to Dr. Brown. I winced as he examined my arm, prodding and poking the tender area.

"Is it broken?" Edmund asked.

"I don't think so," Doctor Brown said. "However, it's very hard to tell. There could be a slight fracture. There's no need to set it, but it should be wrapped well for at least a couple weeks." He turned to me. "And you mustn't do anything to put any strain on it."

"Like washing clothes," Edmund said, winking at me.

The doctor looked aghast at the thought of a lady such as myself doing such menial tasks. I smiled, thinking how wonderful it was that Edmund had been in such a jovial mood. I was happy as well, even with my sore arm. When the doctor suggested I go lay down, I did so with a light heart. He left some medicine with Aunt Mary in case I should have trouble sleeping. I was in good spirits when I kissed Aunt Mary on the cheek and went up to my room. Once settled, however, my happiness vanished and I felt very uneasy. I tried to sleep, to put all that had happened out of my mind, but I just couldn't do it. I was beginning to feel afraid. Had someone tried to kill me? Or was it madness to keep thinking someone would try to lure me off a cliff or push me in front of a carriage? I wasn't sure which would be worse—that someone really was trying to kill me, or that I was making myself crazy thinking about it!

The rest of our visit with Aunt Mary was pleasant, but uneventful. I didn't feel up to going out much, so things were rather dull. About a week later, just as I was beginning to feel better, Edmund suggested we go back home. Although I would miss Aunt Mary very much, I had found that I did not like city life. Many people—Aunt Mary included—enjoyed the noise, the crowds, the hustle and bustle of the busy city; I, however, was not one of them. Surprisingly, Edmund did not appear to like London all that well, either. With a reluctance to leave Aunt Mary, but a desire to get back home, Edmund and I packed our bags and left the following day.

CHAPTER 16

When Edmund and I got back from London, we settled into a comfortable routine. We both seemed to put that scene on the cliffs and in his study behind us and we were good, if not very close, companions. Also, Edmund no longer mocked my Christian beliefs. Apparently his aunt had had a good effect on him. In fact, whatever my doubts were about the marriage, I had at least stopped fearing that Edmund was trying to kill me. It seemed funny even to think it. I couldn't explain why it seemed that there had been three attempts on my life, but I didn't think Edmund had anything to do with it. I felt very peaceful, and my hopes that this happy state of affairs would go on forever were naive, to say the least.

The bubble I had been living in for the week since we had gotten back from London was popped on Thursday night, when Edmund mentioned casually that we were invited to a dinner party at Mrs. Colton's the next evening. Immediately, I could feel my spirits plummet, and all of my old doubts and fears came crashing back. I felt that I had been living in a dream—in this dream, Mrs. Colton and Mr. Denson didn't exist. Unfortunately, they were very real. I said little about the invitation, but I dreaded it very much. I slept fitfully that night. The next morning dawned bright and cheery. When I came down to breakfast, I found Edmund eating eggs and bacon and humming a happy tune. I poured myself a cup of tea and sat down.

"I wish we didn't have to go to this party," I said, sighing. Edmund seemed to read my thoughts.

"Are you worried that Melinda might cause a scene—that she might be too outrageous in her flirtations with me?"

He grinned impishly at me over his coffee cup. I smiled faintly, but his words hit too close to home for me to join in his lightheartedness.

I spent the day renewing my friendships with several of the farmer's wives. I hadn't been around to see them since we had gotten back from London and I was feeling a little guilty about that. Edmund seemed pleased that I took an interest in the estate, and I think it actually helped him in his dealings with his tenants. They had always respected him, but now that they respected me as well, it added to his reputation.

I had told the cook that I would be gone for luncheon. I decided to take along some bread and cheese to the Singer family and perhaps eat a bit with them. When I got there, Mrs. Singer was just setting things out for a meal. The children were glad to see me, if only because they knew I probably had a treat. Mr. Singer was downright courteous. He doffed his cap when he saw me, and the big man was almost quaking with fear that he might do something to offend me. Edmund must be a more powerful man than I thought. I felt honored somehow that he would go to such lengths to protect me.

After I had spent as long as I could away from the house, I went back to try and figure out what I might wear. I finally decided to wear the ivory silk gown I had worn when we were married. I was hoping it might subconsciously remind Edmund of his decision to marry me. Perhaps it would keep him from focusing too much of his attention on Melinda. I also chose to wear Edmund's Christmas present. The diamonds felt cold against my skin.

I let Sara fix my hair. She had gotten very good at it. When Sara left me, I started pacing around the room. I fidgeted with my dress, smoothed imaginary wrinkles, stared out the window, and tried to pray. I prayed for patience and wisdom. I expected Mrs. Colton to have an arsenal of biting comments and scathing looks. I knew Edmund would do his best to try and bait me, and I didn't want to have to make small talk with Mr. Denson.

Finally it was time to go. While I was coming downstairs, Edmund came out of the drawing room. He looked up and saw me, and I saw him raise an eyebrow. He met me at the bottom of the stairs and offered me his arm.

"You're going to give even Melinda a run for her money, aren't you?" he said with a wink.

"Actually, I would prefer to think that my beauty comes from within."

"Are you saying Melinda's beauty is only skin deep?" he asked.

"Perhaps."

He didn't answer; he just opened the door for me and

gave a little bow, directing me to go on first. I rolled my eyes at him and went over to climb in the carriage. Unfortunately, I had never traveled in this dress, and I realized that something about the style of it made getting into the carriage very difficult.

Edmund gave me a playful push on my bottom to help me up and in. I knew he was simply trying to get some kind of reaction, so I just sat down primly and said, "Thank you for your help," as nicely as I could.

This response seemed to please him even more, and he laughed out loud. I shook my head and looked out the window.

"You know," I said, "for such a proud, arrogant man, sometimes you can be very childish."

"Oh, really," he said. "Melinda doesn't think I'm childish."

"Yes, well, *Melinda* would love for you to help her into any carriage," I said sharply.

He smiled arrogantly. "Do I detect a smidgen of jealousy, my dear wife?"

"Of course not," I said sullenly. I had a sneaking suspicion that he was trying to make me jealous, so I didn't say anything more.

When we arrived, Edmund helped me out of the carriage, and held my arm as we walked up the steps to the front door. The doorman announced us, and Mrs. Colton and Mr. Denson came over to greet us. She kissed Edmund on the cheek in greeting and clung to him a little longer than was proper.

"It's so good to see you again. I'm so glad you're back."

Mr. Denson kissed my hand in greeting, but he seemed a little reserved. More people were arriving, and the pair left us for the moment to go see to their other guests. Edmund and I moved over to a corner of the room.

"I wish Nathan and Amelia were going to be here," I whispered quietly.

"You sure are complaining a lot tonight."

I frowned at him, but he went on.

"You should be the happiest belle at the ball—looking the way you do. I think you've made all the ladies jealous."

"Not all of them," I said, looking over at Melinda Colton.

He followed my gaze and smiled. "Oh, I'm sure she's jealous of you. You have something she doesn't."

"What's that?"

"You have me." He smirked at me. The statement struck me as so idiotic, and so far from the truth, that I had no reply. Mrs. Colton looked over at me then and gave me an icy smile. We had a buffet style supper to start with, and after we had eaten, we went into the large room she had decorated for dancing. Edmund left me then and went over to talk to some of the gentlemen. I was surprised when Lady Conrad came over to talk to me.

"Good evening, Mrs. Fitzpatrick."

"Good evening."

"Did you have a nice trip to London?"

"Yes, ma'am, it was very nice."

"This is a nice party, isn't it?"

I nodded, wondering why she was being so nice to me.

"I hope you're happy with the way things turned out,"

she said. Something in her voice made me think she had stopped being nice.

"What do you mean?"

"It seems things have worked out very well for you."

"I don't understand."

"I'm congratulating you on your good marriage. We were all *so* surprised when Mr. Fitzpatrick married you. It was very fortunate for you, my dear. Mr. Fitzpatrick was a very eligible bachelor. I wonder *how* you ever managed it."

All I could do was blink at her as I struggled for something to say.

"Hello Lady Conrad." I was startled when Edmund appeared at my elbow. His interruption saved me from replying, and the set of his jaw made me wonder how much he had heard. He would not take kindly to the assumption that he had been somehow tricked into marrying me.

"I must steal my lovely wife away from you," he said graciously to Lady Conrad. "There is someone I want her to meet."

He held my elbow in a steel grip and led me quickly away.

"Who did you want me to meet?" I asked as he led me over to the punch bowl.

"No one," he said, helping himself to a glass, "but I decided that if I didn't get you away from that spiteful woman, one of us would have probably smacked her."

I giggled. "I can't believe how vicious she is."

"Yes, well, you made a lot of ladies unhappy the day you married me. Speaking of jealous ladies," he said softly, "here comes one now."

I turned to see Melinda Colton gliding toward us. She was a vision in a pale blue dress which set off her bright blue eyes and made her blond hair shine.

"What are you two doing stuck over here in the corner?" she asked playfully. "Our most famous couple should be mingling about, helping to make my party a success."

"What do you mean by 'our most famous couple?'" I asked, stupidly stepping into a trap.

"Why, everyone is still talking about how the two of you were married so suddenly—how you pulled Edmund out of the clutches of half a dozen hopeful girls."

Edmund replied before I had a chance to, and I wasn't sure if I particularly liked his way of changing the subject.

"Melinda," he said, almost purring, "Allow me to be the first to tell you how ravishing you look tonight."

"Well, Edmund, you're hardly the first!" she said, laughing.

"Then let me be the most sincere."

With barely a glance at me, Edmund led Melinda away, cooing softly about the way her hair and eyes captivated men. Perhaps because I felt he was being just a touch sarcastic (and maybe even trying to make me jealous), it didn't bother me very much that he walked off with her arm in arm. At least I hadn't had to respond to her biting comments.

I walked out into the courtyard. I had had just about as much of Melinda Colton's party as I could handle. The air was very cool, but I didn't mind it. I rubbed my cold arms and paced back and forth.

"Are you enjoying the party?" said a voice behind me.

I whirled around to see Mr. Denson standing very close to me.

"The party is fine," I replied. "I just needed a little fresh air."

"I'm sorry Melinda is making such obvious advances towards your husband. I'm even sorrier that your husband seems to be enjoying it."

I gave him a scathing look. I couldn't believe his impertinence.

"I'm sure my affairs are none of your concern."

"Why, Mrs. Fitzpatrick, you misunderstand my motives! I do not wish to offend you. I just feel bad that you should suffer. It need not have been so."

He gave me such a look of longing that I could scarcely contain myself. I wanted to scream. When he reached out a hand and caressed my cheek, I slapped his hand away.

"I'm sorry Mr. Denson, but I am a married woman," I said hotly.

The smile he gave me was faintly mocking. "What's good for the goose is good for the gander, according to the old saying."

I bit off a stinging reply when I saw Edmund standing in the doorway. He looked at me inquiringly for a second, as if wondering whether he was interrupting anything. I must have given him a pleading look because he came right over.

"You look tired, Kaitlin," he said, taking me firmly by the arm. "I think it is time we go." I let him steer me back inside. Edmund made a beeline for Melinda. When he told her we were leaving, she looked putout.

"You can't leave yet," she complained.

"We really must. My wife is not feeling well."

Melinda turned to me with a most hateful look on her face, which disappeared almost immediately.

"Perhaps you would like to go lay down upstairs, my dear," she said in a deceptively sweet voice. "Then your husband wouldn't have to leave the party."

I looked up at Edmund, unsure what to do.

"We appreciate your kindness, Melinda, but we really must be going." With that, Edmund took my arm and led me quickly outside. We had to wait a few minutes while our carriage was brought up.

When we were finally settled and on our way home, Edmund leaned back and sighed heavily. "I must remember that I really don't like those kinds of parties," he said quietly, his eyes closed. I didn't say anything, but I couldn't have agreed with him more.

CHAPTER 17

A few days after Mrs. Colton's disastrous party, Edmund and I were eating dinner when Jeffries barged into the dining room.

"I am sorry to interrupt you, sir, but there is a very agitated couple at the door." He gave a distasteful little cough. "I believe they are tenants of yours. I tried to send them away, but the giant man threatened me." At that he swallowed nervously.

My mind was swirling, but when he mentioned "the giant man," I knew who must be out there. I threw down my napkin and rushed out into the hall. I stopped short at the sight of Mrs. Singer's ashen face and tear-streaked eyes. Edmund bumped into me then gently set me aside. I recovered from my shock and went over to Mrs. Singer. I knew it was uncommon for any type of bond to develop between a tenant and a "lady," but I had recently showed Mrs. Singer how she could have a relationship with Jesus Christ, and that had definitely created a sense of kinship between us. Also, I remembered very clearly the embarrassing scene I had created when I had tried to protect her from her husband. Even now, I felt somehow responsible for her welfare. Suddenly, I realized Edmund had spoken.

"What's happened?" he had shouted.

I put my hand on his arm to quiet him when I saw Laura bury her face in her mother's dress. That's when I noticed that Johnny was not with them, and I expected the worst.

"Where's Johnny?" This time it was my turn to shout.

"That's why we're here, ma'am," Mr. Singer said. He was standing with his head bowed slightly, his hat in his hand. "He's gone, I mean, we can't find him."

We spilled out of the hall and onto the wide portico that led to the drive. I looked around—as if the boy might materialize right there. As I glanced about me, I noticed a slightly acrid smell in the air. I ran out onto the drive and spun around.

"There," I yelled, fear swelling in my chest and making breathing difficult. "The old barn is on fire! Do you think—?" I didn't finish. I was interrupted by a series of barks coming from that direction. Edmund yelled, "Let's go!" and grabbed Mr. Singer's arm. They ran down the lane and toward the burning building as quickly as they could.

Dashing inside just long enough to tell Jeffries to summon help, I picked up my skirts and rushed after them. Mrs. Singer seemed to have been struck dumb in a moment of motherly terror, but then she yelled "Johnny!" and started running after me. She caught up to me within the first fifty yards. By the time we reached the men, they were trying to pry open the big sliding door, but it was jammed. The puppy was running in circles by the barn door, barking wildly.

They stood staring doubtfully at a rope that dangled from the open door in the hay mound. Flames flickered here and there, growing larger moment by moment. Suddenly, we heard a sound that made me gasp and made Mrs. Singer shriek. From the very high opening, we heard a whimpering sob, and saw Johnny's face peek out.

"Johnny!" Mrs. Singer cried, falling to her knees with a wail of desperation. The boy's face had disappeared from the opening, but we heard him cry, "Mommy" and begin whimpering.

Had the boy shimmied up the rope and into the hayloft? I could hardly believe it. Edmund grunted with determination and grabbed the rope. He struggled a little at first, but then he started pushing off the side of the barn a little, and he seemed to be working into a sort of rhythm. I stood in dumbfounded silence as my husband risked his life to save the little boy. It seemed like an eternity, but it couldn't have been more than a minute when Edmund finally climbed through the opening.

I put my arm around Mrs. Singer and said encouragingly, "Edmund will get him down," but I held my breath until he came back to the opening clutching a grimy little bundle to his breast.

He pulled the rope up until he had the end. He wrapped it around Johnny's waist, made sure it caught snugly under his arms, then began lowering the boy down. "Singer!" he called out hoarsely and the big man positioned himself under the boy in case something went wrong. Martin and the others were lugging pails of water to wet down the grass around the barn.

When Johnny was halfway down, there was an ear-splitting crash. To my horror, the hay mound collapsed, taking Edmund with it. Mr. Singer caught Johnny and held him tightly. This I noticed with only a very small part of my brain. I had frozen for a moment when I saw the barn slowly collapse in upon itself, taking Edmund with it. I watched as he disappeared and flames engulfed the spot where he had been. As soon as I found my voice, I started to scream. I ran toward the opening that had been created when part of the barn wall had collapsed.

Strong arms caught and held me, and I watched in horrified silence as Martin and another servant rushed in to get Edmund. Only when they had carried his limp form out away from the fire did my captor let me go. I ran over to Edmund's side, my heart beating wildly. Someone called for a wagon and a doctor. I gently brushed the hair away from a gash on his forehead. A large bruise was already forming around the cut. I gently began to wipe away the blood with the hem of my dress. His face and hands were covered with several severe burns.

Finally, I saw the rise and fall of his chest and I knew him to be alive. I sucked in a great amount of air, unaware I had been holding my breath. I knelt by his side, numb with shock, while we waited for a wagon to carry him home. A little way off, the Singers were hugging one another and crying.

Soon, Martin came with a wagon and Nathan came riding up in a cloud of dust. Someone quickly told him what had happened, and I was glad for I didn't trust myself to speak. Nathan frowned at the gash on Edmund's forehead and the burns on his face and hands. He groped in his bag for some salve. He quickly put some of this on the worst of the burns. "It's better if they aren't exposed to the air," he said quietly, then began checking for broken bones.

I wondered if perhaps I was in the way—kneeling over him like I was, but Nathan didn't ask me to move, and I didn't know if I could have if I'd tried.

"I'd say a possible broken rib or two and quite definitely a concussion," he said to no one in particular.

"Lift him into the wagon very gently." He helped me in first, and four sturdy men lifted Edmund's limp form into the wagon. Nathan climbed in and positioned Edmund's head more comfortably on my lap. It frightened me that he had not regained consciousness.

"When will he wake up?" I managed to croak.

"I don't know. It'd probably be better if he stayed out until we get him settled. He's going to have an unbelievable headache when he wakes up."

"You're right."

I groaned with pleasure at the sound of Edmund's voice.

"What happened?" Edmund muttered, trying to sit up. Nathan put one big hand on his shoulder and pushed him down again. He looked up at me, expecting an answer.

"The hay mound collapsed," I said, finding my voice.

"Johnny?"

"He's fine." I felt my eyes fill with tears. When a tear

dripped on Edmund's cheek, his eyes flew to mine, a surprised look on his face.

"What's the matter with you?" he asked harshly.

With a sound halfway between a sob and a sigh, I turned away from him—not bothering to answer.

"You see that—my dear wife is terribly worried about me." I couldn't quite tell if his voice was edged with sarcasm or pain.

We got Edmund home and the men carried him upstairs to his room and laid him on the bed. Nathan began bandaging Edmund's head and applying more salve to the wounds. I was a little taken aback when he began taking off Edmund's shirt. Edmund opened his eyes long enough to see that I was uncomfortable, then closed his eyes again, smiling. Nathan asked me to help him steady him while he wrapped a bandage tightly around his ribs. I did so, and was thankful that Nathan didn't remark on my obvious embarrassment. Finally, we were done, and Nathan settled him back on the bed.

"Well," he said, "you'll live. I'm a little worried that you might have a concussion. You'll have to watch him closely, Kaitlin." I nodded. "And I think at least one rib is broken, so you'll need to spend a couple days in bed."

Edmund grimaced. I felt that he probably wouldn't want to spend any days in bed, but he was definitely in pain. His face had gone white while we worked to bandage him up, and he was still rather pale.

"Can you give him something for the pain?" I asked Nathan.

He nodded, so I rang for Mrs. Parks and asked her to bring us some tea. I pulled a chair up close to the bed and sat down. If Nathan noticed that the room showed no evidence of having a woman living in it, he said nothing. He probably knew ours was not a usual marriage. Still, I caught myself just before saying, "I'll stay here with him tonight." I didn't want it to be that obvious.

There was a knock on the door. When I called, Mrs. Parks brought in the tea. I poured a cup for Edmund and Nathan measured some laudanum into it.

"I sure wish I could take that in something stronger," Edmund said scowling at me. "But I made a promise to *someone* that I wouldn't drink anymore."

"That's just the pain talking," Nathan said smiling warmly at me, "Well, I'd better be getting back to Amelia."

"How is she doing?" I asked.

"She's very uncomfortable, but I think she still has a couple of weeks to go."

"Please tell her I send my love."

"All right. Good bye, Kaitlin—Edmund."

Edmund grunted. His eyes were closed and he seemed to be trying to ignore me. I sat quietly for awhile, sipping my tea. I ate one of the cakes Mrs. Parks had sent up because I suddenly realized I was hungry.

Watching Edmund lay there with his eyes closed was rather boring, so I went to my room to get a book. When I came back into the room, Edmund was still sleeping—or at least pretending to. I got up and leaned over his bed, my face close to his, trying to see if he was really asleep—perhaps I was trying to make sure he was still breathing.

"I'm not asleep yet," Edmund said quietly.

I was so startled I lost my balance. I gave a little shriek

as I started to fall on top of him. I caught myself so I didn't land too heavily on him. Edmund groaned as the bed shook and I brushed against him.

"I'm so sorry, Edmund. I didn't mean to hurt you; I just wanted to know if you were awake."

"Next time, please just ask me. You don't have to fall on top of me."

"Are you going to be okay?"

"Yes," he said through tightly clenched teeth, his eyes closed.

I sat back down and picked up my book. I wanted to run out of the room, but I didn't. I just kept berating myself for my stupidity and clumsiness. I couldn't believe I had just done such a dumb thing. I wanted to cry, but I didn't. I knew that the moment the tears started to fall, Edmund would open his eyes and see me. I couldn't bear to have him see that his words hurt me.

I spent a long time in prayer after that. Perhaps Edmund's enforced stay in bed would give me some time to talk to him about God. However, I had a vaguely uneasy feeling that I was the last person in the world who would have any influence on him.

The next morning, I awoke suddenly and realized I had fallen asleep in the chair by Edmund's bed. He stirred in his sleep and opened his eyes. He was surprised to see me there.

"What are you doing?" he mumbled.

I ignored him. Instead I asked, "How are you feeling?"

"Fair, I suppose. My ribs hurt, but I really don't think any are broken."

"Do you want something to eat?"

A knock on the door interrupted us. Jeffries opened the door and gave his Master a sheepish look.

"Sir, Mr. Singer is here to see you."

"Send him in."

Mr. Singer burst through the door. He came and stood by the bed, his head bowed.

"Sir, I can't thank you enough for saving my little boy. You risked your life. My wife said that's what Jesus done for me. I ain't a religious man. I ain't never believed in none of that, but when I saw you risking your life for my son, well, it got me thinking that maybe there was something to what my wife said. Anyway, thank you sir. My wife thanks you, too."

With that Mr. Singer left the room. I was speechless. I didn't know what to think. I looked over at Edmund; he had gone pale.

"Edmund, are you all right?"

He gave a harsh laugh.

"Isn't it ironic that I should lead that grizzled man back to religion? It's too much." He would have laughed more, but it hurt too much.

"I think I'm ready for something to eat," he said quietly.

I rang the bell, and soon Sara poked her head in.

"Please send us up some breakfast," I told her.

"I think I'm going to hate staying in bed," Edmund said. He struggled to sit up.

"I need . . ." he said and stopped. I knew what he needed, so I went over to help him to the bathroom. He leaned heavily on my shoulder. By the time he got back in bed, we were both exhausted. I hated to see him in pain, and I could tell by the beads of sweat on his forehead that he was. Breakfast came and we ate in silence. Soon after, Nathan came to check Edmund over. He rewrapped his ribs and rebandaged his forehead.

"Tomorrow morning, I'll need you to rebandage the wound on his forehead. I won't be able to be back until tomorrow afternoon. His ribs will wait till I get here to check them."

"Okay," I said.

He left soon, and Edmund lay back with his eyes closed. Nathan had given him some laudanum, and I knew he would sleep soon.

"Kaitlin, I wish you would find something to keep you occupied. I feel bad enough as it is without having you sitting there watching me like a hawk and pitying me."

"I … I don't pity you."

"Then please, for my sake, go have fun."

Have fun. He said the words so easily yet I knew it would be impossible.

"All right, but at least let me get you some books to read."

"Fine."

I went to his study and found a few books on his shelf, then went to my room and got his mother's Bible. I put that in the pile of books. By the time I got back to his room, he was asleep. I set the pile of books on the bed beside him and quietly left the room. I stayed away from his room the rest of the day. I ate luncheon and dinner in the dining room. That evening, before I went to bed, I knocked on his door.

"Come in."

I walked in and sat by his bed.

"How are you feeling tonight?" I asked him.

"About the same—bored to death. By the way, thank you for the reading material." He gave me a mocking grin, but he didn't say anything about the Bible.

"Well, good night."

"Good night."

I went through to my room and sat down on the bed. I stared out the window at the sea for a good long time. Finally, I undressed and got into bed. I didn't sleep for quite some time.

The next morning, I ate breakfast in my room, then went next door to see how Edmund was. He had already eaten breakfast. The empty tray sat beside him on the bed. He was propped up on some pillows looking at one of the books I had brought him. When I entered the room, he looked up and smiled.

"I'm glad you're here. This bandage is beginning to itch."

I went over and carefully unwrapped the old bandage. There was no infection, and I was glad of that. As my fingers worked to place the new bandage over the gash, I lightly brushed a few of Edmund's hairs off his forehead. The tingling I felt in my fingers raced up my arm and settled in my chest. The feeling growing in the pit of my stomach was foreign to me, but not unpleasant. I lingered over the rewrapping, letting my fingers run through his hair and touch the skin on his forehead. As I looked at the curve of his jaw, the shape of his cheekbones, I had to stifle a sigh. His eyes were closed, but I knew had they been opened, I would have seen the deep blue color, the sparkle that was sometimes there—though sometimes it seemed as though he looked right through me. My fingers trembled as I finished rewrapping the bandage around Edmund's forehead. When I finished, I sat down in the chair by the bed to catch my breath. Edmund opened his eyes and looked at me.

"Thank you," he said.

"Are you feeling better?" I asked, my voice catching a little.

"Yes. When Nathan checks my ribs this afternoon, he may even say I'm fit to get up and move about."

"Good." I rose nervously. "I think I'm going to get some fresh air."

"Fine. Perhaps I'll join you for dinner tonight."

"That would be nice," I said and fled the room. I needed to see Amelia. I decided the walk would do me good, so I headed off down the path.

CHAPTER 18

The fresh air cleared my head a little, but I still felt as though I were drowning in an angry sea. Is that what love was? Is that what love did to a person? I could hardly believe it. It had been coming on so slowly and gradually that I hadn't noticed it. Or had it been there all the time and I had just denied it? Perhaps it hadn't been "God's Will" for me to marry Edmund, but my own. Was *that* the reason I had agreed to this foolhardy marriage? And it was foolhardy, I saw now. To be married to a man who didn't care about you was one thing if you didn't care for him. But to love him? To be married to and love a man who cared nothing for me? It was unbearable. I found myself shaking at the thought. I tried to push all thought aside as I raced toward Amelia's.

Suddenly, a sound to my right caused me to stop. Miles Denson had ridden up and dismounted. I hadn't heard him until he jumped down. He tied his horse to a tree branch and came over. He took in my untidy appearance and red cheeks and raised both eyebrows.

"Is something the matter?" he asked.

"No, I'm fine," I said as I tried to step around him to go on to Amelia's. He blocked my path.

"Don't go just yet, Kaitlin. I need to talk to you."

"What is it?" I said impatiently.

"Kaitlin, you know how I feel about you."

"Please, Mr. Denson. I thought I made it clear to you at your cousin's party that I am not interested in you."

"But I love you, Kaitlin. Melinda and I are leaving for London today. I couldn't leave without trying to make you understand how much I care for you. Edmund doesn't deserve you. He never has. Get the marriage annulled, and we'll be married as soon as possible."

He grabbed me by the shoulders then and stared down into my face.

"Edmund is not a *real* husband to you, is he? I can't believe that he is."

I blushed then and Miles smiled. "There now, it doesn't matter. What matters is that I love you."

He bent his head and kissed me, lightly at first, then his arms went round me and his lips pressed down on mine. At first, I confess, I didn't quite know what to do. Finally, I pressed both hands against his chest and pushed him away. I wiped my mouth as though to erase the memory of his kiss. I resisted the urge to spit.

"I'm sorry Mr. Denson, but I am not interested in your offer of love. As I told you before, I am a married woman. And, I will stay a married woman."

He stepped back then as though I had slapped him. His jaw was clenched and his eyes had a slightly glazed look.

"Very well madam. I surely hope you do not regret this. Have a good day."

He jumped on his horse and rode off without another look at me. Was he threatening me? I pressed my hands to my face and found tears trickling down. I shuddered and started running to Amelia.

By the time I knocked on her front door, I was out of breath. The housekeeper opened the door, took one look at me and said, "Goodness gracious!"

"Is Amelia here?" I panted.

"Yes, ma'am," the housekeeper said, giving me a frightened look. "She's in the parlor."

I didn't wait for the housekeeper to announce me. Instead, I left her gaping and rushed into the sitting room. Amelia was sitting in a chair working on some embroidery. When I burst in, she struggled to her feet.

"Kaitlin, what has happened?"

"Oh, Amelia!" I groaned and sat down on the sofa. She came and sat beside me and held my hand. I turned toward her and burst into tears. She brushed the hair out of my eyes.

"Oh, Dearest, what has happened?"

"Oh, Amelia," I cried between sobs. "I love him. What am I going to do? I love him. And I was coming to tell you. But then Mr. Denson came into the woods. He said he loves me. He kissed me. Oh, Amelia!" I groaned.

Amelia grabbed my arms and gave me a little shake. "Kaitlin, calm down! Start from the beginning. Who do you love? Is it Mr. Denson?" she asked with a confused look on her face.

I started giggling until I hiccupped. Amelia shook me again.

"Kaitlin, calm down or I will slap you."

I took several deep breaths.

"No, dear Amelia, I don't love Mr. Denson. I dislike him immensely. On my way here he stopped me in the woods. He made some advances, professed his love for me, and then he kissed me. I pushed him away as soon as I could. It was awful.

"He's not the one I love. It's Edmund. I was bandaging his head and it dawned on me. I love him, Amelia. I love him so much that it hurts. And he can hardly stand the sight of me. He didn't even want me in his room yesterday. What am I going to do?" I sobbed. I tried to wipe my eyes on my dress. Amelia hugged me for a long while and let me cry. After a few minutes, she pulled a handkerchief from somewhere and handed it to me. I wiped my eyes and nose and took a few deep breaths.

"Well," she finally said. "This does change things, doesn't it?"

I nodded and smiled. What an understatement! It had not been very pleasant living with Edmund at first, but we had come to a fairly agreeable, somewhat friendly relationship. But how could I go on living with him, now that I knew I loved him? What if I slipped and said something? What if he found out how I felt? I couldn't let that happen.

"What should I do?" I asked.

She looked around the room, a puzzled look on her face.

"I don't know what to tell you, Kaitlin. In many ways

Edmund has changed so much since you came. You have been a good influence on him."

"But ..."

"But I don't know if he's ready to love anyone. I mean, I don't know if he's ever really loved anyone before. I think he's too afraid of getting hurt. I think you need to keep praying for him, but be patient. Give him time, and I think he'll come around in the end."

Her words brought fresh tears to my eyes. I knew she was right, but that was not what I had wanted to hear.

"I know you're right," I said, my voice cracking, "but it's so hard." I barely got out the words.

"I'm back, honey," Nathan called from the hallway.

"Oh dear," I cried, "I don't want him to see me like this."

It was too late. He came into the room then stopped short when he saw me.

"I'm sorry to intrude ... Kaitlin! What's the matter?"

"Don't worry, Nathan," Amelia interjected, "It's a female problem."

"Well, I'm a doctor. What's the trouble, Kaitlin?" he asked as he sat down in a chair across from me and gave me a sympathetic look.

"Nathan," Amelia said sharply. She gave him a severe look that said, "Please go away."

"Ah, well. I'm sure you can handle this, Amelia. I'll see you later, Kaitlin. I hope you're feeling better."

"Thank you." He left and I had to smile.

"He's such a good husband," I told her.

"Yes," she smiled fondly. "He is."

"Well, I probably should get going."

"Wouldn't you like to stay for luncheon?"

"I would, but I didn't tell anyone where I went, so they'll be expecting me."

"Okay, Kaitlin. But let's say a prayer together before you go."

"All right."

Amelia prayed. *"Dear Father in Heaven, Please be with Kaitlin as she tries to help Edmund grow closer to you. Help her to know what to do. Give her strength and patience. Help her to find ways to show your love to Edmund. Thank you Lord, Amen."*

"Thank you Amelia, I feel better already," I said graciously.

"Just keep praying and be patient, and things will work out. You'll see."

"I'm sure you're right."

"Of course I'm right," she laughed.

I left then. The sun was shining, and Amelia's confidence had been infectious. God would solve this problem just as He had solved many others. He will be with me. I was amazed at how cheerful I felt as I walked back toward the house. Then, as I came up over the hill, the house came into view and the sun went under a cloud. I felt a shadow of despair creeping slowly over me, and I tried to shake it off. Once inside, I went to the drawing room and picked up the baby blanket I was working on for Amelia. From the way she had looked today, it wouldn't be long now. I couldn't concentrate, though, and I soon threw it down in disgust. Outside, it had begun to rain, so I put off any idea of a ride.

Instead, I went to the sitting room and sat down at the piano. I played until my fingers hurt, but afterward I was somewhat calmer. When I heard Jeffries take Nathan up to Edmund's room, I went to my own room to rest. Later, I decided to check on Edmund before dressing for dinner.

I knocked on his door and he called out, "Come in."

He was wearing slacks and struggling to put a shirt on over his bandaged ribs. His hair was damp, and I thought perhaps Nathan had helped him to bathe.

"How are you feeling?" I asked.

"Pretty good. My head doesn't hurt nearly as much, and my ribs only hurt when I move. Ha, Ha—ouch."

The attempt at humor brought a slight smile to my lips.

"I see you're trying to dress for dinner."

"Trying, yes."

I went over and helped him finish putting on his shirt, though it cost me a good deal of composure. My fingers trembled as I buttoned the buttons, and I couldn't believe Edmund couldn't hear the beating of my heart.

"I must go dress," I said.

"You look fine."

I went through the communicating door and rang for Sara. She helped me dress and fixed my hair, and in a short time, I was on my way downstairs. Edmund was already in the drawing room. As soon as I got down there, we went into the dining room. There was little conversation while we ate, but when we were almost finished, he spoke.

"Kaitlin, I'm feeling like I would like to hear you play."

"All right."

We went into my sitting room, and Edmund eased onto the couch. He lay back and closed his eyes. I played as though he were not there. Indeed, I tried to imagine he was not.

The next few days were extremely hard. At every turn, it seemed that I had to try and keep from staring at Edmund or saying something that might seem strange. I almost lost the battle on Sunday evening. I had managed to avoid Edmund all day, but just before dinner, he sent Sara to find me and make sure I was coming to dinner.

"Good evening," he said casually when I went into the drawing room. "I haven't seen you all day. Are you avoiding me?"

I tried to brush aside his joking. "You could have gone to church with me … besides, I didn't know you wanted to see me today," I said with more playfulness than I felt.

"Well," he said slowly, "Melinda won't be back from London for a few days, so I'm in need of a little female companionship." He smiled at me as though I should appreciate this little joke. I wondered if he was trying to make me jealous, or if he was just trying to pick a fight to get his mind off something that was eating at him.

I decided to try the direct approach. "Are you trying to make me jealous? Or do you want to pick a fight with me for another reason? Perhaps you're bored."

Instead of answering, he smiled enigmatically and led the way to the dinner table. As we ate, we discussed some improvements he wanted to make to the estate. Then, suddenly, he changed the subject.

"Kaitlin," he began, looking a little uncomfortable. He paused and then went on. "When we were in London, Aunt

THESE *Rugged* CLIFFS

Mary and I talked about my mother a lot. We discussed what my stepfather had done, and how upset I had been when I found out the truth. I came to realize that I was glad to know what really happened, that I found a certain amount of peace about the situation, and that I no longer felt bitter because my mother had 'left me.' I was amazed at what a burden was lifted when that bitterness was gone. I have wanted to say something to you about it before, but I just couldn't seem to find the words. Anyway, thank you."

Tears sprang to my eyes, and my throat tightened, but I managed to smile and say, "You're welcome."

An awkward silence followed Edmund's words. I didn't trust myself to say anymore. I longed to go over and put my arms around him, but I tried to hold my emotions in check. Soon, dinner was over. We went into the drawing room, and Edmund asked if I wanted to play a game of chess.

Every time Edmund would stare at the board, deciding on his next move, I would stare at him. It was only a matter of time, I knew, before he would look up at the wrong time and catch me gazing at him, but I couldn't help it. I was also playing terribly, and when he easily won the first two games, he gave me a strange look.

"Is something bothering you?" he asked.

"No. I guess I'm just a little distracted. I'll beat you this time."

Weighing heavily on my mind was the fear that he would learn that I loved him and then when he rejected me, our intimate little chess games would come to an end. However, I concentrated more on that game, and I almost had him in checkmate when I thoughtlessly commented, "I wish things could go on like this forever."

His gaze locked with mine, and I realized that I had voiced my hidden fears.

"What do you mean? Do you know some reason why things won't go on like this forever?"

"No ... I mean ... it was just a comment," I said lamely. My cheeks were burning, and I only wanted to run out of the room.

Edmund made one more move, but it was not a good one, and I had him in checkmate.

"There," I said, "I won one. Now, I think I'm going up to bed."

I stumbled out of the room, my cheeks still blazing from embarrassment. Would he be able to read my thoughts? Did he understand my thoughtless comment?

I think he called after me, but I ignored him. As I rushed up the stairs, I felt a strange surge of pity for Melinda Colton. If she felt for Edmund what I did, no wonder she hated me so much. I made it to my room and flung myself on the bed. Tears flowed freely down my cheeks. I had come so close to saying something that might have really given away my horrid situation. I couldn't bear to see the look of surprise or even disgust on Edmund's face if he were to find out that I loved him. After a few minutes had passed, I heard a knock on my door. The sound startled me. I quickly wiped my eyes with the back of my hand, but I knew I looked like I had been crying. I couldn't let Edmund see me like this. I went over to the door.

"Who is it?" I asked.

"It's your husband. I was wondering if you are all right. You seemed upset just now. What's wrong?"

"Nothing is the matter," I said trying to keep my voice steady. I took several deep breaths; I thought he had gone.

"Kaitlin, I need to talk to you," Edmund said quietly.

"I'm sorry, but I'm not feeling very well right now. Can we talk in the morning?" I asked, pressing my fists against my face to try and keep myself calm.

When I got no answer, the tears began to fall anew. This time I didn't try and stop them. I lay down on the bed and let myself sob. What had he wanted to talk to me about? I wondered. I was torn between relief that he had not seen me crying and despair that I had turned him away when he wanted to talk. What if he had wanted to talk about Jesus? That thought brought fresh tears to my eyes. What if my pride had kept me from helping him find God?

It was a long time before I cried myself to sleep. Fresh tears continued to fall, and I could not get the thought out of my head. What would have happened if I had opened that door?

The next morning, I saw Edmund at breakfast. He seemed to be his old self again, which didn't make me feel any better about last night. The next few days were agony. Although I tried to stay away from Edmund as much as possible, I could not avoid him all together. But, at least he was pleasant, and I was hoping that we would still be able to go on as though nothing strange had happened.

One night, before going down to dinner, I spent a few minutes praying and reading my Bible. It had been an extremely trying day. Edmund had almost caught me staring at him at luncheon, and had wondered jokingly what had me blushing. I could not afford a similar mistake tonight. I asked the Lord for inner strength and greater faith. It was a good thing I had taken time to pray. Little did I know that I would need all the faith I had to make it through the coming evening.

Chapter 19

When I walked downstairs to the drawing room, I put a smile on my face, determined to be kind but to keep stronger emotions in check even if it killed me. Edmund rose when I entered and gave me a slight smile.

"You're looking nice tonight, my dear," he said easily. I smiled and was about to reply when the butler entered.

"Mr. Denson and Mrs. Colton are here to see you sir, ma'am," Jeffries said.

"Good evening," my husband said as they entered the room. "We were just getting ready to dine, would you care to join us?"

I could not help but feel jealous when Edmund issued the invitation. It was not that I didn't want to have guests, just not these guests. I noticed with a certain amount of displeasure the way Mrs. Colton grabbed Edmund's arm when dinner was announced. She turned back to smile at me, and I felt the blood rush to my cheeks. Don't let her worry you, I kept telling myself. He's your husband, not hers. He didn't want her, remember? Yes, but he didn't want me, either. He just wanted to be free of fawning girls and their doting mamas. The words *He didn't want you* kept running through my ears.

Now was not the time to dwell on that matter. Mr. Denson was pulling out my chair at the dinner table. I looked up at him for the first time. He had a smug look on his face and when he caught my eye, he winked and smiled. I sucked in my breath. He was arrogantly mocking me, and I had no idea why. He went over and sat down. I noticed that two extra places had hurriedly been set. As the soup was served, Mr. Denson caught my eye. He smiled again, a rather sinister, knowing smile, and my spine tingled. He looked over at his cousin and some strange look passed between them.

I shivered with uneasiness. I knew something was wrong; something was going to happen, but what? I remembered Mr. Denson's words to me when I had refused his offer of love. *I surely hope you do not regret this*, he had said. What had he meant by that? Was I going to find out?

These musings all took place during the first course. For awhile, there was little conversation. Then Mrs. Colton asked Edmund if the doctor was looking forward to the new baby. Edmund said Nathan was fairly bursting with pride. For a time the talk centered on babies.

"Are you looking forward to having children?" Mrs. Colton asked me. My fork clanged against my plate. I could feel my face turn red again. I looked at Edmund for help but he seemed to be waiting with much anticipation for my answer. He was smiling at me, too, in a mocking way. I tried to speak casually.

"I hadn't really thought about it," I said quietly.

Mrs. Colton chuckled. "You'd think you'd *have* to think about it at some time." She put her hand on Edmund's arm and leaned close to whisper something to him.

I was mortified, but not quite as much as when Edmund grinned impishly at me and said, "You'd think so, wouldn't you."

By the time dinner was over, I was quite ready to plead a headache and go upstairs. But that would leave Mrs. Colton and Edmund alone and I couldn't bear the thought of that. I wasn't looking forward to the evening ahead. I led the way back to the drawing room. Usually, Edmund left the dining room when I did, but tonight he and Mr. Denson stayed.

As I walked, I prayed. I didn't know why, but I was starting to feel more and more uneasy. I prayed for wisdom and patience. I told Mrs. Parks to bring us tea in the drawing room after awhile. Then, I sat down on the sofa and Mrs. Colton pulled a chair close.

She leaned over and whispered conspiratorially. "Is there something wrong between you and Edmund? That is, I don't mean to pry, but you seemed rather upset at dinner. Is there something I can do to help?"

I wanted to scream at her, *Just go away and leave us alone!* but I didn't. I tried to smile at her and said, "I don't know what you mean; everything is just fine. Edmund and I love each other very much."

I regretted the lie as soon as I said it. I was afraid my voice had betrayed me. Mrs. Colton patted my arm in a patronizing way. I wished Amelia were here. She would find some way to help this horrible situation. Finally the men joined us and Mrs. Parks brought in the tea. I poured but I was painfully aware that my hands were shaking.

"My dear, you're shaking," Mrs. Colton said. "Are you nervous?"

"No," I told her, "I'm just a little tired, I think."

Edmund had been standing by the window, but came to sit beside me on the sofa. The two cousins sat facing us. Suddenly I felt as though we were all waiting for something. I wondered if it had anything to do with Edmund—if he knew what the tension was all about.

When Mr. Denson looked at his cousin and she nodded, I knew they were finally ready to spring something on us—or me. I was not ready for it; I don't think I ever could have been.

"We've thought about whether or not to tell you what we've discovered," Mr. Denson said.

"We figured it would come out sooner or later, so you might rather hear it from friends."

I glanced at Edmund with a questioning look on my face. He didn't look at me. Instead he sat, jaw clenched, staring straight at Mrs. Colton.

"As you know, we visited our aunt a few days ago. Well, we decided to stop off and check on things at your home, Kaitlin, since it was right on our way. I know you've probably been wondering how the house is doing and everything."

My face had lit up for a moment at the thought of my home, but then I remembered that they had some sort of bad news. I braced myself for the news of some tragedy.

"What has happened?" I asked hoarsely.

"Why, nothing has happened to the house, my dear. Nothing, that is, except for the fact that it has been sold."

At first her words didn't sink in. Then as I realized what she had said, I went numb all over.

"What do you mean my house has been sold?" I asked breathlessly, trying to keep some sort of control. I looked at Edmund again. He seemed angry.

"How did you find this out?" Edmund demanded.

"We talked to a certain solicitor."

"Mr. Cabot?" I asked.

"No, his partner."

"But you see, Kaitlin," Mr. Denson interrupted, "that's not the worst of it."

"I know this is going to be a shock to you," Mrs. Colton said in a condescending tone, "but when your father died, it was found out that his steward had mismanaged his funds. Your father was terribly in debt. The house and everything in it had to be sold to pay the creditors. I'm afraid there's nothing left for your inheritance."

There was a great rushing sound in my ears, and for a moment I couldn't think clearly. I had gouges on my arms where my fingernails had dug in, but I couldn't feel them. I wanted to get up and pace around the room, but I knew my legs would not support me. I just sat there trying to breathe.

"My dear, you look so pale. I'm sorry to have upset you. And dear Edmund, you look pale, too. This must have come as quite a shock to you," Mrs. Colton said, giving me her most innocently sympathetic look.

"Yes, it has," I said feebly.

"Of course," Melinda continued, "I'm afraid people will

say that it didn't come as a shock to you—that you knew all along and trapped poor Mr. Fitzpatrick into marrying you in a most devious way!"

"That's not true!" I cried, shaking my head. I hadn't thought of it like that. I couldn't look at Edmund to see if this was the direction his thoughts were taking. Would he believe I had purposely deceived him? Would he think that that was what I meant the other night when I said things couldn't go on like this forever—because I was afraid of being found out? I felt nauseous.

"You had everything to gain from appearing to be the rich young heiress of Mr. Fitzpatrick's friend." By now the glint in Mr. Denson's eye and the smile on his face were purely evil. What shocked me almost as much as the news of my father's misfortune was the realization that these people were enjoying my pain. They really hated me.

Please, God, help! I silently screamed. I finally got the courage to look up at Edmund and wished I hadn't. His jaw was clenched, his face pale, and I could see that he was furious.

"So Edmund," Mrs. Colton began, "will you divorce her quietly or will there be a scandal?"

I felt a shudder go through my entire body.

Edmund stood up. "This has gone far enough. This is a personal matter between my wife and myself and I would kindly ask you to not make decisions for me." He spoke quietly, but I was relieved that at least not *all* of his anger was directed at me.

"But, Edmund, we were just trying to help," Mrs. Colton

purred. The words were so hypocritical that they turned my stomach.

"Get out!" This time he fairly shouted. She slammed her cup into its saucer and got up.

With chin held high and one long last look at Edmund, she let Mr. Denson lead her out of the room. Edmund went and shut the door and leaned against it, his back to me.

I sat there for a moment, not knowing what to say or do. I felt an immense guilt for bringing this upon Edmund and yet I wanted him to know I was innocent. I poured myself another cup of tea. I was surprised that my hands had stopped shaking. When Edmund finally turned around, I stood up to face him.

"Please believe that I knew nothing of this. I never wanted to trap you into marriage, especially not because of my financial condition. Please believe me."

"I believe you."

He said it with such lack of emotion that I almost felt as though he had slapped me. I wanted to cry. The color had come back into his face, but his eyes still sparkled with anger. He came over to stand beside me so that I had to look up to see his face. I could almost *feel* how tense he was, just standing next to him. I tried to take a step back.

"I'm sorry to have caused you any distress. I'll leave tomorrow for my cousin's house. I'm sure she'll let me stay while I figure out what I should do. You can send the annulment papers there."

My voice almost broke on the last word. Edmund seized my teacup and hurled it into the fireplace. It shattered and the fire hissed and sizzled where it was splashed with hot tea. That was exactly how I felt inside. He grabbed my upper arms and stared down into my face.

"You'll do no such thing, do you understand me? I'll not have you running off to some distant relative so you don't have to face this thing. We'll get through it and go on as before. There will be no scandal! You will not leave!"

He emphasized the last words by giving me a little shake. Then he turned and left the room. I sat down. I knew he was serious, but I didn't think his was the best plan. I had to get away from the mistrust and the anger. I had to let him get on with his life and not be saddled with a wife who would be known as a fortune hunter. Sitting there, alone, I found the courage to be calm and collected. I could go and pack my bags and leave in the morning before everyone was up. I could do it.

Just then Jeffries came into the room. He coughed a little and said, "I know it is late madam, but a note was just left for you."

I took the note and thanked him as he took his leave. I saw right away that the note was from Amelia, but it was not her usually neat handwriting. It was written as if by a woman in a panic.

It said,

Please come quickly. The baby's on the way. I can't stand the pain. I need you. Please hurry.

Amelia

I went at once to grab my coat. The thought crossed my mind that Edmund would worry if he found I was gone, but I dismissed it. I was sure that it would not worry him *that* much. I was glad to have something else to occupy my mind.

I wrapped a green scarf around my head and ran outside. With my skirts whipping about me, I ran toward the cliff path. It felt like rain, and I knew the shortcut would get me to Amelia faster than if I went by the road. I thought of the time I had almost lost the puppy—and myself—over the cliff and shuddered.

I had grabbed the lantern that now hung by the door, and I was glad of it. The sky was full of clouds and there was no moon. The rain started as I got to the path along the cliff. I had been running, but I slowed down now for fear the path might be slippery.

Just as I was carefully making my way along the path where the cliff face was the steepest, I heard footsteps. Someone was coming along the path behind me. For a second I stood frozen to the spot. The footsteps stopped. Perhaps it had been my imagination.

"Who's there?" I called. Nothing.

As soon as I started walking again, I heard those scrabbling footsteps behind me. I don't know why that sound caused my hair to stand on end and my breathing to come in painful gasps, but I was terrified. Then a voice crashed through my mind and yelled, *Run!* I ran as fast as I could manage, slipping at times on the wet ground. I turned around once and caught sight of a black cloak flapping in the wind. I scrambled as fast as I could along the muddy path.

Finally, my lungs screaming with pain, my legs weak from the effort, I slipped and fell flat on the ground. Before I could get up, I felt hands grab me. I kept trying to crawl away from my attacker, even as they were trying to throw me over the edge. I clung frantically to the grass, mud, bushes, anything to keep from going over. I tried to turn and fight against those shrouded arms, but it was no use. My strength gave out. With one last glimpse of a large black hood, I went over the edge. Even as I fell, I was grabbing at the dirt and brush to slow my fall.

Time seemed to pass slowly—too slowly. It was as if I was being guided by some outside force. I knew God was with me, so I relaxed and let myself roll down the hill—at least, that was what it felt like. I wondered if perhaps I had fallen at a point where the descent was not as steep or if it had simply been a miracle. I kept repeating Thank You, Thank You—and then I hit the bottom.

The dreamlike state I had been in vanished and I ached all over. I knew I was covered with mud, but it was being slowly washed away by the rain that pelted down on my face. My head felt as though someone had been trying to crack it open with a hammer. I didn't think any bones were broken, though it hurt too much everywhere to even move. I lay back and waited for them to find me. Panic gripped me at the thought of lying here for days without anyone caring that I was gone. I wouldn't let fear take control, though. God had protected me and I knew He would not leave me now. With that thought in mind, I blacked out.

I was wet and cold when I woke up again. Rain was still falling on my face, but I could do nothing about it. I tried to open my eyes, but it felt as though a great weight was pressing down on my eyelids. I wondered how long I had been lying there.

A sound from far above sent a thrill through me. Someone was at the top of the cliff. I heard a scrambling sound on the rocks nearby. I opened my mouth to cry out, but no sound came. Suddenly, I felt a presence beside me, felt hands gently touching me.

"She's alive!" I heard Edmund shout.

"Why did you do this?" I heard him say in a low agonized whisper.

He must think I jumped off the cliff on purpose, I thought in amazement. I wanted to cry out and tell him I had been pushed, but the only sound that escaped my lips was a soft gurgle. Edmund's hand brushed the hair off my forehead, and I knew he was bending close to my face because I could feel his breath on my cheek.

"It's going to be all right, Kaitlin," he said softly as his strong arms picked me up. I could hear him talking to me, reassuring me, but his voice started getting farther and farther away. As I was jostled around, I felt a piercing pain in my head, and fortunately, I lost consciousness.

CHAPTER 20

When I finally woke up, I couldn't move. Or, at least, I could move, but it hurt. So I lay still. When I opened my eyes, all I could see was the window. I didn't hear anything. I didn't know what time it was, and for a moment I didn't know why I was in bed. I didn't remember going to sleep the night before. Then I realized I hadn't. Slowly and painfully I remembered falling over the cliff. I saw that dusk was falling, and I was surprised that I had slept the whole day.

When I tried to sit up, a wave of nausea overcame me and I was forced to lay back down. I thought I might at least roll over. Sara was sitting by my bed working on some needlepoint. To my surprise, Edmund was sprawled in a chair by the fire, apparently asleep. Sara looked up and when she saw that my eyes were open she gave a startled scream.

"Oh, my dear! You're awake. She's awake!" When she cried out, Edmund jerked up out of his chair and stumbled over.

He looked terrible. He hadn't shaved, and his face was

covered with beard stubble. When he looked at me, it was with obvious relief. But then he spoke and there was barely repressed anger in his voice.

"What were you thinking of, throwing yourself from the cliff like that!" he growled.

I stared at him. The room had felt fresh and cool when I awoke, but now I could feel a stinging warmth in my cheeks. I couldn't believe he would think I had jumped on purpose.

"I didn't jump." I said after a few moments. In those few seconds, the rest of the nights' events had been replayed in my mind, and I was painfully aware of what he must think of me. He spoke again, as if he had not heard me.

"After I went up to bed, I got to thinking that I may have been too harsh with you. You weren't in your room, though, and when I came back down, Jeffries told me about a note you had received. I couldn't imagine what was going on, but he said that you had quickly gone out. When I spotted your body lying on the rocks at the bottom of the cliff, I couldn't believe you would have been so stupid as to jump."

At some point in this conversation Sara had quietly left the room. I was glad, too, for I was close to disgracing myself further by breaking out into uncontrollable sobs. He had been running his hands through his hair, and it stood on end. His shirt was untucked, and he loomed over me, glaring like some demented gargoyle.

"Of all the idiotic, hysterical things to do. You finally convinced me that my mother was a Christian—that she didn't commit suicide, and now look what *you* did! Were you so afraid of being found out that you would rather end it all than face public disgrace? Did you think I would heartlessly turn you out in the street or did you think I would divorce you and send you away with nothing? What manner of cretin you must think I am that you would rather face death than face *me!*"

There were so many things I wanted to say, but I couldn't find the strength.

"Well, what do you have to say for yourself?" he said loudly, after a short silence.

I gathered my nerve and tried again. "I didn't jump. As I told you before, I had no knowledge of my father's finances, and while I am sorry to have ruined your life, I did not try to commit suicide. I was planning to travel to my cousin's today, but as you can see, I've slept most of the day."

I felt pleased by my summary of events until I saw the look on his face. He choked and snorted all at once and his face turned a rather nasty shade of red.

"Today is not Saturday. It's Monday. You've been unconscious with a fever for two days. Nathan had just about given up hope. He said you could die at any moment." He turned pale and sat down on the side of the bed. "You wouldn't believe how I begged and pleaded with God to keep you alive."

All of a sudden a thought seemed to come to him.

"If you didn't jump off that cliff, what in blazes were you doing at the bottom of it?"

The room started spinning when I began to remember. It wasn't possible, I told myself, it just wasn't possible. I decided to tell Edmund exactly what happened in the hope that he would believe me.

"The note Jeffries told you I received was from Amelia. She was in a panic because the baby was coming and she needed me. So, I grabbed my cloak and a lantern and took off down the path by the cliffs that would get me to her quickly. As I was hurrying toward Amelia's, I heard a sound behind me, and I realized someone was following me. I began to run as fast as I could on the slippery ground, but finally I fell. Before I could get up, hands grabbed me and pushed me over the edge. I struggled, but it was no use. I didn't jump over that cliff, I was pushed."

Edmund's eyes locked with mine in a piercing stare. Finally, he spoke, "Amelia was not about to have her baby. She did not send you a letter."

"Then someone *is* trying to kill me!" I yelled.

Edmund sat by the edge of the bed and held both my hands.

"Look, Kaitlin, I don't know what to think. Something strange may be going on, or you may be trying to cover up your foolhardy decision to throw yourself onto the rocks. Whatever the case, I will try and get to the bottom of things."

"You don't believe me?" I asked, stunned.

"I don't know what to believe."

"Edmund, I'm a Christian. To give up and jump to an easy death would mean giving up on God. I have more faith than that. I believe that God will work things out. I thought you were beginning to realize that my faith in God is real. I know I have been a horrible witness to you, and I am sorry. I don't want to be responsible for chasing you farther away from God. Please believe me. I would not lie to you."

Tears filled my eyes, and I looked away from him.

"I do realize that your faith in God is real," Edmund said quietly.

My eyes flew to his. "You do?"

"Yes. You may not realize it, but you have shown me that your faith is real in many, many ways. You have made some mistakes, I agree, but it was through your mistakes that I began to see how much you really believe. One thing has kept me from God—hypocrisy—and when I looked for it in you, I could not find it. You didn't always act like what I thought a Christian should act like, but you were always honest when you thought you'd made a mistake. I must say that caught me by surprise. And so, I suppose I really do believe you. I don't understand it, but I believe you. There, does that make you feel better."

I began to cry harder.

"What's the matter now?" Edmund cried.

"Nothing, I'm just happy, that's all."

He raised an eyebrow and gave me a strange look. "That's nice," he said in a patronizing way. I didn't mind too much.

"Kaitlin, there's something I would like to tell you ..." suddenly he stopped and shook his head. "Never mind, it can wait. This doesn't seem to be the right time. Anyway, I think you need to get some sleep. We'll discuss the situation Mrs. Colton brought up another time."

The happiness I was feeling evaporated. For a moment I had forgotten about that. I was so happy that Edmund's heart seemed to have softened that I wasn't thinking about anything else. Now, I realized that there were still so many unanswered questions. How could I stay here with Edmund when everyone thought I had tricked him into marrying me?

What would people think about me? What would people think about Edmund? Thinking about the future gave me a headache, so I decided to push all those thoughts aside and get some sleep.

When I awoke again, it was morning, and I was starving. Even though I had been awake awhile the night before, I hadn't eaten anything. I looked around the room, surprised to see Sara sitting by the fire.

"Sara," I said quietly.

She put down her needlepoint and came over to me. "Do you need something, ma'am?" she asked.

"Yes, I'm starving."

Sara smiled. "You don't know how good it is to hear you say that. I'll be right back with some food."

Sara walked out the door as Edmund walked in.

"How are you feeling this morning?" he asked.

"Hungry," I told him, smiling.

"Good, good. I brought you some letters that came yesterday. Probably people writing to wish you well."

"Thank you."

Edmund seemed to choose his words carefully. "I asked Jeffries about the note that was sent to you."

"And?"

"He said someone knocked loudly, but when he got there, all he found was the note attached to a bright strip of material lying on the porch."

"Someone must have left it there to lure me out."

"Perhaps. It's best not to jump to conclusions."

That was easy for him to say. He paused for a moment, seeming a little unsure of himself. "Well, I guess I had better get busy. I'm going to ride around the estate today and see how things are going."

"I wish I could go with you," I said drowsily.

"Someday," Edmund said, and then got up to leave.

Someday, I thought to myself. I didn't really believe it would ever happen. I was still contemplating whether or not I should go visit my cousin and give Edmund a chance to think about whether or not he wanted to be saddled with a wife that was looked on as a fortune hunter.

I picked up the letters Edmund had given me. The first letter was from Amelia. She wrote:

> *Dearest Kaitlin,*
>
> *I was so sorry to hear about your unfortunate accident. Nathan and I are praying for you daily. I know God will take care of you. The baby will be here soon, and I hope you will be well enough then to hold him. When you are feeling up to a visit, Nathan said he would bring me over there so I could see you. You'll have to come downstairs, though, I don't think I could climb up to your room. Please get well soon, Kaitlin, I miss you dearly.*
>
> *Love,*
> *Amelia*

The second letter was not so friendly. It was from Melinda Colton.

> *Kaitlin,*
>
> *How shocked we were to hear the effect our revelations had on you. If we would have known you would try to commit suicide on hearing that you had been found out, we would have tried to be gentler in revealing our information. As it is, I am afraid the townspeople are talking up a storm. Lady Conrad says she knew you were a fortune hunter when she first met you. I'm sure I believe that you didn't know you were penniless, and of course I've tried to tell that to everyone, but people like to believe the worst.*
>
> *I know this is a difficult situation for you, and I hope I haven't made it worse for you by telling you all this, but I thought you would want to know all the town gossip. I do hope you feel better soon.*
>
> *Sincerely,*
> *Melinda*

I reread Melinda's letter and then threw it on the night-stand in disgust. What a horrid, horrid woman! How could she say all she had said, and still try to pretend she was my friend—that she was telling me all this for my own good? I wondered if it was all true. Did people really feel sorry for Edmund and dislike me so much? Tears began to fall down my cheeks and I lay back on my bed, exhausted from the emotional strain. Finally, I came to the conclusion that for Edmund's sake, I must leave. He didn't love me, and I didn't want him to have to do the "noble" thing and stay married to me. Mrs. Colton might be right. Could Edmund ever be sure that I was telling the truth? I didn't want a cloud of mistrust to hang over our relationship. I loved him too much to put him through that. As soon as I was stronger, I would pack my bags and leave.

Later that day, I got up for the first time and began to walk around. Every day for several days, I spent time walking around my room, building strength for my journey. Before too long, I felt that I was ready to leave. Although I hate to admit it, there were tears in my eyes as I packed my suitcase. I hadn't realized how happy I had been the last few months. I almost couldn't bear the thought of leaving Amelia. I had never had such a good friend. With great difficulty, I tried to push away the thought that I might never see Edmund again. It made my stomach hurt and my knees shake. Why had it taken me so long to figure out that I loved him? And why, when I had figured it out, was I forced to leave?

I felt a guilty pang at having packed a few of the dresses Edmund had bought me. As soon as I could, I would try and repay him. Perhaps I could find some type of job—a governess perhaps. I left the wedding ring and necklace he had given me on my bedside table, along with a short note and the address where he could send the annulment papers.

Packing was hard work, and I was still feeling rather weak. I had to sit down on the bed to rest. Sara had come in and tried to talk me out of leaving. When that didn't work, she broke down and began to weep. When I could no longer stand her sobbing, I sent her down to see if Martin could take me into town in the carriage.

Standing up again after the short rest was not easy. I took my suitcase in both hands and made it to the door. I took a last look around my room. I wanted to remember it just the way it was. The hallway was difficult to navigate until I made it to the banister that led to the open staircase. I didn't know how I would make it down all those stairs.

I was half dragging, half pulling myself and my belongings. I hadn't realized how weak I had grown from my days in bed. My head was pounding and I felt a sort of rushing in my ears.

"Where are you going?"

His voice was soft but right behind me. I dropped the suitcase and swung around to face him. I gripped the banister to keep from falling. My chest hurt, so badly had I been frightened, and I didn't want to look at him. He was the one I was running from, after all. It was his mistrust that I couldn't bear. I also realized that I was running from him out of fear. Fear that he would find out how much I loved him and that it would disgust him.

He said it again. "Where are you going?"

I felt tears well up in my eyes and my throat ached from trying to hold them back.

"I'm going to live with my cousin," I said quietly. "I left you a note letting you know where to send the annulment papers for me to sign."

"You aren't going anywhere. The marriage will not be annulled. You will go on being my wife and you will go back to bed and recover."

I couldn't believe he was talking to me as though I were a child. I had a notion of telling him just what I thought, but when I looked up at him for the first time, my heated response died in my throat. He looked outwardly calm, but there was a tightness in his jaw and a funny look in his eyes that made the words stick in my throat.

"Why?" I finally managed to say with as much energy as I could.

"Your father entrusted me to look after your finances. Just because you don't have any doesn't mean I'm going to throw you out into the street. Besides, I feel it's my duty to take care of you."

"Duty," I said dully. The word felt heavy on my tongue.

"Yes, duty. I feel I owe it to your father to be responsible for you."

"Thank you very much," I said with tears in my eyes, "but I won't be anyone's wife out of pity, or because you think it's the 'noble' thing to do."

I turned to pick up my suitcase and walk out on him—proud, defiant—with my head held high, but my body rebelled. I couldn't lift the suitcase. From some far-off place, I could hear Edmund calling my name, and I felt myself slowly falling.

He caught me before I hit the floor.

"I guess I get my way after all," he said softly, carrying me back to my bedroom. I felt humiliated. I wondered if perhaps this wasn't some type of punishment for my prideful attitude.

"Besides," he said as he lay me down on my bed. "I don't think it would be Biblical for me to divorce you on such grounds, and I know you would not want me to do anything of which God would not approve."

I looked up at him. He smiled and I saw that familiar glint in his eyes. He was teasing now, not mocking, trying to placate me. He asked if I would be all right or if he should send Sara to me.

"I'll be fine," I said and turned my back on him. When I heard the door close, I let myself cry. Great quaking sobs shook my body. After a few minutes, I felt drained, but somehow much more peaceful and resigned.

I wondered what his real reasons were for having me stay. Perhaps he didn't want the scandal of sending away a divorced wife. But if I had really tricked him into marrying me I would have deserved it, wouldn't I? Perhaps he was trying to do the noble thing. I didn't want him to be noble. Or perhaps he believed that I had known nothing of my father's finances. Perhaps he pitied me.

Whatever the case, apparently God wanted me to stay. Perhaps it would be sinful to want an annulment simply for the sake of my pride. But how was I to face him, day after day, knowing he might possibly think me a fortune hunter? I pushed these thoughts aside to finally deal with a more frightening matter. Had I really been pushed off the cliff? And why? Or had it just been my imagination that I had seen that cloaked figure? If someone had tried to kill me, who? An idea started to form in the back of my mind. It grew, looming into my consciousness before I had a chance to stop it.

What if Edmund didn't want the scandal of a divorced wife, but wouldn't mind the scandal of having his wife commit suicide because of a guilty conscience? My room suddenly felt cold. I shook my head as if to force such thoughts out of my mind. Thinking such things was absurd. I remembered the conversation we had had when Edmund told me I had been a good Christian witness. His heart really was softening. I must believe that there was hope for him. I would not think of the alternative.

Early the next morning, Edmund came up to my room.

"Kaitlin," he called softly, but I had awoken when he opened my door.

"I'm awake."

"I just came to tell you that I'll be going to London this morning. I have some pressing matters to take care of. I'll be back late tonight or possibly tomorrow morning."

"You'll be gone all day?" I asked sulkily.

"Yes. I'm sorry if you'll be lonely. However, yesterday Melinda and Miles came over to see you. I told them that you were still tired, but that they could try back today. I mentioned that I would be in London and that the servants will be busy cleaning the west wing of the house, so they might be by to give you some company."

"You really think I want to see them after all they've done!"

"I know you don't like them, but I'm not going to stop them if they want to be neighborly."

I was sure Miles and Melinda wanted to be anything but neighborly. I couldn't believe that Edmund had invited those people to come visit me. I wanted to scream at him and tell him that I didn't want them anywhere near me, but I didn't.

"Do you really have to go?"

"I'm afraid I do, but don't worry, I'll tell you all about my trip when I get back."

He left the room, and I sulked. The morning passed slowly. I was sad that Edmund was gone, but I was angry that he had invited Mrs. Colton and Mr. Denson over without asking me if it was all right. Perhaps they wouldn't come after all. It was afternoon now, and they hadn't shown up. Mrs. Colton probably wouldn't want to come if she wouldn't be able to flirt with Edmund. I was disappointed when I heard a knock on the door.

"Good afternoon, Kaitlin," Mr. Denson said as he entered the room. "I see you're resting well. My cousin sends her regards. She wanted to be here, but I told her I was going to visit you alone." He came over and stood beside the bed. He quietly tossed the bell pull up and over the top of the canopy bed, out of my reach. Then he walked over and locked the door. When he saw the incredulous look on my face, he smiled mockingly.

"It'll do you no good to scream," he said. "The servants are all over in the west wing. Your husband conveniently informed me that they would be doing some early springcleaning. He didn't realize his careless words played right into my plans."

When Mr. Denson finished speaking, he came over and sat down on the edge of the bed.

"I was so sorry to hear about your unfortunate accident," he said, patting my arm.

I pulled my arm away, and he grimaced.

"I can't believe you survived the fall from the cliff. I was so hoping you wouldn't make it."

He had said the words calmly, but they caused the hair on the back of my neck to tingle. He spoke softly, but I was aware of something very menacing in his attitude. I began to be afraid, and the fear made my stomach flip and my throat tighten.

"I'm sorry to have to kill you," he said, "It would have been better if you had let me love you." He reached out and touched my cheek and I cringed. For a moment, I was speechless. He couldn't be serious!

"Why?" I asked. The thought crossed my mind that I needed to keep him talking.

"Why do I have to kill you?" he said, pondering. "That's a good question. I suppose it wouldn't hurt to tell you. You see I'm heavily in debt to some unscrupulous men in London. When you first came here, I thought it would solve my problems if I married you. But then you ruined all my plans. You went off and stupidly married Fitzpatrick." He shook his head and chuckled. "Melinda sure was spitting fire that day." The grin disappeared and he scowled at me. "I was not happy about that, either. I had been hoping he would marry Melinda. He would be sure to give her some money, and I knew I could squeeze money out of her. However, it just so happened that in order for him to be able to marry Melinda, I would have to get rid of you. Unfortunately, you were uncannily lucky. That day in the woods, I couldn't believe I'd missed."

"That was you!"

"Yes. And then there was that incident with the dog. You should have gone over the edge you know," he said, giving me a strange look. I felt an icy chill wash over me. Something had kept me from going over that cliff. I remembered that God had been with me then, and I tried to remember that He was with me now, but fear was knifing through my stomach, and it took all my energy to keep from fainting.

"That fool saw me out there with the dog, so I had to get rid of him."

"You killed Jim?" I shivered again, this time with rage.

"Yes, my dear, I did. The old fool deserved it. If you would have just married me, none of this would have happened. I even followed you to London, but that horse didn't finish you off, either.

"Of course, when we found out you were penniless, I was sure Fitzpatrick would divorce you. Then he would be free to marry Melinda. But, I underestimated him. He is an arrogant man. I didn't think his pride went that deep. He would rather stay married to a woman who made him a fool than to admit it." He shook his head.

"I decided that night that I had to get rid of you. I knew you were distraught. Everyone would have believed that you were so guilt-ridden or devastated that you thought suicide was the only answer. They believed Edmund's mother committed suicide, and they would have been quick to believe you had also jumped off that cliff. And still, you didn't die. Now, though, I will make *sure* you commit suicide." He grinned at me and reached to touch the side of my face. I cringed and turned away from him. He grabbed my chin with one hand and before I could even try and stop him, bent down and kissed me. This was the second time he had forced himself on me, and it made me furious. The feel of his lips on mine made my stomach lurch, and I thought I would vomit.

Instead, I bit down on his lip until I tasted blood. His head jerked back, and he hit me across the face—hard.

He licked his lips, grimaced, and pulled the bedclothes back. When I tried to crawl away from him, he laughed and grabbed a handful of nightgown. I turned over and tried to kick him in the face, but I couldn't kick very high or very hard. I was still weak.

He caught my foot and pulled me towards him. That's when I started to scream. He chuckled and said, "I'm afraid no one will hear you."

He picked me up and began carrying me toward the window. I fought with every ounce of strength I had. He almost dropped me once, and I knew that if I had been well, I probably could have gotten away. It was a futile thought. Tears of frustration stung at my eyes as I called out to God for help. When Mr. Denson opened the window latch, I felt a renewed strength. I was fighting for my life! I almost got free when he had to let go with one hand to open the window, but then both hands grabbed me again and I was perilously close to going out. Right now, he was the only thing between me and certain death, and he was quickly positioning things so that he could push me out.

"Stop!"

Help came in the form and figure of my enraged husband as he flung open the communicating door and came toward us. At the sight of Edmund, I saw Mr. Denson pause for a moment, mouth open, unsure what to do. I took that opportunity to push away from him as hard as I could. As I flung myself toward Edmund, I heard Mr. Denson gasp. I turned to see him falling backwards out of the window, his eyes bulging as his hands fought to grip the edges of the window frame. In a moment, he was gone. I covered my ears with my hands to block out the sound of his scream then I buried my face in Edmund's chest.

Soon, I heard screams down below, and Edmund led me away from the window and set me down on the bed. He went over, looked out of the open window, then came over and sat down by me.

"He's dead," he said quietly. After some moments of silence, Edmund said, "I didn't go to London today. I thought he might be the one trying to hurt you, so I told him I would be gone to see if he would take the bait, and he did."

When I had regained a little composure, I blurted out, "What took you so long?" Then I blushed.

It was his turn to blush. He looked a little sheepish when he said, "I got so bored waiting in there to see what would happen that I fell asleep. I'm afraid I'm a heavy sleeper. I can't believe I almost didn't make it in here in time."

I burst into tears and he pulled me into his arms. I cried for a few minutes and then I looked up into his face.

He gently touched my cheek. "Does that hurt?"

"A little." He bent and brushed his lips—oh so gently—along my cheekbone.

"But … I don't understand," I said.

"What don't you understand?"

"You."

His explanation came when his lips crushed down on mine. I was not thinking clearly when he moved his lips to my forehead and then leaned back to look into my face.

"Do you understand that?"

I shook my head, uncomprehending, unable to believe what my senses were telling me. "But you don't love me," I said, "You think I married you for your money, and ..."

He silenced me with a finger on my lips.

"Shhh—read this."

He pulled two pieces of paper from his pocket and handed them to me. I glanced at the signature at the bottom of the letter and saw that it was from my solicitor. The other document was a deed to my home.

With mounting disbelief, I read.

> *Dear Mr. Fitzpatrick,*
>
> *As you are reading this letter, you must have already made the acquaintance of Miss Kaitlin Howard, whose father was a good friend of your uncle's.*
>
> *Yesterday, I discovered that Mr. Howard's estate has been mismanaged dreadfully by his steward, Mr. Jameson. It seems that for the last five years this man has been borrowing money from several banks in Mr. Howard's name and has been using the money to pay household and business debts. All other moneys from Mr. Howard's account have been embezzled by this man whose whereabouts are unknown.*
>
> *Unfortunately this places Miss Howard in a detestable situation. She has absolutely no money and will be lucky if all of the debts will be paid*

off with the sale of the house and its contents. She is not aware of any of this, and I must confess I do not wish to tell her. Perhaps you will have an idea—being a friend of her father's—as to what would be best for her to do.

It may, of course, solve all of her problems if she were to be married ... maybe you know of someone? I don't know how long I can keep news of this quiet. It can't be for long.

I am sorry to place this problem in your hands, but I was worried what news of this sort would do to her, considering her present emotional condition. Perhaps it will be easier for her to deal with the news when she is away from her home and the place of her father's death.

I am trusting you to deal with the matter with efficiency and decorum. Again, I apologize for thrusting this matter upon you.

Sincerely,
MR. JOSEPH F. CABOT

"But I don't understand. Why did you marry me if you knew I had no money? Why do you have the deed to my house?"

He looked at me then and the answer was there in his eyes, but I wanted to hear it.

"Because I love you. I think I loved you almost from the

moment you arrived, disheveled, on my doorstep. I bought your house as a wedding gift to you, but I never got around to telling you."

"I can't believe it," I said as tears filled my eyes.

"Kaitlin, dearest, I never said anything to you because I hated myself for having fallen in love with such a prudish young woman. Especially when I had vowed never to fall in love at all. And, you had made it very clear that you wanted very little to do with men in general and me in particular. The gossip about your reputation simply gave me the excuse I needed to get you to marry me. It was a mad plan I know, but I had visions of your falling in love with me, coming to me and confessing your love … it soon became clear to me, however, that you were still as indifferent to me as ever.

"When I lost my temper and attacked Jim and treated you so horribly when I found out what happened to my mother, I was sure you would never forgive me. And yet, you were there asking me to forgive *you*. I think it was at that moment that my cold, hard heart began to thaw. Even though I found your beliefs hard to understand, your actions really made me think. Yet, I couldn't set aside a lifetime of hate too easily.

"When we were visiting Aunt Mary, of course she saw through my little charade. But, she told me that she believed I was in love with you. She was right. She also told me that *you were in love with me*. I didn't believe her, of course. She advised me to be gentle with you. She said she didn't think you knew you loved me yet. I didn't want to woo you; I had too much pride for that. Instead I continued baiting you, trying to make you jealous. I did give my aunt quite a shock that day, though. I told her I was intrigued by my wife's views on Christianity. I wasn't quite ready to make a decision; my pride was still getting in the way, but I wanted to know how to have what you and she had."

Tears flowed from my eyes as I listened in amazement.

"Then, that day Mr. Singer came in, humbled and thankful—and religious—I didn't know what to think. I knew there was something to this 'relationship' you kept talking about, but I wasn't quite ready to commit to anything. I think I was finally desperate enough to call on God when you were sick. The old, cynical me kept arguing that you had jumped off that cliff, that you weren't any different from anyone else, but a tiny part of me wanted to believe. I finally decided that whatever happened to you, I would accept Jesus Christ as my Savior. When I made that decision, I felt such a peace as I've never known. I'm afraid that when you woke up, the old me got the best of me. I'm sorry I was so rude to you then, accusing you the way I did. I just didn't want to let you see how scared I had been. I wanted to tell you about my new relationship with Jesus then, but there was so much on my mind. I was furious that Melinda and Miles had come, flaunting their knowledge that you were penniless. I was getting close to telling you myself. I hated it that you would hear it from them, and I knew how you would react. I couldn't tell you then that I had known all along. I was afraid you'd hate me for keeping it from you. You don't hate me do you? You do love me?" He seemed so vulnerable at that moment that it broke my heart.

"Oh, Edmund, I do love you. Perhaps I started loving you long ago, but I only realized it after you almost died saving Johnny from that fire. I was terrified that I would give myself away and look at you with love and you would look at me with disgust. I can't believe how blind and stupid I've been. There I was, loving you so much it hurt, and yet I was so afraid of rejection that I couldn't say a thing."

"*You* were afraid of rejection? I was afraid that if I made any advances toward you, you'd run back home like a scared kitten. I couldn't have that, not when you would find out about your penniless state. So, I had to try and wait. At times it was almost impossible for me to keep my hands off you."

He reached up and caressed my cheek.

"Even now I'm finding it very difficult not to touch you. You see," he said smiling, "I want you to be my wife—my *real* wife."

He kissed me until I was breathless. He caught my face in his hands and stared at me for a moment, then he kissed me again with such passion that I knew that I wanted to be his *real* wife, too.

EPILOGUE

Not many days after Miles' attempt on my life, Amelia's baby was born. A little girl. Amelia had so hoped to give Nathan a son, but on the day Edmund and I went to visit them, Nathan was fairly exploding with pride.

"She's as cute as a button, isn't she?" he asked as he placed her gently into my arms. Amelia was propped up on some pillows on the settee, resting. She looked fondly at her husband.

"He's convinced she's the prettiest baby ever born, but that's just a proud father's conceit."

I laughed, but agreed that she was a darling. I looked up at Edmund who was standing beside me. He smiled warmly at me and squeezed my shoulder.

"Did you name her Anna?" I asked.

"Yes."

"Precious Anna," I said softly, "You are a blessed little girl to have parents such as these."

She responded by scrunching up her nose and letting

out a squall. Nathan rushed over, took her from me and gave her back to her Mama. Soon after, we rose to leave.

"Well, we better be going now—we'll give the two of you a chance to rest," I told Amelia, "But I'll be back soon. I'm going to want to see a lot of that little girl."

Amelia smiled and Edmund and I saw ourselves out. We walked hand in hand along the cliff path towards home. The last week had been blissful. Edmund and I took long walks together; we rode together; we even prayed together. Those were the best moments.

At first after Miles' death, I found it hard to talk about all that had happened. I was overcome at times with guilt at having caused his death. After the funeral, two things happened that helped put the past behind us. First, I began to be able to talk through the pain and fear and guilt I had felt. Edmund was a wonderful listener. Second, Mrs. Colton left for London, not willing to stick around after the tragedy and the realization of her cousin's guilt. I'm afraid I was not sorry to see her go.

I had one nightmare—a few days after the incident—and I woke up screaming, drenched in a cold sweat. It was a strange delayed reaction. It almost made it worthwhile, however, to awaken to find Edmund's arms around me, soothing me as he dropped tender kisses on my forehead and whispered words of love.

Now, as we stopped to stare out over the cliffs at the calm sea below, my heart overflowed with thanksgiving to God. Edmund awakened me from my thoughts when he said, "Everything looks so peaceful now. It's hard to believe these cliffs have caused so much heartache."

"I'm glad the heartache is over. Now all I feel is thankful and loved."

"I'm glad you feel loved because you are," he said tenderly.

"By the way," he said as we walked along, "how would you like to have a daughter?"

"I would like that. But I think I ought to have a son, handsome like his papa."

"And will you wake me up in the middle of the night to fix you eggs and bacon?"

"Of course. And will you do it?"

"Gladly," he said as he grabbed me by the waist and swung me around in a circle. "Gladly," he said again, emotion making his voice gruff, and he kissed me as we stood near those beautiful cliffs.

Tate Publishing & *Enterprises*

Tate Publishing is committed to excellence in the publishing industry. Our staff of highly trained professionals, including editors, graphic designers, and marketing personnel, work together to produce the very finest books available. The company reflects the philosophy established by the founders, based on Psalms 68:11,

"THE LORD GAVE THE WORD AND GREAT WAS THE COMPANY OF THOSE WHO PUBLISHED IT."

If you would like further information, please call
1.888.361.9473
or visit our website
www.tatepublishing.com

Tate Publishing & *Enterprises*, LLC
127 E. Trade Center Terrace
Mustang, Oklahoma 73064 USA